KARA

My First Kiss

Kathryn Gillings and Gary Baxter

Cover Design: Yazoo Designs
Interior Layout: Cecily Potter

Printed in Australia

Revised edition 2023
Republished July 2023

Paperback ISBN: 978-0-6458751-0-2
E-Book ISBN: 978-0-6458751-1-9

Chapter 1

$\mathcal{G}$reg Sheppard was one of the last to step out from the warmth of his schoolteacher's red brick bungalow and into the cool of the summer night. He knew his father would be late picking him up, he always was. Heading toward the gate, he stopped halfway down the path, his thoughts halting him into the semi stunned realisation that his life was progressing so quickly now that he was almost a teenager. New experiences every day, new feelings that he had never felt before but tonight, had proven to be extraordinary.

It was a Friday night, the night of the year 7's primary school social held at their teacher's home. Everyone was sitting on chairs arranged in a circle in Mr Bourke's lounge room, heads and eyes slightly bowed, hiding that preadolescent embarrassment.

When Kara arrived, all the seats were taken. Kara simply walked up to Greg and sat on his lap. While Mr Bourke started panicking, and raced to find another chair, Greg was stunned. He was surprised she'd chosen his lap to sit on, and sat there motionless, wondering where to put his hands.

He knew Kara of course, having been in the same class all year, however he'd never had much to do with her. Neither had he ever been this close to a girl, so the action sent a warmth through his body he couldn't explain, but he liked it. It wasn't long before more chairs arrived and Kara was instructed to move from his lap by the nervous teacher. She hopped up looking back at him, and with a smile, moved off to talk to some other girls that had just arrived. It was a while before that new found yummy feeling subsided and Greg returned to normal.

The night had been tame, and typical as first socials go, especially under the sugar-coated eagle-eyes of the grown-ups. By about 10.00 p.m., parents started to arrive, and everyone began to say their goodbyes and leave.

As Greg stood there, on the path, caught in his own headspace, Kara appeared in front of him. She stood right up close, directly in front of him, and kissed him.

Just like that!

Her first connection with his lips was barely a peck—small, gentle, and nearly a matter-of-fact touch, more like a quick kiss goodbye. She hesitated, leaning her head back away from him, but then looked directly into his eyes, straightened and moved forward again. Her soft lips pressed against his—firmer this time, which to Greg, held for what felt like minutes, but in reality, lasted only a second or two. Greg was frozen, he didn't know how to kiss, he just stood there with his lips still puckered, as Kara ran off to her waiting mother.

Throughout the night, they'd never spoke.

Not a word.

He felt a warmth flood his body, screaming out a language he didn't understand. *This must be what love is,* he thought. His heels steadied back to the ground as he pulled himself together and looked around to see a few of the others kids staring at him. They'd obviously seen what had just happened. *This will be the talk of the school next week.*

Greg jumped into the front seat of his father's big Dodge Phoenix that had finally arrived. The street was now empty.

'Did you have a good time, Greg?' his father asked as the car moved away from the curb.

'Yeah, I did dad, it was better than I expected,' was all he could muster. His father was a lovely man but they weren't close enough for this conversation.

While the next day was the weekend for his classmates, it was a workday for Greg. He'd quietly worked a Saturday morning job for the past couple of years, pulling car parts off wrecked vehicles in a car graveyard. Unbeknown to anyone at school, this was survival, not a career as such. On this particular morning, he worked in a complete daze, consumed with the recollection and feelings from the night before.

I must be in love, and Kara is my woman. She's not the prettiest girl in the class, maybe third behind Anna and Karen, and she's not the most popular, but she's mine. My first and only love.

He spent the day with his head in the clouds trying to plan how he could support his beloved twelve-year-old soulmate on the $5.00 he earnt each Saturday. *Love will find a way* he thought, as the Sidchrome ratchet clicked away in his hand.

That kiss unknowingly changed both of their lives. The imprint and the impact of their connection is the mere start of this story.

Chapter 2

*H*e tossed his bag on the floor, shed his Ted Baker suit coat, and wrenched off his tie in the first moments of entering his North Adelaide townhouse. He unbuttoned his shirt with one hand and headed to the kitchen. Today had been a big day. It was a relief to stop and take a breath after what had been a month of solid negotiations. He grabbed a glass and poured himself a wine.

Securing a major tourism event contract always felt good. He was usually keen to share in celebrations with his team but tonight he strangely wasn't interested, finding himself left wanting… something. He didn't know what or why. He wandered around his apartment, as if searching for the release that the peace of coming home after working away normally offered him.

Stepping out onto the balcony, the heat of the day and the usual Friday night city traffic pounded through him, offering no comfort. Aside from the warm feeling building in his chest from the wine, he didn't feel the usual glow of excitement that he craved after closing a deal. He let out a sigh. *The couch it is then,* he thought.

He walked back inside, grabbed the remote, and sank into the soft, tan leather.

Greg looked around his apartment. He glanced at the photos of his daughters on the wall. His thoughts were turbulent. *I must call the girls tomorrow; they'll be wondering why they haven't heard from me this week. God, I miss them.*

The long-past sound of their giggles and chatter in his ears as he carried them, one in each arm, down the hallway each morning echoed in his mind. He smiled, remembering how his wife would laugh as he walked them into the kitchen, teasing and cajoling them into breakfast and the bustle of their morning routine.

We gave them a happy life, he thought to himself.

But life and relationships change over time. Just as history forever tells, there are always leaders and followers. Greg was a dynamic leader. His wife was a committed follower. He was charismatic, ambitious, and social, while she was steadfast, quiet, and shy. As the years progressed, she struggled to keep pace with their increasingly high-profile lifestyle. So, it was no surprise that once their daughters had grown, he and his wife both agreeably moved to a new passage of life for themselves, forever friends, bonded by their now-adult children, but little more than that.

On his own in those initial years after the divorce, he had worked hard to ensure his wife, their girls, and all the family stayed close.

After kicking off his shoes, he flicked the clasp of his watch, resting it carefully on the coffee table. The watch had been such an extravagance back when he'd bought it in celebration of securing his first big contract. Staring at it, and surrounded by all the luxury of the apartment, it reminded Greg that, he could want for nothing more. These days, he had all the toys that any man could wish for, an AMG Mercedes Benz; a forty-eight-foot Riviera Cruiser; his 1200cc Kawasaki motorcycle and connections and networks around the world as director of a renowned event production company. He should not dare look back.

But that was then, and this is now. 'You have a great life,' he scolded himself out loud. He picked up his phone and started scrolling through social media. This was a daily necessity for work, but tonight it was just as a distraction. As he flicked through the newsfeed of the many colleagues and friends, he saw a post from one of his primary school mates, Paul. *I must call him. We haven't seen each other in person since our primary school reunion.*

Primary school. Thirty-five years ago. His mind meandered and then rested on that memory. He could still see her.

They were both twelve years old. Already, he was instantly noticeable; in contrast, she was part of the background. Yet she was the one who dramatically changed his life all those years ago. In seconds, a brief smile and a shudder of delight flickered through him. She had started his engine in an unexpected moment, and his life seemed to continue to fire on all eight cylinders ever since. Probably thanks to her.

The mention of her name this week as a local contact, innocently suggested by the producer for the event he was negotiating, had kept bumping into his thoughts. 'If it's the same lady you're thinking of, she's into community development and used to be married to a local footballer named Werner. They ran a building company here in Clare.' Greg had discreetly smothered his personal interest that had surged at the moment, all the while listening intently to the information about this woman. He put this to the back of his mind. He had work to do.

But tonight, with rare private time for himself, that suppressed desire to find her, had suddenly resurfaced. *God, I would just love to say hi and tell her how that little moment changed my life.*

No longer camouflaged by a white gold band and a married name, her existence was once again revealed and created another possible chance to reconnect. He started a search for her profile on Facebook. He'd done this many times before… all without success. 'Well look at that, its' her!' he said as the lingering memory of those eyes merged with the sight before him. It took him the next hour to compose a message, trying to be casual, but with feeling. He finally hit send. And then waited.

He finished his glass of wine and fixed himself a light meal, he checked his phone every five minutes, listening for that familiar ping.

He half-heartedly watched television before showering. Hours passed, until eventually, he headed to bed, still hoping that the girl who had stayed in his memory all those years would respond to his message.

Little did he know how long it would take.

Chapter 3

*K*ara Werner's husband had finally passed away. Well, in reality, he was still very much alive, but in these past four years since the sudden and dramatic end to their twenty-three years together, Kara had officially laid him to rest. He still lived close, but she was no longer afraid of him. It had taken so much time to put the pieces of her true self back together, like a 10,000-piece jigsaw—slowly and carefully. Her friends, the home she redesigned in the fashion of her new life, her work and her garden offered her comfort and sanctuary. The quietly confident, articulate, caring, sometimes silly and fun woman had emerged from the ashes. Kara had allowed her real colour and style to shine through.

When she finally changed her surname back to her maiden name, it was like she'd passed the test and at last had a licence to drive her own life. She was finally happy.

She didn't know that there was one piece missing.

A very important piece.

What on earth are you doing woman? Should you really be doing this, Kara? Her sensible, mature self, tried in vain to scream at her resurgent adolescent heart, which had driven her to uncharacteristically start throwing clothes, shoes, and make-up into a bag in the middle of the night. Her car had nearly found its own way from her driveway to the main street of the Clare township, before she thought to turn on the headlights. 'Get a grip woman, you need to calm down!' she told herself, as she applied the brakes to slow the speed of her car back to within the town limit. She'd been driving as fast as her heart, totally oblivious to the road, any rules or any of her surroundings.

As she reached Adelaide Road, she turned up the music that streamed from her phone. She needed a distraction from her thoughts, concentrate on driving, get to the city safely and get on that plane.

Try as she might to focus on the 140 kilometres ahead, the beat of her favourite tunes only accentuated the shuddering waves of excitement and fear that kept crashing through her body. She gripped the steering wheel as the sound of his voice and the recap of the messages they had exchanged in these past forty-eight hours consumed her head like a thunderous applause.

'How could I have missed his message? I could've met him two years before now!' she scolded herself out loud.

He was someone she only knew on the thin thread of a heart-struck memory from decades ago. After all this time on her own, someone arrived unexpectedly with a powerful jolt into her world. A man who'd searched for her, supposedly having held her in his heart for decades. It was unbelievable. Electrifying and frightening all at the same time.

It's crazy. It's ludicrous! The thoughts crashed along at a pace now faster than her car, and the conversation with herself continued.

Yes, he is a long-lost friend. Well… sort of. You know who he is, or rather who he was all those years ago. Maybe? There is the fact that, you kissed him—once or sort of twice. But you were only kids. He was so cute then and doesn't seem to have changed much. But you did only see him for two minutes at the chance meeting on the day before you got married. That was over twenty years ago! You really have no idea who he is or what you are doing!

Kara had been both surprised and secretly aroused by finding his message and the open, honest conversations they'd since shared during the past two days. She'd warmed instantly to his voice. He emitted a tone that conveyed both strength and softness, like whipped cream—cool, gentle, calm, yet all the while, so powerful and sultry. Kara kept mentally replaying the text messages and conversations she'd had with him over the past couple of days. *I still can't believe how I missed his message when he first sent it!*

She'd been sitting in the chair at her beloved Michael's hairdressing salon, enjoying the welcome 'quiet time' between tinting and rinse.

Kara always loved the enforced relaxation time that her time in the 'chair' gave, so she'd often just flick through magazines or casually through Facebook on her phone, just some little indulges away from work. Tonight, she'd welcomed this time to check her new tablet. It was only then she noticed a message and a new friend request. She'd never paid much attention to those requests, as few were legitimate friends, but this one surprised her.

What? It can't be? She read it again. *Oh my God… how have I not seen this before?* Michael picked her physical response through the mirror—her wide eyes, a smirk and rather awkward expression that had appeared. A mix of secrecy, excitement, and embarrassment all at once.

'Okay… what's got you grinning there, Kara?' he asked.

'Oh. Oh, nothing really… well…?'

As she looked up, she spied his inquisitive stare fixed on her that commanded an honest response. 'I've just found a message from a boy— I mean— he's a man now, who I knew in primary school. He's evidently been searching for me for a while!'

'Let me see. Wow, he looks hot,' Michael said as she held up the tablet for him to see. 'You crushed on him in primary school, didn't you? I would have!' Michael said. The comment was no surprise to Kara. Michael caught her confirming blush—before she even said a word.

'Oh, alright— yes. I did. Lots. But he never spoke to me.'

'Well go on then—make up for that, you're a grown-up girl now, send him a message!' said Michael with a naughty grin.

'Stop that! I'll think about it. Now come on, let's get this hair finished!' Kara said with a laugh as she snap-closed her tablet.

While usually loving the banter she shared with Michael, and with whom after 13 years as a hairdresser and confidante she could implicitly trust, tonight she just wanted to get home and indulge in her own discovery. The power of a simple message.

Hello Kara,
I've been trying to find you for awhile now, about twenty years actually. You have been hiding pretty well. I'm going to be working near you tomorrow, and I thought I might just try again. I would love to catch up, even if just for a quick chat tomorrow as you are a special memory to me (30 years ago). I wonder if you remember?
Greg Sheppard

But that was sent over two years ago.

'How on earth could I have missed this?' she kept asking herself. She immediately started a message in reply, wanting desperately to apologise for her oversight.

However, it took her until after 11.00 p.m. that night to respond. She was trying to find the right words, wanting her reply to sound casual yet interested. She wanted to confirm she understood what 'special memory' he was referring to, but all the while not wanting the real thrill of his contact to be revealed… well, not just yet.

Her heart was thumping with beats faster than the music as she gripped firmly to the steering wheel, as much to steady herself than the car. Her body had taken over as she imagined what may happen in the next two days. Sudden tremors and waves of sheer heat and pleasure kept rising from between her legs, throbbing and pulsing vibrantly, throughout her whole body.

She thought this was nervous excitement, her mind not yet realising what her body already knew. She was becoming aroused by just the thought of this man sending her sweet and suggestive messages, let alone the possibility that within twenty-four hours she could be making love to a man she hardly knew.

It would be the first time in over four years she'd been with a man. She hadn't refused to stay in his room. The body shivers and delicious vibes kept escalating.

Chapter 4

$\mathcal{G}$reg awoke and glanced around. Yes, those familiar white sheets. It was Wednesday morning, and he was close to half-way finished with this project. He was lying in bed in yet another strange hotel. This was the part that he both loved and disliked about his job. As director of one of the country's most successful advertising and event management companies, he had spent years, always on the go. The constant planning, travel, and schedules were gruelling and tiresome, but there were benefits and she was lying next to him.

He gently climbed out of bed and went to the bathroom.

Returning, he slipped carefully back under the sheet. Lying on his back, his head turned to look at her. She was still asleep. He loved seeing her tousled blonde hair across the pillow, the evidence of last night's passionate lovemaking. It had been amazing—so hot, slow, deep, and tender. Tess was a special and beautiful woman. They had met a couple of years ago at the launch of a campaign for her now former husband's computer company. It happened that her husband had assigned her to help Greg, the event production manager, to offer any 'assistance' he needed.

She had such a mixture of hidden and yet obvious appeal. Later Greg had explained to her, 'You struck me instantly with your beauty, while trying to be so inconspicuous that I couldn't help but notice to you.'

Despite being so willing to help, as she casually chatted away, he also noticed how she looked and felt out of place with her fast-paced and upwardly climbing husband. She was clearly smart and attractive, however, had lost her voice and self behind his glitzy ambition and the blueprint he'd inadvertently laid out for her to fulfil as the director's wife. Greg quickly picked that she had hidden strength, dreams and desires of her own.

Greg could not shield himself from being attracted. She was not only exquisite on the eye, but had picked the glimmer of the star, seemingly shouting out to shine, behind a dark shroud. He simply smiled, listened and started to share snippets of his own life.

In a matter of days, she'd felt so comfortable with Greg's genuine interest that her guarded covers slipped away to reveal her natural beauty and maturity. The two of them couldn't help become friends, confidantes and then lovers. The mutual attraction was instant, deep and powerful. They attempted to restore themselves to life before they met, Tess with her husband, and each with their children, they both suffered a period of abstinence and contrition.

Their forcefield connection could not be denied. After barely another six months, each of them broke free of their former lives.

Despite the near insatiable appetite for each other's company and their heated attraction on every level, from the outset, they'd committed to retaining their own individual lives. However, by the time the eventual divorce from her husband was finalised, Tess and Greg found themselves hungry to spend more and more time together. Such was their bonded attraction, that these days, it was whenever they could. Today, she was to be wrenched away from him, as, she was heading back to Melbourne, to check on a shipment for her homeware business while he still had the TV shoot to finish here in Sydney.

Tess was lying on her side, facing away from him. Greg stretched out, deliberately allowing his arm to brush across her back, and turned his body towards her, his toes gently moving up and down the silky flesh of her legs. She stirred, her body twitching and moving ever so slightly.

He loved this time, the beginning of 'morning after' sex, so sweet and possibly the most intimate, like taking a breath as you climbed into a hot bath. He loved the delight and anticipation, just knowing that within minutes, he would again feel the rise of the heat and resurgence of the passion from only hours before. He started by brushing soft kisses down the nape of her neck and across her shoulders.

Greg knew she was awake even though she hadn't spoken a word. He waited for that blissful moment when she eased her body closer towards him, slowly edging her butt cheeks to press against his thighs, casually brushing across his groin, to feel him already getting hard. She arched her back slightly, allowing her legs to part just enough to give him access to her.

This minute said it all. It was the beckoning invitation that Greg loved most. 'Now' and 'please' her body called. As he gently lifted her head to cradle her in his arms from behind, he slipped between her legs and just inside her… feeling that already wet invitation and acceptance of his first thrust, waiting to hear her barely audible first gasp. This was a feeling like no other.

It was only then that he whispered, 'Good morning, beautiful,' before pushing inside her again. She arched further to have as much of him as she could and it wasn't long before they both sang the song of ecstasy. Greg loved the start of each day with this delightful woman beside him.

Spooned together with Greg's fingertips brushing up and down her back, Tess was lost in the afterglow of her orgasmic awakening. Jolted back into the day by the alarm, she turned to kiss him and then reluctantly headed to the bathroom, mindful she had a flight to catch. Greg reached for his phone and booked her a cab, knowing full well she'd forgotten to organise one last night.

Tess gazed into the bathroom mirror of their hotel suite, hands pressing onto the bench. The reflection staring back at her with her vivid Mediterranean blue eyes was finally one that expressed her radiance.

Her golden hair looked even prettier these days now that it fell naturally, allowing its length to graze below her shoulder blades. Her body still defied its age; while still firm, it was now energised in all the right places, and her skin was ever so much softer than before. As was her smile.

She knew why. Feeling loved and cherished had transformed her more than any clothes or stylist could ever imagine or provide. He alone had been the catalyst. Greg had inspired the woman she now saw in front of her. His love and attention had raised her confidence and energy, giving her the strength to establish her own business too. He was the reason she felt so alive and happy today and every day during the past two years. Her eyes shone.

She wished she didn't have to leave. Whether travelling or at home, it was the same feeling after each time she lay with him.

Like early this morning.

Tess had heard the bathroom door click, rousing her awareness it was morning and he was awake. Laying still, daring not move or breathe faster, in fear of breaking the feeling of excitement in anticipation of his first touch. She could feel his adoration for her glow through every pore of his skin.

She waited. She wanted him… as she did all the time.

Why wouldn't she?

Whenever with him, his reverence was near overwhelming and completely irresistible.

She loved him.

When they parted these days, it just got harder. Thankfully, they would be reunited in a few days when they both landed back home in Adelaide.

Chapter 5

By lunchtime on set, Greg had the production crew in place, and all displays, models, props, lights, and sound equipment was ready. With full running sheets, everything was ready for the director and DOP, director of photography to take control and start the shoot. He'd done everything to this point, but to his relief, it was the start of the 'breathe time,' as he called it, when he could step back for a couple of hours or days. It was his standby time before stepping in once again to take charge and manage the bump out of the event.

It had been a relatively easy afternoon, and that night he enjoyed a casual dinner with a couple of the crew at a local Thai restaurant. They'd even sorted some minor changes on the set, which they'd planned to deal with in the morning. He left them in good spirits in the restaurant and walked back to the hotel. With Tess gone, he knew the first minutes back in his room would feel empty, but he also needed a quiet night on his own. Besides, he always carried the glow and pleasure of their time together, even when they were apart.

It was just after 11.30 p.m. when he entered the hotel lobby. His phoned pinged with that familiar message tone. Without thinking, he swiped the phone and opened the messages. A quick glance had him stopping in his tracks. If anyone had seen his face, they would have spotted the rare image of Greg Sheppard in a state of disbelief.

Kara Gilbert had finally replied.

Greg entered his room, poured a glass of wine, and quickly returned his attention to his phone. He read the message carefully, then read it again. It really was Kara, after all this time. *Wow, I can't believe it. It's been years since I messaged her.*

He had been searching for her for years, and she had never been far from his thoughts. At the recent school reunion, he imagined her walking through the door as cute as she was on the day she'd kissed him, back when they were twelve. In his fantasy, she'd walk up to him and without speaking, kissed him again. But she never attended the reunion.

He would often bring up her name in conversation when he met up with old friends, to find out where she might live or if anyone had seen her. Whenever his work took him to the Clare Valley, he would ask locals about her, as he knew that was her family's region. Despite his enquiries and research, he'd never found her.

His memory drifted back to a couple of years ago, when he'd been engaged to arrange a tourism event in the South Australian wine regions, with a focus on new winemakers and restauranteurs. He'd spent a couple of weeks in the lower north of the state around the Clare area, her hometown. He'd visited wineries and met the townsfolk and worked with a host of people arranging launches and the promotional campaign in the lead up to the region's Gourmet Weekend later that year. Unexpectedly, one of the regional development officers assigned as the producer of the event, mentioned her name in a conversation as he was driving Greg around Clare Valley.

He'd passed a comment that Greg should look at the promotions plan that Kara Gilbert developed for one of the community projects she had managed.

'Kara who?' Greg had asked.

'Kara Gilbert. She's a local and works in community development across the state. Kara's done quite a bit of work for us over the years. She's such a lovely person. I think you two would get on well.'

Greg had commented on how he'd gone to primary school with a Kara Gilbert from up this way many years ago. The conversation had continued, and Greg had gently probed with questions, discovering she'd been married to a local builder and footballer named Werner and had only recently divorced. From what he could gather, she had remained single and still lived in the area. The regional development officer had casually commented that she was well respected and not a bad looker either.

After stumbling onto this new information, Greg had decided he would make yet another last-chance attempt to find her. Checking Facebook, he'd discovered her page, and while her settings were private, he'd thought it couldn't hurt to at least send a message.

But there had been no reply.

He had all but resolved in his own mind that she must be happy with her life and didn't want or need to complicate it with him.

So be it, I can't do anymore, he'd thought at the time.

Until tonight.

Kara had replied to his message.

Well hello, Greg!
I must apologise. Fancy replying to a message from over two years ago. Talk about leaving a person hanging! I must confess that I never check the Messenger Request section of the app, and I only came across your message tonight. I am so sorry!! It's lovely to hear from you. I haven't really been hiding, just moved back to the country so many years ago and spend most of my life driving and travelling around the countryside. If you are still living and working in South Australia, we've probably been passing each other close by for years! What brought you to Clare? How did you track me down? Now, Greg, my memory is quite good (in fact, I don't think any woman ever forgets their first kiss). Hope life is good for you and one can we can catch up for that quick chat.
Regards, Kara

She hadn't ignored his message. She just hadn't seen it. As simple as that. After all this time, he'd found her!

Greg waited until morning to reply, but as he lay in bed that night, he couldn't stop thinking back to the memories of her. In reality, it was only one vivid memory. It was an event that lasted for only a minute in time, barely that, now over thirty-five years ago. But it was a unique memory that had stayed with him as if it had happened yesterday.

Greg had replayed that scene over and over in his head many times. He had never forgotten Kara. The imprint of how this quiet girl and that kiss had made him feel as a young twelve-year-old had been everlasting. A simple yet poignant 'rite of passage' moment, which awoke a new young man in place of the boy he had been before. Apart from a brief and unexpected encounter some eight or nine years after that night, Greg had not spoken to her or heard from her again.

To Greg, Kara remained this unknown girl who had impacted him the most from his childhood years. While he really hadn't thought that much about her since then, from time to time, he recounted how Kara would float back into his thoughts as the one who initiated a moment in his life that had rather profoundly imprinted on him.

Kara Gilbert had turned the key. She was the one. This was the first kiss he had experienced with a girl.

He'd instantly fallen in love, and for the next two days, the twelve-year-old was planning how they might spend the rest of their lives together. 'It's just curiosity,' he told himself. It's been decades, and if you meet her, it closes a childhood fantasy. Still, he couldn't wait to reply.

Hi Kara,

It's so nice to hear from you. I must say the lack of reply was most disturbing. I knew you still lived in Clare and have been trying to find you each time I visited the area. Sometimes we must have missed each other by minutes. I travel around the country setting up events, TV ads, and promotions and have been involved in the advertising for the Gourmet Weekend in your area each year. Now about that kiss!! It may not have been your first, but it was most certainly mine. I wasn't sure from your message whether you actually did remember it. I can remember it like it was yesterday. I can describe the event in precise detail.

Greg.

Life had moved on considerably since all those years ago. He had been besotted with Kara in the initial days after that kiss, but only for the time that you would expect a young man to feel after such an unexpected intimate experience. Especially one that a girl had initiated. A first kiss would always be a milestone. Perhaps for Greg and Kara it meant a little more than what they both understood or needed at the time, as both unknowingly they were the only two who had unique circumstances in those preadolescent years. She was an only child, and he was the eldest and only boy. Both lived in a single-parent family, which, in those times, was a life foreign to most of their classmates. Dealing with the loss of a parent because of separation or divorce was rare in those days and often misunderstood, with the impact on the children in a family often never being noticed. But perhaps years later it was too easy to analyse, and it probably wasn't worth fussing over their brief connection either. Somehow, for whatever reason, perhaps only a secret crush, the spark had been ignited by Kara in a most unexpected and quite unique way. Well, it was a first kiss!

His life had moved on in the predictable direction—high school, studying, dating (lots of that!), and all the desires and pleasures that a good-looking young man could attract. He had definitely worked hard to make his own mark and establish a career, and he'd created all the traditional markers of a successful life. But that wasn't as easy as it sounded. An achiever, he had a quiet determination to work hard, depend only upon himself, protect his sister, build a life that was better, be successful, do no harm to those he cared for, be financially sound, and ultimately be happy every day.

Some years later, when young by today's standards, he had married a girl who complimented and supported him, a caring and dependable woman. She gave him the support and foundation necessary for a man with a demanding career, high expectations, and a drive to learn, experiment, and achieve. She had also given him two beautiful daughters and was the perfect mother and homemaker. He loved her for her nurturing qualities and their children—indeed, a unique gift.

The years after they divorced were hard work. He'd desperately missed the comfort that a family life had wrapped around him, despite it having crumpled to a predictable shell in later years. In those alone times, when his need for a tender, caring soul consumed him, Kara was often one whom his thoughts had drifted to. He had searched for her ever since. To no avail.

A couple of years ago, he had found Tess. This was the woman who had truly imprinted on him as a man. She grabbed not only his lips and the dreams of what was thrilling and possible; she had grabbed his heart. Like the butterflies inside, which had fluttered strong for Kara for only a few days as a young boy, this woman in his adult years had truly captured them. Her hold was where his wings had willingly settled, with an all-consuming passion and what he felt he had searched for all his life.

What had started as a casual encounter had quickly and unintentionally grown to be so much more. While they'd agreed to being 'friends with benefits,' every moment he spent with her was an ultimate pleasure. Not just hot, lustful, and satisfying, but reflecting the shared pleasure he craved in an intimate partner. Their mutual respect, the common views, subtle jokes, shared interests, and a physical connection encapsulated the love and attraction that just flowed and glowed through them both. Sure, since his divorce, he had found some lovely women with whom he had regularly shared some exciting and satisfying times, each of whom held a special connection with him. He'd stayed friends with them all, but once he found Tess, she was always the one who was the magnet he was drawn to and for whom he would eventually forsake all others.

He'd recently felt that he really didn't need anything or anyone else anymore. He was satisfied, excited, and truly fulfilled the entire time he and Tess spent together. He always felt so happy. After these past couple of years, both now free to be together, sharing their constant, yet semi-detached lifestyle, he'd been thinking seriously that it was time to suggest shedding one of their apartments, start slowing down their careers, and enjoying more of each other. Although he still had the occasional lady while working away, he had come to a place where he felt that she was really the only woman he wanted, needed, and adored. He had finally found what he felt to be true love with Tess for the first time and had told her so not that long ago. But there was a small disturbing thought… *So why did you continue to look for her? For Kara?*

Before he could answer himself, Greg heard his phone signal another message. It was from Kara.

Dear Greg,
How can we keep missing each other for twenty+ years? I am really so sorry we haven't had a chance to connect until now! We will have to plan a time to meet somewhere soon and have a decent catch-up. So please let me know when and where that could work for you. Hey, it was definitely my first kiss! Still a strong and special memory indeed. xx

She does remember me, and without a second thought, he replied.

The fact that you can remember it and it was your first as well has given me butterflies. I feel like a little boy again.

With that simple reply from him, the first spark was lit.

> You're a bit of a romantic, aren't you? That's so sweet.

> You have no idea!

> So hey, when can we catch up?

> I'm working in Sydney this week until Sunday. But sometime soon after that would be great.

Later the same day, when Kara found a moment to herself— he was her first thought. No. The truth was, she had been thinking about him all day.

> So sorry for the late reply. I've been in meetings all day. Well, let's hope we can catch up sometime soon. Here's my phone number. Call me sometime to arrange to meet. Hey, BTW, thanks for connecting. I've been smiling warmly all day. K x

Greg wanted to call her straight back, but he waited.

That night he called and despite talking for hours, it barely felt time enough to catch up on the enormous gap of years that had passed. If anyone had heard them, it could be mistaken that these two had remained in touch and were close friends for years, such was the relaxed and natural flow of their conversation.

Greg shared that he was living on his own, but he knew he had to be open about his current relationship with Tess and so he told her all about his plans to soon seriously commit to her. Kara had told him bits of how she came to be divorced and how she was now settled into life after a most difficult marriage. She was enjoying being free to make her own decisions and wasn't looking for any serious relationships and loving how she'd been connecting with old and new friends. Their spoken words were saying these things, but even over the phone without even the touch of a hand or meeting in person, there was already some inexplicable and magnetic attraction.

It didn't stop there.

Friday morning, Greg awoke to the memory of the previous day's contact with Kara and their long phone call. He sent another message.

I'm glad I made you smile. I so loved our chat last night.

Well, I'm tired this morning. My sleep was disturbed with thoughts of you all night!

The day was full of a constant exchange of messages between them, which turned rapidly into suggestive, fun, electric, and pure unadulterated flirting.

By about the twentieth message, Kara couldn't resist.

You know, I've actually been looking at flights to Sydney? How crazy is that? I've not ever been on set for a commercial film shoot, and besides, I'm not sure I can wait until next week to see you!

Well, you could cash in on free accommodation, stay with me and get to see the final stages of filming...

Kara was a bit taken aback by her own instant reaction. She could feel herself blushing. *What is happening here? Did he say what I think he said, that I can stay with him in his room? In his bed or on the couch? He's told me about his long-term plans with this Tess lady, who sounds gorgeous, and yet here he is, inviting me to stay with him.*

As for you, Kara, what are you thinking? You are doing the same! She had to admit she was secretly quite excited and didn't want this to stop. She replied, trying to be cool, when in fact she was feeling nothing of the sort. She was already captivated.

> Not so sure about the pace here, Mr Sheppard? Yesterday we said "Hi!" and now without so much as the touch of a hand, we are talking about sleepovers? Phew!

> I'm sorry. I hope I haven't scared you off? I'm so not sure why I said that. Would you like me to organise a room for you?

> No, and, no, you haven't scared me off, but hey, we probably shouldn't be doing this?

It was as if both Greg and Kara had paused with the same thoughts. There was a good thirty minutes before his next reply.

> This is strange, I know. You know my plans, and so I can't commit to anything, but that hasn't suppressed the excitement this has generated.

> I know. I feel the same.

> Okay, I was going to save this for our "date," but I was so in love with you after that night all those years ago, that I spent the whole of the next two days thinking we would get married and spend the rest of our life together. Well, I was only twelve, remember? So now in my imagination, we have already met again, wined, dined, and kissed, and we are already there.

> Now I am seriously blushing. After being a one-man woman for so many years... and having spent so much time on my own, you will probably be disappointed. I'm seriously out of practice. I did like where your thoughts were going though!

Well, maybe we could just keep practising? Blushing... already? We haven't even had phone sex yet!

Phone sex, God, are you experienced in that too?

There was a long time before his next message. Greg knew he had a choice here, and despite his first impulse to say, 'Well, perhaps I've got carried away here, Sorry. The whole surprise of finally finding you after so long has been rather exciting. So, let's find a time to catch up for coffee or a drink when I get back...'

But instead, he sent:

I wish I could kiss you again now.

Before she could reply, her phone rang. It was him. They talked more. Lots more and by the end of the call, Kara was madly booking a flight to Sydney. It was then that the trembling started.

Kara arrived at her Aunt Sarah's unit in Adelaide just before 3.00 a.m. She was rather surprised at how unperturbed and excited her aunt was after she settled down from the initial panic of her unexpected dramatic arrival. 'It's all okay. No one has died,' she reassured her.

'Well, I thought it was either someone had a serious accident, or it was a man! Kara, darling, I must say it's about time!' Sarah said with a somewhat devilish smile.

Kara frowned, trying to smother her with an expression of 'settle down,' and saying, 'Look, he's just an old school friend. Let's not get too carried away.' She didn't want to share too much for fear of exposing how excited she was.

Chapter 6

*K*ara repacked her bag after grabbing a couple of hours sleep, and by 8.00 a.m., she was in a cab on the way to the airport. Now she was really starting to get nervous. That morning as she stepped out of the shower her reflection in the mirror jolted the realisation that only one man had seen her naked in the past twenty-five years. What made it worse, her confidence was pelted by her own research. She'd checked out all she could find about Greg on the internet. Repeatedly, articles, images, events had flooded the screen search—he was everywhere.

Shit! This man is famous and surrounded by models and celebrities all the time. He hasn't seen me for over twenty years, and oh my god, now I'm old! In the mirror, her eyes found those of the naked woman that stood in front of her. She tried to read them; *what sort of woman is she?* This lady was much older than she imagined. Sure, wrinkles were forming in the corners of her eyes and across her brow. Her breasts weren't too big or too small, but showed the signs of motherhood of two children, years before. Her figure wasn't too bad—but what would a man think looking at this woman? What would Greg think?

Her husband had never noticed her, well never appeared to, and to be honest she didn't care what he thought.

She hadn't made love to anyone in four years. No, she hadn't had *sex* with anyone in four years. It was decades since she had made love. *Or hell, had she ever?*

She closed her eyes and the older woman in front of her slowly disappeared. She imagined Greg looking at her beautiful slender naked body with an uncontrollable look of want and desire. She gently let her fingertips caress her breasts as she pictured him naked walking toward her. Her eyes slowly opened, agonisingly wanting him to be there—but then no, the older naked lady had reappeared. She sighed, then turned and looked at the clothes that laid on the bed and thought, *you can only be who you are. We are both the same age after all.*

She resolved that this would probably just end up as a rather awkward meeting, a polite catch-up over coffee, and after a while, having both satisfied their curiosities, they would simply get on with their lives. She stopped, hugging her bra to her chest and said to herself, 'I can do this.'

She finished dressing and decided to treat this like a Sydney shopping trip with a friend.

Another message interrupted her anxious debate with her thoughts.

Hello there. What time is your flight? Getting excited?

I board at nine here. Excited? Yes, definitely. Bit nervous too.

I'm a bit scared too.

You scared? Of what?

Scared you won't like me. Scared you won't have a fun time, and scared hearts might be broken.

> For a start, I wouldn't be coming if I didn't like you! Not long now. I will message you when I arrive in Sydney.

> I can't wait.

The messages had relieved some of Kara's doubts, rekindling her desperate desire to get on that plane. At pace, she collected her case and raced to the airport.

Finally at the security bag check, and waiting in line, she'd put her bag in the tray and then, just as she approached the security officer, she realised she was still wearing her boots.

'Oh damn! Sorry, I suppose you want my boots?' she asked him. He looked up at her, at first with a serious look on his face, and then with a warm grin.

'No, all of you!' They both laughed as he pointed for her to continue through to the metal detecting machine.

Once through into the airport lounge, she messaged Greg.

> Hey, what have you done to me? Made me glow somehow? The airport security guy just hit on me!

> I guess that makes two of us.

His reply was all it took for that delicious, fiery feeling to spread through her body again. She felt it now. *He wants to see me, and I have never wanted to see someone so badly in my life.*

She headed to gate twenty-one and waited to board the plane.

The cab ride to the venue seemed to take forever, but thankfully with each kilometre, Kara felt a little calmer. Having exchanged a few messages to check location, her arrival time at the airport, and confirm where they would meet, her panicky fear of the unknown faded, and the tingles of anticipation felt more like this was a fun adventure. She could not predict what may or may not happen, and she shouldn't try, having now decided to just go with the flow, and enjoy the ride. She wanted to catch up with him as a long-lost primary school friend, and this thought was the one she tried to hold on to as she pulled up at the entrance gate and alighted from the cab.

Feeling nervous and excited, Greg tried desperately not to look at his watch or pace as he stood waiting at the venue gate. When Kara had messaged him to say she was arriving in about ten minutes, he'd felt a sudden wave of excitement. He had waited for this moment for so long. The twelve-year-old girl in ponytails that had kissed him all those years ago was now only minutes away. This was a strange and unusual situation, he thought. They'd chatted, flirted and now she was on her way to possibly sleep with him. *What could go wrong?* he thought, raising his eyebrows.

She stared out of the cab window, searching for the first glance of him. She recognised him instantly and smiled as she saw him look at his watch then back towards the taxi. She fumbled to pay the driver, trying to hurry, but paused and took in a deep breath before exiting the cab. Taking her time to settle, she focussed only on collecting her bag from the boot of the taxi, straightening and taking in the surroundings. She turned, focussing her gaze on him. She smiled with her heart pounding as she walked up to him, her eyes not leaving his. She was desperately trying to read his thoughts. First impressions are everything and she wanted to know his. She approached him slowly, the last metre nearly an effort, as if the air was thick, or filled with reverse magnetism. Finally, their lips touched, she kissed him lightly. Sparks tingled through her as if she had touched a live wire. His lips were soft and had left hers, before her eyes opened. *Please don't let that be the last*, she thought.

'Welcome to my work, Kara. I can't tell you how excited I am to see you.'

He leant toward her to place an entry pass lanyard over her head, then took her bag, and escorted her inside. This was a thirty-five-year, 'hello again' in the waiting.

Inside, she was fighting to suppress the thundering nerves that had risen, but drawing on her professional self, she stood tall, outwardly calm, and found her smile.

When he reached for her hand Kara's heart nearly exploded in her chest.

'Come, I'll show you around.'

Greg introduced her to his workmates and showed her how the construction was coming along. They grabbed a sandwich from the café and Kara bombarded him with questions about the industry.

Finally, Greg said, 'Have a wander around, I need to be in a quick meeting now. The pass will get you anywhere. What say, I meet you back here in an hour and then we can go?' he reached over and kissed her not waiting for a reply.

I could really get used to him doing that, she thought.

Kara slowly relaxed, finding herself genuinely enjoying her time exploring the world of events and Greg Sheppard. There were moments when she nearly forgot he was the sole reason she had travelled here. She loved meeting people and discovering their roles.

She felt a warmth being here that she couldn't quite put a finger on. Was it because she was in a different world, a world of stage and film and big dollars, that was so far away from her own, or was it the realisation that probably in a few hours' time this man will take her in his arms and make her a woman again, something she hasn't been for a long time? Just then that horrible pang of sensibility burst through her mind's vision. *What if it's a disaster, I really don't know how to make love? For twenty-five years, I have just laid there while a fat man had sex. How do I start, what do I say?*

This thought was broken when she heard her name being called. She turned to see Greg smiling at her, his whole expression made her melt. *God, that smile would make any woman weak at the knees.*

'I'm done here for today, so shall we get going?'

She nodded, fighting to stop the trembling from starting again. This time it wasn't nerves. Greg took Kara by the hand. Somewhere in that moment, they left everyone, letting all guards and the years behind, finding themselves laughing as they strolled off swinging their arms like young children in a schoolyard.

As they approached his car, she thought, *did he get a separate room for me, or have we just begun our night as two strangers jumping into bed together?*

As if reading her mind, he touched her on the arm and looked into her brown eyes. 'I've booked a room for you at the hotel near mine if you would feel more comfortable, absolutely no pressure.'

'Thank you, Greg, I appreciate that. Let's just grab a drink and see how we go, shall we?' She smiled, and her eyes were sparkling. Mixed emotion flooded her head. *'Don't overthink it,'* she said to herself.

When they arrived at the hotel, Greg took her hand and bag and headed for the elevator. He opened the door of the top floor suite and invited her in. Greg wasn't too sure how he should steer this, but realised he would quickly pick up if it wasn't going well.

Sitting on the lounge with a drink in hand, the conversation was light and flowing. Greg enjoyed hearing more about Kara's life and how her work had changed in recent years. She was fascinated about all the aspects of his work. But all the while, she couldn't stop thinking about how she wanted to touch him.

With each sip of wine, her need to have his lips again on hers flourished.

Greg checked the time, 'Hey, Kara, it's getting late. Shall we go and grab some dinner?'

'Yes, that sounds good.'

'Do you mind if I grab a quick shower? I won't take long,' he said, fully aware she hadn't mentioned anything about a separate room yet.

'Sure,' Kara said, as she took another sip of wine. She stood and wandered around the suite. She heard him turn on the water as she strolled taking in what she could learn about him. She glanced into the bedroom and could see his leather bag, a small music speaker and exclusively labelled clothes folded over a chair. She turned, her wine glass still perched on her lips, when she noticed the bathroom door was ajar. The temptation was too great. She had to sneak a peek. From where she stood, she caught more than she expected. Her eyes fixed on the mirror, which perfectly reflected Greg's naked body in the shower, she nearly bit a chunk out of the glass. When they had first met that morning, she had immediately noticed how good he looked. At about six feet in height, this slim, fit, clean-shaven man was fashionably attired and it was clear he was strong and agile. But now, to see his bare body in the flesh was something else.

My God! He's so hot! His body defied that of a man in his mid-forties. His butt cheeks were round and firm, he had strong, tight thighs, and legs tapered in a shape that suggested he was an athlete rather than an event manager. His shoulders were broad, tapering to a slim waist.

The tremors had returned, now indistinguishable between fear and lust. Kara was torn between her embarrassment, nerves, and the overwhelming desire to just walk into the bathroom and join him. The decision was soon made for her when she heard him turn off the taps, she stepped back out of the bedroom and scrambled to sit on the couch. She shook her head and let out a slow long breath.

Greg emerged from the bedroom dressed casually in jeans and T-shirt.

Standing in front of her, he bent down, bringing his face close to hers, and looked her in the eyes. 'Thank you for coming all this way, I can't believe you are really here.'

It was in that moment, that Kara knew she wouldn't be needing another room, her loins were now in charge, her body was preparing for a guest and he had just knocked on her door, loudly.

'Well, come on then,' Greg said, 'let's get you some dinner; you must be starving.' He took her hand as he straightened up and helped her to her feet. He felt Kara's resistance to move.

She just stood there. Suspended on the spot.

She couldn't hold it together anymore. Her heart was pounding, and she was moist right through to her jeans. They couldn't leave the room yet. The impulse was too overpowering. She had to have him now.

As Greg turned, she said, 'Perhaps we can have a late dinner?' as she slowly started unbuttoning her shirt.

When Greg glanced at her, a look of surprise flickered across his face, at the reveal of her bra. He turned and moved to stand in front of her and slowly pulled her close, and it was then he kissed her. Time stood still. He discarded her shirt and bra then she removed his T-shirt.

Kara ran her fingers across his chest, then pressed closer to feel the warmth of his body and the hair on his chest caress her breasts. She felt him stiffen through his jeans as he pressed against her. She had to let him escape. She undid the button on his jeans as his tongue teased her mouth with care and precision. She undid his zip and soon found him filling her hand. Through the kiss she heard him moan as she stroked his length.

She had no recognition of how they had shed the rest of their clothes and found their way to the bed until that first feeling of his touch inside her. His long fingers made the first deep entry into her body. He brought her to the edge within seconds, and she couldn't help but give herself to that goddess of pleasure. It overtook her with vibrant delight. It was so intense; she could feel her body pulsing against his fingers, long after she had crested that wave of ecstasy. While still lost in that cloud of pleasure, she felt it. His power. Firm and strong, his hands took her by the hips and slid her forward. Lifting her legs and placing one on each of his shoulders. He allowed her to feel the first touch of his resplendent erection. He offered her only a little at first, teasing her. She looked up at him, her eyes open wide, she had surrendered herself totally to him.

He leant forward over her, one hand brushing the hair away from her eyes, the other held him suspended at only a stare's distance from her face. His eyes took in her every detail and vulnerability.

'I have loved you for nearly all of my life.' He uttered the words so softly, it was almost to himself.

She blinked and let her smile and eyes slowly reply. Her body was begging for him now. It was only then, that he lowered himself slowly into her.

From the first inch of him—every part of her accelerated to a pace she couldn't control. She was nowhere and everywhere all at the same time.

For a split second, he paused, suspending all motion. He had held onto the desire for this moment for so long. As she arched and reached for him, he gave her all of him, driving forward hard in one defining thrust.

Her eyes shot open as if she had been stabbed and let out a scream that might've matched the violent thrust of a sharp blade. Greg rode her hard, pushing deeper than any man had ever been before. She was a helpless passenger as the fire exploded again inside her, convolutions pulsed through her as a second climax erupted.

Her body was now almost limp, exhausted from the passionate lovemaking. He stopped still deep inside her, her body clenching him, as each pulsing wave gently faded. He lowered her legs and she realised he was still hard inside her.

To Greg, this was a dream come true. To make love to his childhood sweetheart after all these years.

He thought of the years he tried to imagine what it would be like had their lives been different and she did become his at twelve. He desperately wanted to explode and fill her with his love juices, but he wanted to give her all she could want and self-control was what he was good at.

She kept thinking: *How is this possible? How is he still going?*

This was nothing like she'd ever experienced, neither as a young woman so many years ago nor in all her married life. He didn't stop.

Her inhibitions left her totally somewhere during the night. She couldn't tell exactly when. All she knew was that this feeling was like nothing she had felt before. It was exultant. This is what she had heard and read about but never believed was possible and had certainly never experienced.

Pure sex. It seemed to express the intimacy yet had a light-hearted pleasure that redefined a real and clear sort of love. Not in a traditional sense, but more like a song or piece of music felt through a physical connection and rhythm. Combining all the different types of love into a moment.

Despite this, it all felt so raw, real, and amazing to Kara. This was sex as exciting, innocent, and pure as that first time they kissed after the school social. Physical intimacy was their connective tissue. It had just taken thirty-five years to get beyond second base! They liked each other, were attracted and held a bond of only seconds, but that moment from decades ago was unique to them alone.

Who cares if this only lasts for these moments or for longer? Do you really need anything more than the chance to feel this, even if just once in your life?

Her body yielded to him again, uncontrollably.

Right then, she was his priority. She felt as if she were a delicious taste that was being savoured. When he spoke to her, his tone and murmurs reflected the sheer pleasure of their bodies in discovery and then bonding every inch of their flesh.

Kara found her voice, despite having never uttered a word when having sex before. She moaned loudly, 'Oh my God, oh my God, oh my God.' Escalating and lost in his stimulating touch, she suddenly called out his name.

It was in that moment she felt Greg's whole body tighten and quiver, as his thrusts became even deeper and faster. And then she heard it. It was a sound so powerful and yet lyrical. It built in tone, volume, and strength and resonated through him. Even before she felt the hot, wet flow of his seed inside her, she felt the groan that seemed to grow from a breath building deep inside him. Nearly as if he was in pain, she could feel the sound that rose through his whole body, build, heighten, and escape in a long, deep, resounding moan. Kara felt and heard every part of his orgasm, given like a gift to her in a way that said, thank you. The sound penetrated her as deep as the throbbing flesh that pulsed inside her.

This was a sound that forged deep within, right to her heart, and she already knew she wanted to hear it over and over again. They spent the next few minutes comforted by the warmth of each other's bodies. Gentle caresses and soft kisses assisted in their return to the real world.

Greg and Kara somehow extracted themselves from each other, dressed, and headed off from the hotel to finally grab a meal. They walked to a nearby entertainment precinct and found an Asian restaurant offering a late sitting; in fact, it was the only place still open. With most patrons having left for the evening, it was quiet, and before long they had the place to themselves.

The conversation flowed, with Greg sharing a little more about his work, the sort of food they liked, which was similar really, and they joked about their annoyingly attentive waiter, hovering over their emptying plates, obviously keen to close up for the night.

They started back towards the hotel, walking hand in hand. Kara couldn't help but smile inwardly as she noted they were now holding hands for the second time that day, which was sweet and yet oddly out of sequence, especially after a couple of hours of hot, amazing sex.

Back in the hotel, Greg turned the music on. The moments after entering the room became a blur again for Kara, until they were both naked, hard, wet, and feeling every inch of each other's bodies again.

Their lovemaking was broken intermittently by lying naked on the bed, chatting quietly, and finding out more and more about each other. There was still so much to discover—songs they loved, memories of school friends from years past, places they had each enjoyed, the best holidays, favourite pastimes, and mostly retracing their steps through the years. Greg told Kara about his many attempts to look for her, and both shared their secret pleasure of how they eventually found each other.

'You know, I really have searched for you for years. Since our school days,' Greg said as his fingers stroked her cheek. Stopping, he cupped her face between his two hands, holding her gaze to his. 'That message you found, wasn't the first time. I looked for you often, especially at the reunion. I spent the night hoping you would be the next person to walk through those doors and…' His voice faded.

'And what?' Kara asked softly, her own hands now resting over his, her eyes wide in anticipation.

'And… I was hoping I would be the reason that you came.'

The words hit her like a slap. She'd never forgotten the panic and regret she felt about that night. From the day she received the invitation, she had planned to be there. Greg had secretly been the foremost thought in her mind. While admittedly only a curiosity, she had never forgotten him. She felt crushed as she realized how much he had hoped she would be there, and that he had no idea how hard she had worked to get there.

Kara had carefully mentioned it to her husband, describing it as a rare chance to catch up with old girlfriends. She had explained that it was just one night and made it sound like more of an obligation and no different to his old scholar college events. She'd even offered to arrange a babysitter if he had somewhere else to be. She kept gently and carefully reminding him to ensure she had clear passage to attend. How lame and stupid that seemed now, that she had needed permission. She finally got a green light and was so excited. As fate would have it, on the day before the reunion, her daughter succumbed to an ear infection. A sick little girl needed her mum. She couldn't attend. The memory cut into her.

Kara gripped his hands, pulling them down to hold them against her heart. 'Oh, Greg, I'm so sorry. I had arranged everything to be there, but my daughter got sick at the last minute. God, that sounds lame, but it's the truth.' She paused, then said, 'Maybe, just maybe, it was meant to be? It would never have been as exciting as this reunion right now.' She leaned forward and kissed him. His returned tender kisses told her he'd already forgiven her.

It was well after 1.00 a.m. when they both finally found sleep, knowing that Greg needed to be back on location before 7.00 a.m. Well, they at least tried to sleep. For Kara, just lying next to Greg was intoxicating and electrifying. Feeling the warmth of his body and the sound of him breathing next to her, as he drifted to sleep or tried to, she just wanted to keep touching his bare skin, savour the smell of him and to devour him. These feelings were inexplicably raw, uncontrollable, and overwhelmed her. Her body kept demanding more and more and wanted to give every part of herself to him.

She tried desperately not to allow their bodies to touch, as they both needed to sleep. She turned and laid on her side, faced away from him, so she could gently curl up next to him, barely touching. Greg rolled towards her, his arm reaching across her breasts, gently resting over her body to hold her. He wriggled closer and then breathed into a peaceful sleep. The feel of his leg nestled behind hers, the comfort of his cuddling arm, and his breath rhythmically whispering on her neck felt so good. She was in heaven in just that moment. Her hand rested on his thigh, gently caressing as they lay in this sleepy embrace.

It took only a moment before his steady breathing turned into kisses down her back. His fingers circled her nipples and then his palm shifted to cradle her breasts. Her breathing hitched as her arm reached behind her to stroke him.

They were both once again aroused. She turned to lie on her back, and he positioned himself above her, his body just inches from hers. This time, their connection was slow, tender, and deliberate. He moved gently, rubbing his penis along her labia, between her thighs, teasing her up and down. He stopped to enter her only enough that she could barely feel him inside her, before pulling back and looking into her eyes as if waiting for permission, then entering her ever so slightly again. All the while, their eyes were wide, locked, even more deeply connected than their bodies.

Kara writhed in expectation. He kept tempting her, denying her, and building her arousal all at the same time. She desperately wanted to feel all of his thick, pulsing flesh inside her again. But something urged her to hold him back. She needed him to know she wasn't afraid or as innocent as she might appear. She waited until she could feel the tip of him just touch between her legs again, then raised her open hand to his chest and pushed him gently, whispering, 'You can't come in yet. Just watch. Stay where you are. I'll tell you when.'

He moved back, a little surprised, and then watched as her left hand reached to slide down the length of his shaft. Then her fingers moved to her own lips, parting them wider. Moving her index finger of her right hand, she found her sweet spot and rubbed herself, firmly but slowly.

He watched as her eyes closed. Her finger circled faster, her breathing even deeper. Her hips rose, and he motioned to enter her fully, but she stopped him once again.

'No. No, not yet.' Her voice was deep and hushed. He held his position, his arms trembling to hold himself above her, watching her. He wanted to have her desperately. After some minutes, just when he thought he could wait no more, her eyes opened and locked with his. She just called out, 'Now. Oh, now!'

'God…!' He didn't need to hear it again. She took every inch of his penetrating force in one huge jolt. Her hips rose to meet him, begging for more at each thrust and then holding at that pause of suspension before a crescendo. Both of their bodies shuddered tumultuously. Each of them cried out, letting orgasmic moans escape in unison. Neither could distinguish who owned the sounds this time.

By morning—or rather, only a couple of hours later, Kara slipped quietly out of bed, not wanting to make him late for work, knowing that she was painstakingly slow in the morning getting ready. She headed to the bathroom, but not before stopping to look at the sleeping man she had kissed so many years ago. Smiling to herself, secretly praising the little girl inside for that bold kiss, all those decades ago.

What a reunion this turned out to be.

Chapter 7

*L*ittle did she realise, she had missed the opportunity of experiencing the most heightened lovemaking of all with Mr Sheppard, having unknowingly denied him the pleasure of his favourite 'morning after sex'.

Well… at least on this occasion.

She spent the day at work with Greg at the Convention Centre. The film set for the commercial was so much fun and just added to the total escape for Kara. Greg had been concerned it might bore her, as there was always lots of sitting around; however, he noticed that she seemed quite at ease, wandering around the whole complex, chatting to members of the crew, asking questions, watching and taking it all in. By the time they struck the set and loaded the vans for a quick departure, Kara could easily have been mistaken for being part of the crew herself, lugging boxes, winding cords, and joking with them all as they packed in readiness to head off to the next event.

It was close to 6.00 p.m. Greg had been busy for the last couple of hours, checking that all the equipment was loaded, the return delivery schedules were correct, and bidding farewell to the director and other *'suits'* that were still there wanting to speak with him. Kara had just enjoyed being able to help quietly in the background. She checked her watch. *Damn! Time to go.*

Kara's bag was in the production caravan, and she made a dash to get it before she booked a cab and said goodbye. This was the part of the day she was dreading.

Greg saw Kara standing in the caravan's doorway, her bag and leather jacket in hand. Something in that moment told him he couldn't let her go just yet.

People rarely surprised him, but Kara was not quite what he had expected. She had arrived dressed in nothing overtly sexy or suggestive. She seemed rather shy and yet subtly exuded the shared excitement of their meeting. Greg had sensed a slight nervousness and wasn't totally sure she would even dare enter his hotel room, given her life story and having spent so long on her own. He met the Kara he had predicted, at first. Yet he'd not expected how openly and confidently she engaged with his team and was keen to learn about the many facets of his work.

He honestly thought in respect of how long she'd been alone and from their chats on the phone, that he would need to carefully initiate any advance. But from the second she removed her shirt, she had transformed. Bold, lustful, and wanting, she had initiated, responded, and was near insatiable, loving his every touch and wanting to give him pleasure.

This woman was not like anyone he had encountered, and he could sense there was much more to discover.

He dashed up to her. 'Is it that time already?'

'Yes, sadly it is,' said Kara with a gentle smile.

He took her bag and jacket from her and placed them on the ground before turning her around. Taking her by the hand, he led her back inside the caravan, closed the door and pulled her into his arms.

'Please take a later flight, Kara. Wait and fly home with me.'

Kara dared not look at him, or else she couldn't resist. 'But I've already got a booking…'

Greg just smiled. 'Leave that to me to sort out. Please, just say yes.'

'Okay, yes.'

Seated together on the plane, their thoughts spoke volumes, but outwardly they were quiet. They were both tired. They sat as close as they could be, Kara pensively resting her head on the side of his shoulder for most of the trip while Greg casually brushed her cheek, rested his hand on her leg, or just held her hand. Neither wanted their connection to be broken. As they got closer to home, the evening somehow became engulfed by that dreaded, 'Sunday night feeling,' the reality that, 'everything Monday' was looming. Their landing was the reminder that the end of their time together was imminent.

Back in Adelaide, there was no real discussion about it; they just knew there was now only a bit more time left together before goodbye. They found their bags on the carousel and walked outside, hand in hand, shoulder to shoulder. They casually jumped into a cab, and when Greg gave the instructions to his address, Kara uttered no protest. She didn't really want her time with him to end.

They spoke little more than their gasps or moans of pleasure that night. They conversed in tenderness, lust, and the touch of their bodies. Kara couldn't describe it, and no one would really understand or realise the true effect of this connection on her—or Greg, it was emotional. Passionate. Intimate. The sex was urgent and powerful, their bodies connecting as if in fear that either of them might disappear at any moment, yet it was sensitive, gentle, sensuous lovemaking all at the same time. They were both lost and found. They were technically strangers to each other who held a foreign yet simultaneously intimate understanding of each other, whose combined flavour was more delicious and beyond what they had originally thought their meeting could ever possibly be.

For both of them, it was a subconscious, genuine, and unique form of attraction, expressed through such intense sex and the touch of each other that really could not be described. As they both later found, this whole serendipitous time spent together was for the two of them, the first spark towards ignition. But of what exactly?

Neither of them had any idea what they had started.

It was hard for Kara to say goodbye, but it had all happened so casually. On the surface, both had made everything feel accepting and strangely normal. Greg had made her coffee, and they sat together chatting about what they each needed to do that day. Kara had dressed, gathered her things, and despite his offer to drive, at her insistence, he reluctantly booked a cab to collect her and take her to her aunt's unit. Their goodbye was simple—a kiss, an embrace, and a thank you, with their eyes and gentle smiles towards each other saying everything else. Without them even realising, it was another simple kiss in a driveway, some thirty-five years since the first.

Monday at 7.30 a.m., Kara arrived at her aunt's in a cab. She fumbled for her keys, opened the door, and entered the unit quietly. *I hope Aunt Sarah is still asleep.* Kara wanted to just slip upstairs, shower, change into her work clothes, and sneak out again, avoiding too many probing questions. She dared not speak to anyone yet, for fear of interrupting or breaking her replay of every second of this past weekend. For once, as was her wish, Kara could regroup, pack the car, and head off to her workday uninterrupted.

Greg was back at his townhouse feeling unusually unsettled. This was only ever intended to be a casual, fun weekend with a long-lost girl from years past. He'd spent a number of similar lustful weekends with interesting women during his life, each connecting in some special way associated with his work or interests, mostly opportunistic hook-ups because of a life that was, for the most part, transient.

However, the meeting and time spent with this woman somehow stirred some most unexpected thoughts and feelings. Kara wasn't a breathtaking beauty. She was attractive but not in a way you could pinpoint. More likened to a woman in her early thirties, her body was amazing—slim, gently muscular, and with gorgeous breasts. She exuded a sexual aura, but she seemed oblivious to it. Perhaps it was this sheer naivety that spoke to him, an unusual combination of intelligence yet innocence, a sense of sexy fun mixed with an awkward nervousness that spoke through her big brown eyes. Her strength was unusual, not only in character but through their intimacy. She had ignited sexually in response to his every touch. Greg resolved that his lingering attraction was most likely due to the fact their hook-up had happened so unexpectedly. That the anticipation and build-up to a full-on weekend of great sex and company had added to the experience and overwhelmed him. Yet, he was sure there was much more to her.

His ringing phone startled him from his thoughts of Kara. At seeing Tess's name, a wave of guilt fluttered over him. He took a deep breath and released it. *It's done now. You found her, you had fun, and it's over. Tess really is the woman for you.* With that thought, he swiped his phone to answer. 'Hello, babe.'

Kara had driven the nearly two hours to Clare, getting to work in a delightful euphoric daze, and daydreamed through her first meeting of the day, trying desperately to concentrate on the discussion.

'You're all set for the project briefing and presentation in Melbourne on the 24th, aren't you, Kara?'

'Oh. What's that? Oh, yes, of course,' she replied to Lainie, her regional director. Feeling somewhat guilty for her total disengagement throughout the past three hours, she exited the conference room and headed back to her office. After closing the door, she dropped into her chair and searched for her phone.

Her mind had been focussed on just one thing since she had arrived at work. There was so much to thank him for. It was nearly an hour later before she hit send. For some reason, finding the words and the best way to describe her feelings about the past weekend and her gratitude were unusually hard to compose. Eventually, she sent a rather long email.

From: Kara Gilbert <karaG@bmail.com>
To: Greg Sheppard <Greg@PrecisionEvents.com.au>
Subject: Thank you

Dear Greg,

I don't have the words to express how much I enjoyed our 'reunion.' Wow! My only regret is that it has taken so long for us to meet again. What I could not have ever known at the time, but I know now, is t THAT KISS was not only the first, but the most important of my life. It brought you back into my life, especially at a time when I only now realise, that I needed someone most. You have given me more 'first time' memorable experiences and feelings than you will ever know. You will not only hold a special place in my heart, but you are now its hero. Thank you for rescuing the buried glow, passion, and feelings in me. You have awoken me, and I am not scared anymore to be intimate with someone. I am even starting to think it may be possible to find love again someday. Maybe.

You were so kind, generous, and such a gentleman throughout the entire trip, and I hope you already know how much I enjoyed your body! Please know you are most welcome to call in and say hi and share a meal with me anytime you might wander into Clare again someday. I loved getting a chance to glimpse into your world of work, and it was such a pleasure to experience your success and expertise firsthand. Thank you so much for persevering to find me and for our time together. Friends for life, and I remain a new, but lifelong fan.

Yours,

Kara xx

It was well after lunch when Greg had received Kara's email. He responded immediately.

From: Greg Sheppard <Greg@PrecisionEvents.com.au>
To: Kara Gilbert <karaG@bmail.com>
Subject: Re: Thank you

My dear Kara, to spend the weekend and be intimate with such an important person in my life is truly a dream come true. I could never have dreamt how amazing it could be. While we were making love or even just when we were talking, I had to pinch myself that I was finally with the girl who had been in my thoughts for so many years. Thank you for trusting me and spending the money to enable us to get together, as I

know it cost quite a lot. But most of all, thank you for thirty-five years ago, making this one little boy—the happiest boy in the world. You will be forever in my heart.
Love, Greg.

So ended their reunion week. Greg had given her a gift. It was the last piece of the jigsaw.

Chapter 8

It was a week later, and Kara couldn't resist sending Greg a text to say thank you once again and how much she owed him for giving her such a wonderful weekend in Sydney. There was no reply. While a little disappointed, she had not forgotten their initial conversations and knew full well that her sudden appearance on the scene was really no more than an unexpected and fun distraction for Greg. He told her openly that he was embarking on a committed relationship with a woman named Tess.

'This was the best and most unexpected gift, Kara. Don't spoil it. Let him go,' she told herself.

Another two weeks later, Kara landed in Melbourne at the Marriott Hotel. She was making final preparations for a presentation about South Australia's community development initiatives. The presentation would take place in the ballroom at Crown Plaza the next night. She'd spent the morning with her team going through the final details, then was free for the rest of the day to wander Melbourne. She loved this city and having time to meander along the Southbank and through the arcades in the shopping precinct. She'd arranged a catch up with some friends who were coming to meet her in the hotel lobby around seven that evening, to first take her to a cool new underground bar and then to dine at their favourite restaurant.

Dressed and ready by 6.00 p.m., she headed to the bar to enjoy a quiet wine while waiting. Suddenly her phone rang. It was Greg. 'Hello.'

Kara gulped and quickly regrouped. 'Hi there. How have you been? This is a nice surprise. To what do I owe the pleasure?'

'Well… It's been a busy week, but tell me, how are you?'

'I'm fine, thanks. Well, I'm a bit nervous to tell the truth. Tonight's fine. I'm about to go out for dinner with some friends. More worried about tomorrow though. I'm not as prepared as I'd like to be. I've got to give a presentation at an event tomorrow night, in Melbourne actually. What's going on with you?'

'Oh, sounds like you're busy. I'm sorry, I really don't need to burden you with this, but, well…'

He paused, and Kara could sense by his tone he was uneasy and somewhat agitated…

'Hey there, what's up? Is everything all right?'

'Well, you know how my life has taken me everywhere around the country and the world, really?'

'Yes. Of course.'

'So, being on my own for a time and being on the road so much, I've often had times to meet and connect with a few nice ladies.'

'Yes, well, that's understandable. You seem to be on the road all the time,' Kara said, suddenly realising the full meaning behind what he was saying. He had enjoyed other similar 'distractions' like her, it seemed. Her mind was racing, not sure of what to say.

Eventually, she asked quietly, 'So, are you telling me you have several ladies with whom you sleep with in every place you go?'

'No! Not everywhere. I do some events at the same place each year and over time, I have made some closer friendships with people who I've met up with, whenever I visit their city or town. Yes, sure, I've enjoyed the company of some special women, but only while I'm there. There are one or two who sometimes have travelled to see me at other nearby events, so I saw them more often, but mostly I saw each of them only once a year. But not much recently, since I've spent most of my time with Tess.'

Kara had listened intently. This was unexpected, but also not. *He's telling me the truth. Respect it. As much as you'd like it to be, the two of you are not committed to each other.* She breathed in. *Don't overreact, Kara.*

'So, thanks for telling me. Is everything else, okay? You sound worried about something.'

'So, you're not shocked? You're not upset about all of that? I just want to be honest.'

'Shocked? Well, maybe a little, but no, not actually. I'm just not sure why you thought you needed to tell me all of this though. You were clear from the start that my contact with you was completely 'out of the blue' and things have got more serious with Tess. That our meeting was, in fact… what did you call it? Oh, that's it, "a most exciting distraction." So, while I would love to see and enjoy more of you, apart from that, your life is your business. But thanks, I appreciate you being so honest with me,' she said still not understanding why he needed to tell her.

Greg was quiet for a moment, leaving Kara to wonder if there was something else behind that pause. 'So, is there something else? Why did you call me, Greg?'

'Okay, well, I'm in a bit of a delicate spot, and it sort of involves you. One woman I have seen each year for the last few years in Sydney has got upset with me. Really angry, in fact. A few months ago, I told her I had become involved with Tess and it wouldn't feel right if I saw her intimately anymore. Initially, she was cool with that.'

Greg kept talking, now at a faster pace. 'She knew I'd be in Sydney this past month but had been resigned to the fact that we wouldn't catch up in the same way we did before. But she was working at the Convention Centre event and saw you there with me. She has since messaged me a few times and she's threatening to whip up a bit of trouble for me here at work, not ideal, but I can deal with that. I wanted to let you know because she obviously went digging and found out who you are and has threatened to call you. She can be very vindictive, and I would hate if she caused you any trouble.'

Kara stopped and thought again for a moment before responding.

She took a deep breath and then said, 'Look, first thing, please don't worry about me. You know we aren't meant to be anything beyond reunited friends. I'm fine. You can tell her and Tess whatever you need to about me. Don't stress. I'm cool, and we aren't necessarily ever going to see each other—well, not in the same way, anyway. You've been so open about your life with Tess. I get that.'

'Thank you. You are so sweet. I've been worried about what this might do to you and—' He paused '—er... Tess. Tess knows about the other partners I've had, as naturally, that's something that has happened a bit in both of our lives, but we have also been careful not to give each other that much detail about our separate encounters in recent times. As we've only just talked about wanting to spend more time together, she won't understand and will be extremely hurt hearing from a former lover and our recent reunion from someone else. She needs to hear about us meeting up—from me. I don't want to cause that grief for her or anyone. I'm also genuinely sorry for getting you caught up in this mess.'

Kara's heart skipped a beat, but she knew that was her own feelings reacting. He had enough to deal with right now.

'Greg, don't be worried. It's okay. This past girlfriend or acquaintance—or whatever you call her—clearly loves spending time with you and doesn't want to lose you. She won't risk never having contact with you. Maybe she'll calm down if you tell her what she really wants to hear: That you will really miss her. That she'll always have a special place in your heart and memories. You can be honest about me in that we are long-lost school friends who have only just stumbled across each other, and it was genuinely unexpected, and that I was just finding out about your world and work life. That your life is and will be with Tess now and you've told me the same thing.'

'I hope you're right. Thanks so much for understanding. I feel bad. I shouldn't even be talking to you about this, especially about other women, after just spending a special first time with you.'

'Well, it's a bit out there perhaps, but I'm quickly realising I can never predict what life will throw at us!' Kara said.

'You really are a sweetheart. Oh, and good luck with your speech tomorrow night. Hey, why not call me and let me know how it goes after the dinner?'

'Thanks. I might just do that. It'll likely be too late to call you afterwards though, 'cause if I get through it, I could be taking advantage of some party time!'

'Fair enough. Seriously, you can text me, and if I'm still awake, I'll give you a call. I would love to hear about it. Besides, it's the least I can do.'

'Thank you, Greg. I'll see. Hey, look, I'm sorry but my friends are here to take me to dinner, so I'd better go now. In the meantime, just chill and take care.'

Kara had little time to reflect on the call or even think about the events surrounding Greg. Her dinner that evening was fun and ended up being a late night. The next morning, she allowed herself the luxury of a bit of a sleep-in before the day charged into leading a workshop session, a day full of meeting and greeting delegates, making final touches and rehearsal of her speech, setup of the presentation equipment, and finally getting to her room to dress for the conference dinner. Just as she gathered her bag and notes and approached the door, her phone pinged. It was Aunt Sarah.

> Good luck for tonight, darling. Hope it goes well. I'll be thinking of you.

She hurried a thank you response and said she would call in the morning. Just as she was turning the phone settings to vibrate, her phone buzzed with another message. This one was unexpected. It was from Greg.

> You'll be great tonight. Thanks again for yesterday.

Kara paused for a moment. No. No response needed this time, Kara. She just smiled and headed out the door.

It was almost 1.30 a.m. by the time Kara eventually got back to her room. The evening had been full-on but hugely successful. Despite feeling rather drunk from a number of champagnes, the long day and the spirit of the night after her presentation left her still feeling wide awake. Kara proceeded to the bathroom, removed her makeup, and undressed. After wandering aimlessly around her hotel room, she sat on the bed, stacked the pillows for a backrest and checked her emails and Facebook. She was feeling restless and still running high on adrenalin from the day.

Perhaps I should get dressed again and head downstairs to one of the casino bars? You never know who you might meet. Oh, don't be silly, Kara. Just get into bed. It's been a huge day.

She then remembered yesterday, her eyes turning away from her phone to the blank wall as images of Greg filled her mind's eye. *Should I?* Without even thinking of the time, she grabbed her phone.

> Hi, Greg. You were right, it was a great night, and I'm still buzzing to be honest.

Within a minute, the phone rang.

'Hello, sexy. So, tell me about your night. Did it all go as planned?'

'Hi there. It was great, couldn't have gone better! Sorry to message you so late. I sort of just wanted to tell someone. Anyway, what are you doing up so late, or did I wake you?'

'Couldn't sleep. I was thinking about you… and maybe a bit of work.'

Kara started laughing. 'You have so not been thinking about me!'

He joined in her laugh. 'Okay, well, I am now. Hey, it's nearly 2.00 a.m.! You must be tired. Are you in bed now?'

'Yes, sort of. I'm lying on top of the bed. I was trying to decide whether to go downstairs and have a last drink, and then I got to thinking about you. Oops, sorry, I shouldn't have told you that.'

'And what made you think about me?'

'I was wondering how you got on with your post-Sydney drama? I hope everything has settled down.'

'I called her after we spoke, and she was much calmer. You were so right. She just needed to hear from me. I spoke with Tess too. She knew about her from before, but we talked this through. I also told her about you and I'd finally made contact and met up for an evening together. While I knew she was hurt and upset, she said she understood, especially always knowing I've been searching for my "first kiss girl."'

'I'm so relieved for you all. It must've been hard to tell Tess. I'm pleased you did, and all is okay. She's clearly a very special lady. I'm sorry. I really have been a complication you didn't need, haven't I?'

'Don't be silly! You don't need to apologise. I'm not doing anything I don't want to. Like now, I'm lying here enjoying a nice glass of Mudgee Shiraz and talking to you.'

Kara's body twitched. 'I've already had plenty to drink tonight, but if you want to chat for a while, I was thinking about a nightcap. Wait, there's a little bottle of Shiraz in the minibar,' Kara said, standing up.

'I have all night, so grab a drink. Do you have a nice room?' Greg asked.

'Yes, a suite. They've spoilt me. I'll send you a picture once I get a glass of wine.'

Greg checked his phone and looked at Kara's pic. He could see her legs, feet, and toes lying on the bed and the view of her room, which was a beautifully appointed suite.

'Nice room there. A lot better than mine.'

'Oh, come on… I've shown you mine; you show me yours.'

Greg sent his picture.

'Can you see my glass of wine?'

Kara looked and smiled instantly. He'd obviously snapped himself using the reflection from the mirrored robes. She could see Greg, his head resting on the bedhead, half sitting up and lying back on his bed. He was fully naked, the faint light from the lamp on the bedside table casting a golden glow across the hotel room. He was smiling, holding up his wine in one hand and the phone in the other. His legs were relaxed, gently lying apart.

Kara did notice the glass of wine in his hand; however, her eyes kept moving between the image of his smiling face to the rest of his naked body, which clearly showed that taking a naked picture of himself may got him a little aroused. He looked so relaxed, inviting, and totally hot. Kara badly wanted to be lying right there next to him.

Instantly, her face flushed, followed by the radiant warmth inside her that only he seemed to create.

'You are so naughty!' she said with a giggle.

'Why?' he said cheekily. 'Well, you make me feel a bit naughty, Kara. Besides, there's something about being on your own in a hotel room, lying naked and talking to a hot lady that makes a person quite aroused, don't you think?'

'Yes! I know what you mean. Something about a hotel room does always makes me feel rather naughty.'

'Are you feeling naughty now?' he asked.

'Let me see?' She said in a quizzical tone. 'I'm lying here almost naked, half drunk, a glass of wine in my hand, staring at a photo of a naked man, and talking to the best lover I have ever had… nah, not at all!'

Greg smiled. 'You've got me quite aroused now.'

The champagne, the successful day, and the image of Greg lying alone on a hotel bed combined with the allure of his voice, was all it took.

Suddenly, a bold Kara just blurted out, 'Is that so? Can I see how much?'

Greg was taken aback. Cautiously, he said, 'Sure, if you would like?'

'Yes.' Her tone matched the sensations rapidly stirring inside her.

'Okay, hold on a minute.'

Ping! The next image arrived. Oh my God! He wasn't joking about getting aroused.

Propped up against the pillows, he was naked and outstretched on his bed. He was now fully erect, and the image was so clear and close, she could see the veins bulging up and down his shaft. She had never seen a close-up photo of any man before. Not like this. She smiled as her body tingled.

'Oh my God, that's huge! You weren't joking about being aroused, were you?'

'Like what you see? Is it making you wet, Kara?'

'Yes...' She gulped. 'Very.'

'Have you felt it, or do you just think you are?'

'Oh, I'm feeling it.'

She paused. 'Hey... what are we doing? We shouldn't be doing this. Should we?' The words were right, but her tone gave her away. Her body wanted more.

'Probably not, but... I already feel like I'm there with you. Would you like to hear what I'd do to you if I was really there?'

She didn't hesitate in her reply. 'Yes, I'd like that.' Greg's calm, sultry voice purred in her ear.

'So, imagine the lights are out, just lighting from the streetlights through the window. I'm kneeling with one leg between yours, my hands are feeling across your breasts, brushing across your nipples;

they are erect and hard. My hands are gliding over your stomach and then drifting slowly up and down your legs…'

Kara could barely let more than a gasp escape, so heavy was her breathing now. Her body quivered as her fingers softly rubbed herself. She listened intently; he was already there, right above her.

'My hands slide up your leg, up and down, over and over. I let my fingers edge closer to your wetness each time. I find you. You are so swollen and wet. I slip my fingers inside you. Oh God, you are so hot. I love how warm and moist you are. My hard-on is touching your thigh; it's pressing against you. I feel you spread your legs further, inviting me to have more of you. I want to be inside you. Do you want me?'

'Yes,' she murmured.

'I'm only just inside you. Can you feel me slip in and out of you again and again? I'm just teasing you; I'm not letting you feel all of me yet. I'm just edged into you… Can you feel how hard I am?'

'Yes. I can feel you.' She let two of her fingers push inside her.

'God, I can feel you. I'm pushing deep inside you now. God, you feel so good. You are so wet and tight around me. I'm pushing into you deeper and deeper as you rub yourself. I love seeing you touch yourself.' Hearing her breathing deep and fast, Greg asked, 'Are you close?'

'Yes.' She could barely gasp her reply. 'I want you. I'm going to come; I want to hear you explode in me.' Then she heard that deep, guttural, orgasmic moan resounding in her ear. He had come vibrantly.

Kara's body shuddered uncontrollably, the phone falling from her hand as she grabbed for her breast while keeping two fingers from the other hand pushing firmly inside her, moving in that beckoning motion on her G-spot until she could take no more. A cry escaped her as that rush of turbulent heat radiated from her core, making every muscle clench and pulse.

Kara lay there panting as she groped for the phone but could not speak. The exchange of deep breaths was all that they shared through the phone for the next minute.

After what seemed like ages, it was Kara who finally murmured, 'Well, so that's what phone sex is? Wow, another first for me!' She giggled. 'Hey, thank you. I really am so pleased you called.'

'It was my absolute pleasure, Kara. Thank you once again. Sweet dreams.'

She could barely whisper a soft, 'Goodnight Greg,' before ending the call.

Kara fell asleep almost instantly. Greg Sheppard filled her dreams that night.

Chapter 9

Now a month since her secret escape to meet Greg, there hadn't been a day that passed without a mental replay of their weekend together, especially after their little Melbourne phone encounter. Despite this, she had returned to her usual regime of walking, working, gardening, and keeping in touch with her friends. Outwardly, she perhaps smiled a bit more, and her clothes were new and a touch more revealing. She walked with a more confident step, and to others around her, Kara appeared different, younger and glowing.

Inwardly, the Kara who returned from Melbourne had a vibrancy that radiated throughout her body. Seduction, sex, and the effect of Greg looked and felt good on her. It was indescribable. She felt horny all the time. All the time. Try as she might, she couldn't stop thinking about him or her own sexual needs and wants. Feelings she had suppressed and denied were thundering inside her. She was a mess.

Later, it would be easier for Kara to understand more about why she reacted the way she did post Sydney and Melbourne.

At that time, if Kara had considered the whole event in the usual objective, analytical, and reasonable style that she'd always applied in her life and her work, she may have recognised that she was experiencing the usual chemical and emotional imbalance normally reserved for adolescents after their first heightened sexual experience.

Kara had been physically, chemically and emotionally catapulted through decades in only a couple of weeks. From a casual reconnection with a lost friend and sweet first love, she had been instantly jolted into the reality of exhilarating intimacy that was real, raw, romantic, and orgasmic. Kara Gilbert had been picked up as a mature woman and dropped 'heart first' back into the stages of innocence usually reserved for young love and first heartaches. She was 'crushing and lusting' all over the place! It was no wonder that she would check her phone, looking for messages, or find photos of Greg on the internet and stare longingly at them each day. She read and reread messages they had exchanged and daydreamed about their time together. Kara now longed to reach the end of each day, lay in her bed, touch herself, and sleep, escaping into her dreams filled with romantic and erotic fantasy.

She had resisted the daily temptation to message him after her return home from Melbourne, especially knowing that she had no business in his life. He had enough complications without her. It was best she kept right away.

Lamely, she attempted to regroup. Kara had vowed never to contact him again, repeatedly reminding herself that this was only ever intended to be a casual encounter. Her head kept saying she was simply so grateful they had found each other and enjoyed a sexy, fun reunion. She could handle this; she was cool. But she wasn't. Not at all. She wanted him so badly. He had unexpectedly and profoundly touched a hidden part of her.

Maybe just one more time?

She'd been having such erotic dreams featuring Greg. She would find herself jolted awake during the night, dripping in sweat, panting hard and shaking all over from her fantasy encounters with him. So arousing and vivid, she was shocked to find herself drenched between her legs.

'My God! Surely, I didn't. This must stop, Kara,' she told herself. She knew she had to see him just one more time, feel him fill her body just once more.

It must be the last time. It had to be. She messaged him.

> Hi, Greg. Sorry for the message, but I wanted to thank you. Since my first taste of phone sex, I can think of nothing else and would love the opportunity to tell you a story. I need to return the favour.

Greg had half expected her to contact him. He secretly had also tried to deny that he hoped she would.

> That sounds great, Kara. How about tonight? I'll grab a wine, relax on my bed, and you can share your story.

> Great, how about nine o'clock?

> Hear from you then x

Kara called at 9.00 p.m. on the dot. 'Hi, Greg, I'm a little embarrassed now. Are you sure you want to hear this?'

'Don't be,' he said. 'I'm looking forward to hearing what you have imagined. My wine and I are ready. I'm lying on my bed, the lights are dimmed, and I'm all yours.'

Kara drew in a deep breath. She wanted this call to be as perfect as possible. 'Okay, here we go!'

'You're sitting on the lounge naked, resting back, your eyes closed, and you're just relaxing. I've taken a liqueur bottle, it's Kahlua, and I quietly kneel in front of you. I open the bottle and rest it on the floor next to me. I move in closer towards you, gently wriggling to position myself to kneel between your legs.'

She paused, her next words slowing, and her tone deepened. She wanted each word to infuse through the phone to him, in the way the liqueur and the scene inside her was warming and arousing her.

'Keep your eyes closed. Both of my hands gently caress you up and down the inside of your thighs as I run my tongue over your penis. I keep doing this over and over. I'm not stopping until you are standing erect and hard.

'Are you getting hard?' she asked softly.

'Yes, very,' was all he could murmur.

'The liqueur bottle is now in my hand. I take a small mouthful and roll it around in my mouth until I feel it warm the soft velvety liquid. I'm leaning forward and let the liqueur drizzle from my lips and over you. It runs in the fold of your groin. Your body is shivering from both the sudden feel of the warm liquid on your flesh and the unexpected delight of it.' She paused, allowing him to soak up her words. 'I'm starting to lick and suck up the liqueur. My lips and tongue are again all over you, tasting you everywhere. I take all of you into my mouth and start to suck harder and faster. You taste delicious. I'm drinking you into me. The liqueur is sweet, and you feel so warm. You are a cocktail like no other. I want to taste every drop. I want you to come, come in my mouth.'

Kara had shed any thought of embarrassment. She was lost in her fantasy of his liqueur-coated penis in her mouth and savouring him.

She heard him erupt.

His rasping reply was simple and clear. 'Oh God! I want that for real, Kara!'

In the afterglow of their phone sex, they spoke for ages. Despite what they both knew should not happen, a 'one last time' meeting was arranged.

Greg was leaving for a holiday overseas on a well-deserved break, and Tess would accompany him. On their return, he was moving to base himself at Tess's townhouse so they could spend more time together and officially become a couple. Kara suspected it would be their last chance to make love or to connect in any intimate way.

Kara knew she would have to let him go.

They'd arranged to meet at the Hilton Hotel in Victoria Square on Friday night at 7.00 p.m. Kara set about planning a simple but lovely romantic and sexy evening. If this was to be the last time, it needed to be memorable—sophisticated, elegant, and yet still as sweet as their first kiss. A suite at the Hilton, Sparkling Shiraz on ice, for starters, his favourite Barossa red wine and soft romantic music playing. She organised dinner to be brought to their room to keep their meeting intimate and private, but also giving more time to make this a memorable last physical connection between the two of them. She wanted to tantalise him with a reference to the Kahlua story, but she secretly hoped that they would spend most of their time making love, kissing, cuddling, caressing, and talking for hours. She knew this will be bittersweet though; butterflies with knife sharp wings fluttered in her stomach, reminding her this would be the end. This would be her last night with the man who found her, ignited her, and made her become a renewed, sexy and confident woman.

The old Kara was gone. The new Kara had arrived thanks to one night with Greg Sheppard. But after tonight, he would be gone again to another woman's arms. A woman he loved and allowed to share the rest of her life with him.

She wanted to enjoy him, of course, but even more to thank him and say goodbye in a way that was as memorable as how they first met, all those decades ago.

'Is this really a good idea?' she asked herself. Her thoughts kept somersaulting. She knew her heart was on a precipice. At the moment it was just lust and the uncontrollable need for sex with this beautiful man. *What if she fell in love? What then? But, how would she really know, if she did? What did true love feel like anyway? Or was it already too late?*

Thoughts of tonight's evening with Kara kept flicking into Greg's thoughts all day, sending bursts of excitement through him. He really liked her, and she held a strange connection to his heart from the past. She held that same refreshing fascination that came with each new woman he had encountered over the years.

However, this time he was uncharacteristically uneasy. There was something so differently intoxicating about this woman. She seemed to think like he did. She was sensitive, yet strong and genuinely and enthusiastically interested in what he did beyond just their sexual connection. Her easy and enjoyable company somehow resonated.

He had expected the rush of messages that he received from her after their first meeting, as was the usual response after any time he'd slept with a woman. He was highly sensitive to the knowledge that Kara would possibly become attached to him initially, as there were so many profound 'firsts' for her—the first time someone had sought her out as a woman for years; her first sexual encounter since her marriage ended some years ago and her first taste of a world that was such a contrast to her relatively insular country life.

What he had not expected was what seemed an insatiable love of sex and how it had been trapped and locked away inside her for so long.

It was like the woman on the outside had buried the true woman within.

Kara Gilbert had emerged since they had connected. She'd become stronger, even without her knowledge. She had a hidden powerful desire, lust, and an insatiable appetite for much more than what her outward demeanour portrayed. He found her attractive and intriguing in a way he had not felt before. But he knew that it had to end before hearts were broken.

What are you doing? You're leaving in a week on a holiday with Tess, for God's sake! He had a plan for the new chapter in his life, and he had just decided to make a special commitment to Tess, the woman he believed he genuinely loved.

'No more distractions after tonight for you, Mr Sheppard!' he told himself sternly. But as he'd always done with his work, he committed 100 percent to what was in front of him and gave it his all.

This evening would be all for Kara, for one last time.

Chapter 10

Greg opened the door of room 812 at the Hilton. Kara was sitting on the end of the bed, wearing a simple white satin slip dress, her legs crossed, a glass of sparkling Shiraz in hand. She gave him a smile that took his breath away.

She stood as he approached and whispered, 'Hello.' Their lips met for a greeting kiss. 'Let me get you a drink.' Kara's voice was soft and mellow, matching the background music. She handed him the menu for dinner.

'If we order now, we might have dinner at about eight thirty, if that's okay?'

'Sounds perfect.' Raising his glass, he chinked it to hers, his gaze remaining completely fixed on her since entering the room. 'You look beautiful, Kara.'

Kara's eyes widened, and a blush rose in her cheeks. Her eyes darted away ever so briefly. Such a simple statement, but Kara couldn't remember anyone ever saying that to her. Her heart beat increased slightly making her thoughts falter for a second. *Oh my God… I never want tonight to end… and its only just started.*

'Um, how about we try the mushroom arancini and the pork belly for the main?' she suggested, changing the subject.

'That sounds delicious.'

As she turned and moved to the phone to dial for room service, she breathed in deeply, attempting to gather herself.

With their meal ordered, and her breathing and heart somewhat now settled, she lifted her head and turned to stand close in front of him. Without a word, she led him to sit on the bed. Starting at his feet, she removed his shoes, socks. working her way, up his body, slowly and carefully removing his pants and the rest of his clothes. She didn't speak until his last article of clothing hit the floor.

'I'm sorry, Greg, you won't get to taste Kahlua tonight—only me,' she whispered in his ear as she gently pushed him back to lie on the bed. His body twitched as he looked up at her and smiled.

Her eyes were glistening.

Greg Sheppard was a beautiful man. Lying there in front of her, his outstretched body naked and relaxed, he was breathtakingly proportioned, toned, and tanned. His body begged for her to reach out and touch it, tempting her fingers to stroke every dark hair on his body. She dared not look too long for fear of changing her plan. She only wanted to look just enough to commit this moment as a long-lasting memory.

Kara climbed onto the bed, positioning herself to kneel between his legs. She reached for the body oil on the bedside table and put a generous amount of the silky oil over her fingers. Leaning down, she started at his ankles and slid her fingers ever so slowly up the inside of his calf, over his knees, and up to the delicate inner skin of his thigh. As her fingers reached the top of his thighs, she allowed their tips to trace along the crease of his groin, below his balls, and rim around deep between his cheeks. His body twitched slightly as a small gasp escaped him. Before he could respond further, she gently bit the inside of each of his legs then kissed a trail up his body, grazing her lips up his thighs, over his groin and to his stomach. Her erect nipples brushed over him as she slipped up his body.

Kissing him softly on the neck below his chin, she moved to sit astride him. 'This is all about you tonight. Savour every taste and touch. Breathe it all in,' she whispered in his ear.

Greg let out a sigh, and a wry smile appeared as his whole body relaxed a little more.

Gliding back down his body, Kara knelt between his legs to kiss his shaft. She alternated between sucking and licking, allowing her tongue to trace the tip before taking him into her mouth completely. Drawing him down her throat, as deeply as it could go, she tasted. Up and down, she firmly repeated the motion, taking her time, enjoying her ministrations. When his breathing deepened, showing he was close, she stopped. Wanting to tease him and draw out his pleasure, she slid down his body and knelt at his feet once more. Starting the whole sequence again, massaged up from his ankles, over his calves to the inside of his thighs, her mouth trailing kisses, licks, and love bites as she went. Arriving at his groin, she drew him again deep into her mouth, sucking up and down a few times before continuing her path up over his body to his neck and lips. She repeated this cycle of caressing and kissing again and again, building his arousal each time.

When his hands gripped the sheets and his heavy breathing quickened, she knew it was time. She leaned forward and whispered, 'I want you to watch me.'

Pulling off her dress, she exposed her naked body to him. Greg's eyes connect with hers as she stood astride him on the bed before trailing down to her glistening wetness. Kara glided her hands down her body, stopping between her legs. Giving him a show, her fingers circled her clitoris. As a tingling sensation grew within her, she stimulated herself harder and faster. Her body pulsing and shivering, she neared her climax, barely able to hold her balance as she touched herself.

Greg stretched his arms up her legs as far as he could reach, clutching her thighs. 'Come to me.'

Kara dropped to her knees, and Greg pulled her down on top of him. Holding her butt cheeks in his hands, he guided her, so she took all of his resounding pleasure in one plunging movement. A cry escaped her as he pushed, upsurging into her, stretching her body to accommodate him. He trembled in suspense as he found an intense rhythm.

Rolling her to her side and cradling her in his arms, he thrust into her from behind. He pushed her legs down so they were lying with the full length of their bodies touching each other, spooning and connecting as close as they could be. Until then, the only sounds were their breathing, both heavy and rasping.

Kara's orgasms came in waves. She grabbed her breast in one hand and reached behind her, pulling his smooth butt towards her as hard as she could with her other hand. She wanted to feel all of him and for him to feel every wave of her pleasure as she came.

Barely able to speak, Greg groaned, 'God, I'm going to explode.'

Their bodies shuddered uncontrollably for what seemed like forever. After his breathing had settled, Greg rolled onto his back. 'Wow! My God, I love watching you touch yourself. That was amazing.'

A knock on the door had them frantically grabbing robes. With the aroma of sex in the air the two waiters with knowing smiles, dressed the table and presented their meal in five-star, full-service fashion.

Greg thanked them both as they left, the second waiter giving him an unmistakable grin.

They dined semi-naked, thoroughly enjoying the moment. This was just as Kara had imagined. It was perfect.

After dinner, Greg delighted her by saying, 'Kara, you know, I have a little surprise for you too.' He stood and grabbed his jacket, taking out two silk scarves and a blindfold from the inside pocket.

'Oh! So, you've brought dessert, have you now?' she asked cheekily.

Smiling, he took her hand and led her to the bed, laying her in the middle. Using the scarves, he tied her wrists to the bed legs, firmly extending her arms. He kissed her softly on her cheeks and mouth before gently sliding the blindfold over her eyes. He took a sip of wine and moved to the bottom of the bed. He placed his glass on the floor, then kissed her toes and ankles before tenderly sliding his lips all the way up to her knees. His hands slowly spread her legs, giving him full access to her inner thighs with his tongue and lips. Quivering, she emitted soft groans as his mouth and fingers worked their way to find her to be still glistening wet and starting to pulse. He started pleasuring her in earnest, his tongue finding her firm clitoris. Licking and sucking, he explored all of her. Her moans increased with each taste and stroke. It took only a minute before she climaxed, and he felt her every muscle and nerves twitch.

For Kara, this was another first. She'd never come this way before. Every inch of her body trembled, her senses heightened by being bound in darkness, directing her full focus on the pleasure of his touch. He untied her and held her in his arms. they lay cuddling together for what seemed like ages.

Greg eventually drifted into a deep sleep while Kara lay there completely spent. As she watched him sleep, emotions flooded her, and tears trickled down her cheeks. She didn't want to lose this moment. She didn't want to let him go, but she knew she must. He was committed to another.

But I'm sure he won't forget tonight. Well, I hope not.

At 5.00 a.m., an alarm woke them with a jolt. Greg sat up to lean against the bed head. 'I set the alarm for as late as I could, I'll need to get going,' he said as he leant over to kiss her before he hopped out of bed. He started to dress while Kara lay there watching him. 'I've got a film crew arriving at six thirty,' he said as he buttoned his shirt. 'Are you okay?' he asked.

'Yes, just admiring the view,' she said with a sleepy smile.

Kara slid out of the bed as well and headed for the bathroom.

They were both soon dressed, and within fifteen minutes, they were stepping out of the lift into the car park. Greg knew Kara's car was only two spaces from his as he'd seen it when he arrived. He walked her to her car as she unlocked it, opened the rear door and placed her two bags on the back seat.

'Thanks, Kara.' Greg kissed her quickly on the cheek, checked his watch and walked back to his car. He hastily jumped in and started the engine.

By the time Kara had started her engine, Greg had already reversed his car out and was driving off. She didn't even get a final glance.

Despite Kara also hurrying to leave the room, she wasn't in any rush to get home to Clare.

During the drive, she kept replaying and reliving the events of the night before. It had been electric. The intensity had built from the moment he had entered the room until they were both utterly spent. 'That was awesome for a novice, Kara Gilbert,' she said out loud as she headed for the highway.

When she was about halfway home, she heard her phone ping with that familiar tone. It was Greg.

While she recognised the assigned tone of the sender, she absolutely did not expect the message that came with it.

Thanks for a great evening.

There was now an ignition of a different and unexpected kind. Kara pulled over to the side of the road and read the simple five-word sentence. Then she read it again. Then it hit her, like awakening from a vivid dream. A wave of new feelings erupted within her as reality smacked her like a lightning bolt.

'A great evening?' Her tone was both incredulous and spiked. 'A great evening? So that's all, Mr Sheppard?' Kara's insides burned. 'I have a "great" time when I go to the movies or catch up with a girlfriend. I have a "great evening" when I go out for dinner! A great evening?'

After all the messages full of subtle innuendo, enticement, and every romantic thing a woman wanted to hear, and after she had given so much of her heart and soul into planning their time together, she got only a 'great' rating? *Seriously?*

'Girl, you've just been rated like a takeaway meal!' Kara was ranting, both inside her head and aloud as she restarted the car.

She chose a fast, hard, and angry song on her playlist to match the hurt inside her, turned up the volume, and drove.

By the time she got home, those last eighty kilometres of driving had given her reflection time and she had settled a bit. *You silly woman, Kara. It is time to wake up, grow up, and be real here.*

What were you trying to do? You wanted sex. But you've been lying to yourself. You do want to feel loved. You crave a little personal attention and to feel special. Now you've felt all of that. He's given you a taste, and now you just want more. You can't have it, and what's more, you knew this was all he could give you. Stop thinking and behaving like an adolescent.

He had said you were an unexpected distraction from the outset—albeit a live, raw, and now sexy one, but a distraction from the main game and no more than that. You must let this go.

When she entered her house, she found her phone and replied to Greg with a simple message.

I'm home now. Thank you too.

She couldn't find the words that needed to be said just yet. She had to wait a little longer for the pain that her heart had released to subside. Suddenly overcome with exhaustion, she slipped into escape mode. She undressed, climbed into bed, and only then did she let the tears flow until she fell asleep.

As expected, when she awoke in the evening hours, she was greeted with the hollow thud of the memory of the day and a terrible sense of loss, but she remained calm. Kara's 'grown-up self' had returned, and she could now reflect on the night before in a far more rational way.

Kara, you planned everything for the evening, except for the final goodbye. A lady should always know when to exit and do it gracefully. You didn't prepare yourself for what you originally planned this to be. You knew this was the finish line. Staying with Greg until the absolute last moment was silly. He had to get to work, if you think about it, you know he'll message you when he has the time, as he has always done.

Kara knew that these mixed emotions were not about the text from Greg at all; it was all about her. The realisation and regret that she had lost so many years forsaking her own needs, suppressing desires, and discounting her feelings. Now she must accept their return, control them, and deal with letting go of someone who had reignited her passion and made her feel special for the first time in her life. He had given her a gift of discovery by revealing the underlying spark that had lain dormant inside her for years. Something she once had as a young woman, that she had not even realised she had lost. With that realisation, she knew how to respond to him.

Dear Greg,
Sorry this is a rather long message. I must sincerely apologise, and I am quite embarrassed and ashamed of myself for having put you into a most awkward position. You have been honest and upfront about your life and your future plans and that our reunion, while so special, was ever only intended as a one-time thing. So, here am I, the usually cool professional woman, shocked by my reaction to connecting with you. Perhaps not having experienced someone "liking me for just being me" in such a long time, and the way you have been so lovely by being genuine, safe, tender, and caring, that this somehow ignited a reaction of an infatuated young girl again. While I planned to send you only one message a week after we met in Sydney to say thank you, I kept sending you cheeky messages, trying desperately to keep seeing you. When you replied "yes" to last night, I surged into overdrive. I feel bad for having deliberately tempted you into another night, right when you are leaving with Tess. I have also quickly learned that you are sensitive and kind and don't like to hurt people. So please know that you do not need to think or worry about me or handle me. I admit it will hurt like hell, but my current feverish, passionate desire for you will eventually subside. I will be the sensible, mature forty-five-year-old who now truly accepts your love for Tess, your plans, and our goodbye with respect and grace (can't really say with dignity after some of my explicit messages can I?) and without any more selfish contact. Whatever you want is the most important. So, of course, I will always be here if you wish to call or share what's happening in your life, as any close friend might do. Regardless, you need not ever reply. I already know the words. Mine are too many now too. Forever in my thoughts. With gratitude and much love, Kara.

Kara hit Send and instantly there was that familiar sound of a message from Greg. Damn! Their messages had crossed.

> Sorry, I had no time to talk or share in a proper goodbye, but I really wanted you to thank you for an amazing evening last night. I could not stop looking at you, seeing you so totally absorbed in the unbelievable time we had. It felt so special that you had given yourself to me so unconditionally and offered so many ways to pleasure me with such confidence and passion. I cannot believe how lucky we both are that that cute little twelve-year-old girl decided to kiss me. We not have a bond for the rest of our lives. But for now, I need to clear my head (as best I can) and focus on the plans ahead. It's time. I know you will always be "one call away" as I will be for you. So, for now, see you later. I will love you always and you will be in my thoughts, dreams, and heart forever. Greg xx

Kara read the message, as the tears poured down her face. This time she knew they were shed as much in relief as in loss. She had sent the right message. Ping! Greg had obviously read her words.

> Kara, what a beautiful heartfelt message. Thank you. I'm so sorry. Are you going to be okay?

Kara knew she could not let this labour on. So, she sent a last message.

> Greg, I'm all good. I have shed a few tears here, but I am fine. Have a wonderful holiday and a very Merry Christmas. Maybe we can grab a coffee at the Gourmet Weekend next year so I can catch up on how your travels and life has been. You do not need to worry about me again.
> Take care, Kara. xx

Greg had realised that he and Kara had each sent their messages at the same time. He had been somewhat surprised and touched by Kara's honesty about her feelings and her acceptance that it was time for goodbye. It was such a raw and emotional message. He had taken so much time to compose his message to her.

That morning, it had startled him when he awoke by not only the alarm but also the wave of guilt about Tess that came over him when he looked at Kara lying next to him. Finding the words that he knew he needed to say to Kara was even harder after such an amazing evening and how she had totally indulged him in her sexual pleasure.

Uncharacteristically, he was momentarily torn, confused between his feelings for Tess and the unexpected pleasure of Kara. He didn't want to hurt either of them.

Greg had always been a master of compartmentalising and organising his life and his loves. He could place all his life parts into separate boxes, only opening the lid to the one required for the occasion and devoutly giving his full attention to whatever, that part of his life entailed. Every separate job, mates, family, lovers—what was desired or needed to be done was given 100 percent. Then he would close the lid to that box and open the next, each time giving his all. Perhaps it was this unwavering drive, attention to detail, and full commitment in the current moment, which contributed to the success in his professional life and why he was such an attraction to any woman he encountered. If you were with Greg Sheppard, he truly made you feel special. That morning, confronted by confusion, he raced away to concentrate his attention on work and reclaim his usual sharpness and clarity. Some hours focussing on tasks at work was what he needed to find the order again and settle his thoughts.

'You were the one who had opened the box to find Kara and knew it was only ever going to be for a brief encounter,' he told himself. 'Feeling guilty is the signal that it is time for this to be over, closed, and filed away.' It took until the next morning, but he finally drafted the message to close the chapter that was Kara Gilbert, that girl who had lingered in his thoughts since his youth.

While filled with sadness, it relieved him somewhat to have received Kara's insightful message that told him she had already come to the same conclusion, accepting this would end, before he had even needed to say it. One thing was absolutely right—Kara Gilbert was truly a thoughtful and sincere woman.

Despite knowing this was what should happen and now resolved to move on, it was still with a heavy heart he sent his final message.

> Kara, though I may never hold you again, I will never forget you. Special memories forever. Greg xx

Kara breathed out a heavy sigh. She just stood motionless for a time, staring into nowhere. *You can do this, Kara. It is time to let Greg Sheppard become just a beautiful memory.*

Before she reconsidered, Kara deleted all his messages from her phone. All except the first.

Chapter 11

Tess Merchant's life had transformed since meeting the enigmatic Greg Sheppard. There was a resounding glow and confidence that emerged in her because of them having become lovers. While secret at first, they could contain neither her transformation, nor their obvious attraction for long. She and her husband had drifted apart long ago, as was obvious to Greg when he first met them.

It was only when her husband's affair with their computer company's marketing manager was revealed that Tess finally found the courage to admit to her own affair. She wanted a life of her own, desiring to spend much of that with Greg. While the exposure of each of their illicit affairs brought heartache and some painfully turbulent months, the dissolution of their marriage was accepted, and their divorce settled relatively amicably.

Tess had a newfound energy and independence, and armed with this, she had returned to complete her degree in interior design, at the same time gaining employment with an international home décor import company.

No longer held back by the supporting role that she played as part of her former husband's life, she had shone as the star in the new life of her own. The 'Sheppard effect' had continued to work its magic on Tess in these recent years. Shedding inhibitions and kilos, a bolder and unassumingly beautiful woman had developed. She was absolutely breathtaking, with long blonde hair that she no longer tied up but would let flow and frame her face, accentuating the fresh brightness of her Mediterranean blue eyes. Greg's attention added undiscovered attributes. With renewed confidence came a woman whose walk was a little taller, her clothes were sexier, and she smiled all the time. Oh, and her fantasies and sexual desires became nearly insatiable.

With the freedom to make her own life decisions and the expanse of her working life, which took her all over the country, she relished in the attention of all around her. There was so much to enjoy through a new lens and outlook on life. Most of all, she loved her time with Greg as open friends, all the benefits and none of the dramas.

With the start of December came the time when both Tess and Greg could best step away from work for a break, as most agencies considered this was the downtime for marketing and promotional events and warehouses were stocked due to Christmas and the end of the year looming.

They were both looking forward to this holiday. Especially Greg. Despite all of their travels together, it was always something about work for one or both of them these days. Even though they had now spent many more close times together in their 'sort of' relationship, he and Tess had never enjoyed any decent trip or real extended holiday together that was just completely about them.

So, this was a long-overdue and much-anticipated trip to the Cook Islands. They had decided to make this a decent nearly four-week holiday to a destination that guaranteed sunshine every day. Although each had different ideas of what they might enjoy, the one common expectation was it would definitely be a sexy holiday. It would be a time for relaxing, bonding, and soaking up each other's company. Pure unadulterated fun and pleasure.

Tess knew it was important to spend some uninterrupted time with Greg. She was fully aware he'd been frantically managing several large-scale events for major clients in recent months, but she had detected that he had been somewhat distracted of late. The intimacy and passion were not quite what they had been, which usually never seemed to be affected by his work. Fleetingly she had wondered if his per chance encounter with Kara had a more profound influence on him than he realised. She quickly dismissed this to nothing more than timing and workload. Between both of their schedules they had spent only a few consecutive nights together in the past month. Besides, their discreet, separate 'one-off dates' with others had never affected their connection before. So regardless of the cause, Tess was determined she would make sure that their 'heat switch' was turned back up to smouldering hot before they returned home.

She would smother him with affection and attention both morning and night. She so badly wanted that wild passion and lovemaking to find its way back to how it was. Tess had wondered if part of the excitement for Greg was that he was secretly screwing someone's wife, and that the thrill may have faded now that they were both single.

Tess dismissed these thoughts and turned her attention to the fun and weeks ahead. She and Greg would have over three whole uninterrupted weeks together, starting tomorrow!

Tess hastily shed her work clothes, to step into holiday mode, and grabbed her travel bag. She ensured her passport and favourite lingerie and fragrance were packed and ready. Any other packing would be easy, as clothes would be mostly unnecessary for the majority of the next few weeks.

Greg was surprised when he realised how close the holiday really was. *Bloody hell! Where the hell did November go?*

Having blissfully lost time enjoying the most unexpected discovery of Kara, he had uncharacteristically paused his forward planning. Now regrouped, he knew he needed to turn his full attention to Tess. After all, he now felt so sure that this was the first woman that he could ever truly love and the only one since his divorce with whom he had even considered wanting to spend the rest of his life with. She was perfect for him, and he believed, increasingly, she was the one he could seriously commit to again.

Greg's approach to planning was always ten steps ahead, so there were things to be organised beyond this holiday that he wanted to do to express how much Tess meant to him. His inner stopwatch clicked into gear. He would never forget that day in April when Tess came to him, kissed him deeply, then looked into his eyes and said, 'It's done. I officially have no ties as of an hour ago today, apart from how much my heart and body want you right now.'

On April 30th, it would be two years since he heard those words and felt the woman he was falling for melt into his embrace. It was a day he would replay over and over in his mind. She was now emotionally and legally free from her past. He decided to give her a gift.

Back then, nearly two years ago, he had organised a surprise for her, an event to celebrate her birthday, which had fallen amidst the final stages of her divorce, but moreover to celebrate that their lives could now be theirs to enjoy as they wished. His surprise had started with an elegant dinner of their favourite meal—duck. After an extensive internet search, it was no surprise that Sydney was the place to find the restaurant with the finest duck cuisine in the country.

A restaurant booking was made, and so started his creative plan. First was to tell Tess to keep the day and day after free, letting her know she would only need an overnight bag.

He booked business class flights out for the Friday and afternoon flights back for the next day. Their accommodation would be at the Shangrila Hotel right at the Harbour's edge for the night. Included in their hotel package, he made sure she had an hour in the hotel spa, ensuring a luxuriating treatment and a massage to add extra finesse to her weekend.

To make sure she would feel spoilt from the start, before they departed Adelaide, Greg visited the airport and spoke personally to the staff at the Qantas lounge. He explained his plan to the two ladies on duty in the lounge and asked if he could have a free entry pass for Tess, so she could meet him inside without him having to invite her in as a guest. His romantic plans hit the spot, along with some Sheppard charm and a cheeky smile. He secured a pass without a blink!

Next, he had to arrange a way to get Tess to the airport. He sat and penned three separate messages, placing each note in an individual envelope. Then he booked Jim, his favourite limousine driver to collect her from her unit. Greg explained to Jim the importance of this trip and handed him the three envelopes. Jim listened carefully and noted the instructions about exactly when they were to be handed to his passenger.

The messages were clear, simple, and intriguing.

The first: 'Belated happy birthday! Grab your bag.'

This was to be handed to her when Jim arrived at her door.

The second envelope was to be given to her, once they had approached the city. It said: 'Please join me for dinner at Australia's number one duck restaurant.'

The third was to be handed over, once they'd reached Sir Donald Bradman Drive, when it would become obvious, she was heading for the airport. It simply contained a boarding pass and the Qantas lounge pass in it.

Everything went to plan. That was all it took. While Tess suspected a plan, had packed a bag, and had kept her days free, she was still totally surprised and overcome with excitement. It was the best gift she had ever had.

She had found Greg sitting in his favourite seat in the lounge, waiting with two glasses of champagne on the table in front of him. He stood as she approached, her smile and beauty almost bringing him to tears. She was breathtaking. He kissed her softly and invited her to sit.

'You are a wonderful and most naughty man. I loved the envelopes!'

When they boarded the plane and took their seats, they were served another glass of champagne. They spent the trip talking, touching, and enjoying the excitement of what else was to come. They arrived at Sydney airport and both only having carry-on luggage, they descended the stairs to find a driver holding a sign that read 'Greg and Tess,' adorned with assorted love hearts. Tess looked at Greg, her hand covering her mouth. 'Is there anything you haven't thought of?' she said.

By the time they had checked in, and entered their room, Tess was so ready to play and have some of Greg.

'No, no, no!' he said. 'We don't have time for that now. We still have a lot to do before dinner. Come on, we have to go!'

Tess was rather surprised, but even more excited to find out what would come next.

Greg kissed her and led her out of the hotel, heading to the Westfield Tower, a place he knew that had many exclusive dress and clothes shops. After a few moments, Tess relaxed again as they chatted, window shopped, and stopped to grab a drink at one of the little bars along the way. Once they arrived in the Centre, Greg led her to level two where all the designer boutiques were in one place. He stopped, standing still in the middle of the walkway outside of the stores, outstretched his arms, and turned around slowly. 'Okay, visit as many places as you want. Find a dress for dinner tonight. This is your birthday present, my love.'

The smile erupted and didn't leave her face. She took his hand and visited a number of stores and tried on many dresses with lots of banter, giggles, and fun shared between them, yet she found it hard to choose. Greg thought she looked beautiful in them all. Eventually, they found themselves at Max Mara, and Tess tried on a simple, sleek, mid-length, sleeveless champagne-coloured dress. The minute she walked out of the change room to show Greg, he said, 'Wow! That's it. You look divine. Do you like it?'

'Yes, I love it, babe,' Tess gushed.

As Greg started towards the counter to pay for the dress, he stopped. 'You'll need shoes to match.'

Tess just beamed, and after trying on several pairs, a choice of some elegant pumps, the same colour as her dress, was made.

Checking the time, Greg said, 'Hell, we really have to get moving. Our booking at the restaurant is only just over an hour away.' Greg hailed a cab since they needed to be back to the hotel to shower and dress in under thirty minutes.

They raced up to their room. Tess stripped off in front of him, the temptation almost more than he could take. She gave him that look and headed for the shower. As she entered the bathroom, Greg called out, 'Hey, babe, there's one more thing. Tonight, you are only allowed to wear what we bought today, just the dress and the shoes!'

'Okay!' replied Tess without hesitation.

They arrived at the restaurant only ten minutes late and were quickly seated; a bottle of wine and a full serve of Peking duck was ordered. They sat next to each other, enjoying the view from their seats that faced the window, the position perfect for Greg to run his fingers up and down the inside of her leg. Despite his fervent temptation to touch her, he decided to hold the sexual tension and only teased her a little throughout dinner.

The meal was amazing and the wine superb, but they were both keen to leave once they had finished eating, each wanting to get started on what they had been desperate for all day. In the first moments in the cab on the way back to their hotel, Tess turned to Greg and whispered, 'Thank you,' placing her palms on his cheeks as she brought her lips to his. The soft, slow kiss soon turned hot and passionate, with their hands frantically feeling each other's body. They were oblivious of their surroundings.

Greg's fingers found her sweet spot. She was so wet. With her new dress riding high on her thighs, she spread her legs further, inviting him to pleasure her more.

The cab driver was clearly struggling to drive now with him frequently checking his rear-view mirror. It was in that moment that Greg realised she was quite turned on by a bit of voyeurism.

She didn't hold back with either moans or allowing her body to writhe.

The cab arrived at the hotel, and before he alighted, Greg threw the cabbie a knowing nod and a wink, knowing full well that he had enjoyed the trip as much as they did. Upstairs, they were again locked in an embrace and kissing passionately before the door had even closed. Greg reached behind her and slid down the zipper of her new dress, allowing it to fall from her body to the floor. Her shoes where already gone when he lay her on the bed and continued to kiss her passionately; they were way past slow and teasing foreplay now. Tess almost tore his clothes off, and within seconds they were both fully naked and Greg on top of her. Her legs wrapped around his waist as if she would never let him go. She pulled him into her. He filled her completely with a fiery passion. It was only seconds until her orgasmic screams filled the room. Greg didn't move, still fully inside her, he waited for her breath to calm enough to kiss her. He could feel her clamp him as each wave shook through her body. He slowly started again building to the pace where she had lost all control. He felt her reach the point of no return, where her body again commenced its preparation to deliver its ultimate pleasure.

Tess called out, 'Come with me, fill me.'

Greg now sweating, increased the tempo, using all the energy he had left. Her release was so powerful he felt her juices flow from her body. He needed nothing more to now give her all he had; the delivery was so powerful he felt it surely must have hurt her. Each pulse of his semen thundered through his body delivering an explosion of colour to his mind's eye and a feeling that part of his soul was being transferred to her. As the last drop left him, he felt the vibrant waves from Tess slowly fading.

They were completely spent. Greg fell to the side of her with no grace at all. They both lay on their backs, their eyes closed still floating on the orgasmic cloud they were both riding. Greg reached for Tess's hand and said with an exhausted breath, 'Happy birthday babe.'

When they returned home, Tess told him how much she absolutely loved her gifts and the amazing time they had. She couldn't imagine anything surpassing that surprise.

Subsequently, 30th April had since always remained their special anniversary day. So now for this year, he wanted to make sure his anniversary plans surpassed their last anniversary weekend and it would be eternally memorable.

Chapter 12

*G*reg was in the airport lounge waiting for Tess to arrive. With plenty of time to spare, he had been casually scrolling through Facebook newsfeed on his phone and found himself drawn to look at Kara's page as he had done a number of times before he had sent her that first message. There were only a few recent posts, mostly about events she was hosting in her area. Nothing personal.

He glanced through some of her photos, stopping now and then to look at her. His thoughts drifted back to their wild and passionate reunion. She was such an innocent, yet incredibly sexy woman. Somehow, he kept hearing the words of her last message. I'm all good… You don't need to worry about me.

Greg forced himself to regroup. Enough of the past now! He was looking ahead, and time was now of the essence.

His first call was to a jeweller and then the owner of a restaurant at the Bay. He sent them confirming emails after each call with a few more details of what he wanted and the deadline dates. He was about to call Tess's boss when he spotted her entering the airline lounge.

Along with every other male in the lounge, Greg admired the beautiful woman approach him. She still made his heartbeat faster every time he saw her.

She placed her bag on the seat next to him and kissed him. 'The traffic was crazy. I didn't think I would get here.' Greg looked past her to see many men still enthralled by her. Her tight white jeans and cobalt blue blouse made her look like a supermodel.

He handed her a glass of champagne. 'Oh well, you're here now. We have loads of time, and, hey, we are now officially on holidays.' She accepted the glass from his outstretched hand and took a sip before smiling widely and kissing him. Their holiday had finally begun.

The laughter, caresses, and whispers just flowed, building on the excitement of their thoughts of what was to come. Waiting for the plane, they engaged in their favourite pastime of people watching, imagining, and creating the fantasies and lustful possibilities of seemingly everyday people. Forget the job roles, their marriage status, or how many children they might have—no, Tess and Greg cheekily exchanged what the surrounding people might be like in bed. Would they last? Might this be their only or first partner? How fiery might they be? Were they loud, fast and furious, or innocent and awkward? Who was passive? Submissive? Did they enjoy sex at all? This always got them both aroused as they each imagined a fantasy in their minds.

The flight seemed short as they talked the whole way. Beyond their obvious physical connection, they never tired of talking to each other as they bounced from topic to topic. This was perhaps the natural ingredient and true essence of their attraction to each other.

Once the plane landed and they disembarked, the warmth and welcome of the islands hit them like a comforting blanket on a frosty night. Greg let out a sigh at the feeling of rightness, knowing that every part of this holiday would be amazing.

With their small cases in hand, they sped ahead of their fellow passengers to grab an early cab.

Their hotel on the beach looked even better in real life than the pictures on the internet. While a resort or five-star accommodation had become the norm for Greg's work life, this was different. This time it was all about rest and indulgent pleasure with the love of his life.

They had arrived early, well before check-in time, but the receptionist handed them keys, telling them their room should be ready any minute. A quick call to the cleaner confirmed she was just finishing. Like a teenager, Tess almost skipped down the path to the room, she was so excited. It had been a long time since Greg felt like this with Tess. They had both stepped into a new world. There was nothing else but each other. No work. No family. No phone calls, email, demands, interruptions. It was complete freedom from their everyday lives.

As Tess clutched his hand and led him through the doorway, he took a second to picture in his mind what the next few weeks had in store for him. Here was a sexy woman leading him to a place where he knew he would give and receive the most divine experience. There was no other place Greg wanted to be. *I really do love this woman,* he thought.

'What's the rush, babe? We have three weeks.'

'You'll see.'

He loved her excitement; this was his Tess. The sparkle in her blue eyes said it all. He now knew they wouldn't be leaving the room anytime soon.

The instant the door of their room clicked closed, she turned to him, pulled him into a hard embrace, and whispered a phrase from his favourite movie. 'Take me to bed or lose me forever.'

They undressed each other, taking turns removing each other's garments one by one, their lips hardly parting. Once naked, Tess fell backwards onto the bed, her legs falling apart, and she pulled him between them. The anticipation of this moment, escalating since their departure was all the foreplay they needed.

Greg would never tire of this vision—when her head tilted back with that huge breath as he entered her. This was when she was the most beautiful, never more perfect. Their connection said everything about them. The synchronicity of their bodies when he was at full stroke had their lips perfectly level. At every point of touch, they melded and blended. He was sure they were the perfect couple.

He softened his pace a little making each entry a slow but deep ecstatic pulse so he too could feel her entry into that point of ecstasy, his own pleasure mirrored in hers. Tess didn't try to suppress the sound of her climax as it built or the groan with each stroke. Greg wondered who could hear them making love. He was sure Tess didn't care.

Neither of them heard the cleaner return to the room to put the forgotten chocolates on their bedside tables. The cleaner, a young local woman, had rushed into the room at her usual pace to place the chocolates before the next guests arrived, assuming no one had yet checked into the room.

Greg and Tess were oblivious to her presence as she rushed down the small corridor and entered the bedroom proper. She was now only a pace from the end of the bed. The cleaner looked up in horror and let out a low scream, created from whatever air was in her lungs at that second, not loud but desperate as she suddenly realised her mistake.

Greg, fully exposed and feeling vulnerable, froze. The cleaner dropped the chocolates as she sprinted for the door, slamming it behind her.

'Don't stop,' Tess panted out, still on the brink of an explosive orgasm. Instantly responding to her command, he put the event behind him, and soon the feel and sound of her pleasure consumed his full attention as she shuddered uncontrollably beneath him. He also unleashed a resounding moan and he also exploded inside her.

Once the last wave of ecstasy had subsided and her breathing had started to return to normal, Greg moved to lay at her side. He softly caressed her body, his fingers running over her as far as he could reach, sending tingles through the rest of her body. It was a lovely way to come back to the real world from what she described as an escape like no other—her interplanetary travel.

As reality returned, he remembered the incident with the cleaner.

'That was a bit embarrassing, wasn't it?'

'That was funny. What do you think she saw?'

'She saw everything—a full view of me, pumping into you, that's for sure!'

Tess's response surprised him somewhat. 'It was quite a turn on, don't you think?'

'Well, if I was prepared for it, maybe. Yes.' He hesitated before asking his next question. 'Hey, did you like the idea of someone seeing us fucking?'

There was a moment's silence before her reply. 'Hmm, well, yeah, a little. Actually, yes, I think I do. We would have looked magnificent, you know.'

They laid together quietly for some time, content, luxuriating in the simple indulgence of each other. After what seemed like hours, but, was only minutes, they finally rose from the bed. Greg picked up the chocolates from the floor and they showered, dressed, and headed for the bar to get a drink. Greg couldn't stop thinking about how Tess had treated the whole cleaner thing.

God, there is so much I still don't know about this woman!

It wasn't long before the sun was setting, and they had consumed quite a few drinks. Greg placed his hand on Tess's shoulder. 'Hey, I have a plan. Let's go and have some dinner, then we can change into our swimmers and find a nice quiet spot on the beach.'

'Sounds good to me,' replied Tess trying her best to appear sober.

They returned to their room, changed for dinner, and headed for the restaurant area in the resort. They found a nice place with Italian influence and were soon ushered to a table with a view of the moonlit golden beach.

The day had been a complete dream come true. The lead up, the flight, the conversations, flirting, teasing and the escape to a place that elicited nothing but pleasure. Greg had drunk quite a bit of wine and was now completely relaxed. Lost in the joy of the occasion and the beautiful woman seated in front of him, his guard was down. The effect of the alcohol, the amazing day, and his total happiness in that moment had his usually hidden, soft, and true emotions surfacing. His mother had always said, 'The real person comes out after a few drinks.'

Without realising, he had let himself drift to a place he thought he'd buried decades ago. His mother had left him and the family when he was five. Perhaps it was that broken bond with his mother that made this moment so important. He had always kept every woman he encountered at arm's length, but now, for the first time, he found himself in a space where he had allowed love to penetrate his heart once more.

Tess noticed him soften and was shocked when she saw a tear form in the corner of his eye. 'Oh, Greg… baby, what's wrong?'

He looked up at her, he wanted to say, 'Nothing, it's just being here with you and all of this.' Instead, the buried memories that he had compartmentalised into a 'Do not open' container had spilled out. 'Why do you think my mother didn't love me? Why did she leave me when I was five? Do you know the only photo I have of her shows her holding me by my arm, not even by my hand, and she wasn't even smiling? If she loved the little boy in front of her, her firstborn, why didn't she show it? Maybe I was a mistake, a burden she didn't want or need. Even kids by mistake are still loved and wanted you know.'

Greg's tears trickled down his face as Tess silently struggled with seeing this man—the strong, cool, successful entrepreneur who always exuded confidence and control—pouring out his heart about supressed pain he had kept to himself for over forty years. Tess wasn't sure how to respond. All she could say was, 'Of course, she loved you. Maybe she had a lot going on in her life then too and just didn't know how to show it. Maybe she didn't know how much you needed her?'

They sat in silence for a moment or two until the main course arrived, which was the distraction they both needed.

Greg, feeling embarrassed and exposed, used the silence and another sip from his wineglass to settle his emotions. It had felt like an eternity, but in reality, it was only a moment before he regained his composure. Without looking at Tess, he carefully refilled their glasses and started to eat.

Tess was relieved but didn't take her eyes off him. After a while, Greg was the first to speak. He apologised for his little emotional, wine-induced, outburst and then quickly changed the subject to how amazing the start to their holiday had been. Once again, they found the rhythm and were chatting and laughing as they had been most of the day.

They finished the meal and returned to their room, taking the rest of the wine with them. They changed for the beach and seeing Tess in her new blue-and-white-stripe bikini took his breath away. Tess was not a young woman, but she was fit and trim with the most perfect athletic figure. He loved her tight bum, shapely legs, and full breasts. Her nipples, size and shape were obvious through the thin material.

They strolled down to the beach and eventually stopped in a secluded place where their own inlet pond had formed as the tide receded. While only shallow, it was simply perfect for them to lay next to each other and enjoy the still warm trapped water touching their bodies.

The day's events gave them much to talk about, but for most of this time, they just lay close, enjoying the peaceful sensation of the warmth of both the water and their bodies. Seeing Tess looking so relaxed and stunning, surrounded by the backdrop of this glorious place, he thought nothing could make the moment any more perfect… until a delicious idea prompted him to ask, 'Tess, how would you feel if this was a nudist beach or a nudist resort like in Bali?'

Without hesitation, she replied, 'Fine with me. That's something I could do!'

Greg gulped as he took in her answer. That was not quite what he had expected her to say. For the most part, Tess was a conservative lady. He had learnt more about Tess in the last twenty-four hours than he had in the last two years.

His heart raced with anticipation as he wondered, *how far can I take this?* 'Tess, why don't you take off your top here on the beach?'

Tess turned to look straight into his eyes. 'Really?'

Greg, almost trembling from the excitement, just nodded.

Tess held his gaze for a moment before turning her head away to look straight ahead. Greg drew in a breath, thinking, *damn! Maybe too much too soon.* He scrambled for words to make this situation right.

Before he could utter a sound, Tess spoke. 'Would that turn you on, babe?'

'You know it would!'

Then to Greg's amazement, she reached behind her back, unclipped her bikini top, and ever so slowly slipped the fabric away from her body, teasing him, tempting him with the slowest of reveals. As she finally outstretched her arms and let her top drop to the sand next to him, she gradually turned her body to face him. Greg's whole body started quivering excitedly, so aroused by the combination of the surprise of her response to his request and the public viewing of her breasts and the now deliciously inviting erect nipples.

God, and I thought this couldn't get any better! He resisted the overwhelming temptation to latch his lips and hands onto her breasts, suck them, squeeze them, kiss and stroke them. Mustering control, he allowed his fingers to reach out. He caressed her cheek before leaning forward to kiss her softly. 'You are so goddamn beautiful. Thank you, babe.'

Tess smiled before kissing him deeply. They both knew it was possible that the people just a distance away from them could see them, but neither cared.

During the second week of their holiday, Tess and Greg had booked a short flight to Aitutaki Island for a day trip, a place renowned and regarded as the most beautiful and romantic place in the world with its untouched crisp white sand and turquoise clear waters, bordered by deep green palm trees. Aitutaki was absolutely breathtaking and rendered most visitors speechless when they arrived, transporting them instantly into paradise. These feelings similarly engulfed Tess and Greg as they stepped from the plane almost straight onto the beach. Standing hand in hand, side by side, they looked around and then at each other. They just stood there, completely immersed in the beauty of this little island. It was Greg who broke the silence. 'Oh, how perfect is this? I'm bringing the most beautiful woman in the world to the most beautiful place in the world.'

Tess turned and hugged him with a strength that surprised them both. A tear ran down her face as the enormity of the moment overwhelmed her.

'How could this holiday possibly be any better?' she murmured. 'I want this to last forever, this moment. I don't want to move an inch. Please, please never take me away from here.'

As the tears began to freely flow, Greg held her close, allowing her to sob on his shoulder. Tess was so happy that it nearly hurt.

Greg smiled as he comforted her, knowing he had given them both a holiday to remember. They both had been touched and openly emotional during this break, right from the first days of this special time spent together.

Eventually, she pulled back and chuckled, a little embarrassed. 'I'm sorry. It's just too much.'

'Don't be sorry, babe. This is what you deserve, and more.' He kissed her tear-drenched face.

They made their way to the bus to start their tour around the island. Tess tried to fix her face with her fingers, knowing the mascara must be everywhere. Greg helped a little, wiping her cheeks and reassuring her until she looked composed and tidy once again.

The tour guide welcomed his guests to the island of 1800 people and ran through the format of the day before their flight back to Rarotonga at 5.00 p.m. that evening. As they sat in their seats, Tess looked around to inspect the other passengers. Greg assumed she was about to start their people-watching game, but then she whispered in his ear, 'We are having sex somewhere on this bloody island before we leave, and you need to make sure it happens. Don't disappoint me, Mr Sheppard!'

Greg glanced around the bus, noting that he and Tess were probably the youngest on board with most looking to be aged well into their late fifties or sixties. 'I don't think a sex stop was on the list of activities the tour guide mentioned.' He gave her a knowing look and grinned. Both of them knew that Greg would always rise for a challenge.

The bus stopped at one amazing place after another before reaching the lunch spot in the little coastal town. Greg had again been a little surprised by Tess's bold request. Barely able to take in all the features of the tour, as his mind was consumed by trying to work out how on earth, he could fulfill her wish.

Bloody hell! How, where, and when can we do this? He was determined to make this day all it could be for her and not return home with any thoughts of, 'If only we had…'

They had stopped many times to capture the full experience of the beautiful island, but stops were brief. Before long, they had finished lunch and started the return journey back on a different route to the airport. Then Greg heard the guide announce the magic words: 'The next stop will be at the lagoon, what I consider the highlight of the island.' They would stay there for about twenty minutes to ensure everyone got a chance for photographs and to really take in the beauty.

'Okay, this will have to be it.' Greg told himself.

As the bus approached the park, he furiously scanned for a suitable location. When he spotted the area to the left of the car park, he found what he was searching for.

The bus turned into a parking bay, and Greg leaned towards Tess.

'Stand up now and walk to the front of the bus. Get ready to run.' The minute the bus stopped and the door opened, they were the first off. The other passengers disembarked behind them, all heading for the crystal blue water and white sand, while only some noticed Greg and Tess running in the opposite direction. As soon as they reached the first row of trees, barely out of sight of the people on the beach, Greg pulled Tess close and kissed her passionately. Knowing their time was limited, he lifted her skirt, pulled down her white lace knickers and slipped two fingers inside her. She pushed down, inviting his fingers to do whatever he wanted.

Tess scrambled to undo his shorts, and before they had dropped to his feet, she had him firmly in her hand. Their bodies fell to the sand, Greg on his back and she astride him. Her sweet spot found him with ease, taking all of him completely in one move. She didn't rise up and down, rather she pushed herself down hard onto him. She ground her hips moving back and forth, with him remaining deep inside her like a pulsing force between them the whole time. It was intense and brutally passionate, they arrived together with Tess drowning out any other sound.

Still astride him, Tess collapsed forward to rest on his chest, her head nestling into his shoulder as he wrapped his arms around her, both breathing hard still.

'You never disappoint me, my darling!' Tess whispered, and he squeezed her tighter.

'Let's go. We can't miss the bus; it's a bloody long walk back!'

They scrambled to their feet. Greg pulled up his shorts while Tess madly straightened her dress and hair. She collected her knickers from the sand, shoving them into his pocket before they ran back to the parking bay hand in hand.

Everyone was already on the bus as they sprinted back. Greg and Tess paused to take one long slow breath to compose themselves as they stepped back onto the bus. Tess's hair was a tousled mess, there was sand all over Greg's back, and both were still puffing and panting.

'I think everyone knows what we've been up to,' he whispered.

'And its running down my legs, 'she whispered back.

They smiled all the way back to their hotel.

Chapter 13

Over the days that followed, Greg and Tess luxuriated in the sun. Each day, they walked to a different spot along the endless beach across the pristine white sand. They swam naked in many of the secluded peaceful lagoons, often finding themselves the only people there. This added even more delight in the exclusive indulgence of their escape.

Their evenings were filled with long conversations, along with plenty of teasing, joking, and dining. They soaked up moments where time was unimportant. The only thing that mattered was each other's pleasure. There were many hours fulfilling this intimately and sensually too. The sex they enjoyed was amazing and far-reaching, each time a contrast from that of fast, ferocious, and exciting, to slow, gentle and tender.

They had little contact with many others during this time. A casual hello to other hotel guests, a chat to waiters, or the usual pleasantries when visiting sights or exploring shops. One evening though, they chatted with a similar aged couple that happened to be seated next to them in the lounge bar. The couple, Matt and Sarah, were also Australians and on a sexy getaway. They were obviously enjoying their own type of intimate couple-escape holiday. Greg and Tess could see a similar look of excitement in them. They compared stories of their adventures and Greg admitted to the sandy sex on the recent bus tour.

By the end of the second week, they would steal away to the beach each night where they would lie naked, enjoying their last wine and the recap of each day. Tess was becoming bolder, daring, and more confident about displaying her body and growing sexuality, expressing her fantasies and desires with him each day. Her growing openness and desire to explore mesmerised and endlessly aroused Greg.

He had come to realise his devotion to Tess. While he had already started planning their anniversary celebration, he felt he wanted to make it a much bigger surprise. A lifetime memory celebration for, and of this lady. While Tess had gone out to walk and check out some shops, Greg grabbed the opportunity to remain at the hotel and steal some time to better organise the event for when they returned home. April would arrive all too soon.

Knowing she would be away for a couple of hours; he grabbed his laptop and checked his emails. He hadn't opened them since his arrival on the islands. He wasn't concerned about work, but more so, he wanted to check the progress of his plans for the surprise for Tess. He had received confirmation that the mooring immediately alongside the restaurants was reserved for him on April 30th with the only condition being that he was berthed before 5.00 p.m. Fabulous!

He checked his work schedule. While he had a morning meeting on that exact day in April to sort details of an event launch, he could easily have time to get his boat to the location and get himself and everything ready for his special night. He quickly updated his calendar to show that he would be unavailable for the rest of that day.

His mate Paul, the jeweller, had replied to his initial message that Greg had sent from the airport. Paul indicated he was happy to undertake the work and said he could fit in with Greg's proposed timeframes.

Greg had initially asked him to design a diamond and emerald dress ring, something exquisite, for him to give to Tess as an expression of commitment and to remember their first two years. But now Greg had his heart set on a much bigger plan. He sent a detailed message, describing what he was after and requesting some design options. The ring had to be perfect, a true statement piece. He knew exactly what he wanted. It was to be a three-diamond ring with a large 1.5 carat diamond as the centrepiece with a smaller 0.75 carat on each side, princess cut and square bevel edge on a white gold setting and yellow gold band. He requested a couple of design drawings and asked for details to transfer funds for the deposit.

Greg then checked the websites of all the restaurants at Holdfast shores. He scanned each cuisine, menu, rating, and location, searching for a place offering superb food, elegant service, and in serviceable proximity to where his forty-eight-foot cruiser would be berthed. Eventually he found the perfect option: an Italian fine-dining restaurant situated right in front of where the boat would be parked.

Greg emailed, outlining his plan and asking if he could visit in the week immediately after his return to discuss the options for each course and confirm the menu. Greg was impressed as he'd received an immediate reply. They arranged for a meeting to confirm the finer details of the menu and wine selections. The manager had also offered to provide the waiting service he wanted, offering to set the rear deck table of his boat with a silver service setting. Greg's only mistake was that he mentioned to the manager that 'it didn't matter what it cost' to make it perfect. Something the manager noted with enthusiasm.

Tess had recently been engaged by a retail chain, on a three-month contract to revitalise and promote their homeware range, and would still be working there on that day. So, Greg dialled the number of Tess's manager.

As April 30th fell on a Thursday, a workday for them both, he needed to ensure Tess could leave a bit early or at least exactly on time, and would be forgiven for arriving late the next morning. It was a brief call, with Greg having easily appealed to Tess's manager—a lovely woman who was completely blown away with

Greg's description of such a romantic gift for Tess. She agreed to make sure her day was easy and assured him she was happy for Tess to arrive the next day whenever she was ready.

His next message was a booking for a limousine. He contacted Jim, the company he always used for his events and organised him to collect Tess from her work. By this time, he'd now received a reply from Paul with several ring designs attached. He knew which ring was perfect for Tess the second he saw it. It was exactly what Greg had in mind. Paul had explained in his message that the stones would need to come from a supplier in New York. Greg asked if there would be any chance, they might be held up. Paul confirmed that it was plenty of time as they would almost be overnight. So, without hesitation, Greg confirmed the design choice and transferring the funds for the deposit.

By the time Tess returned, Greg was calmly seated on the balcony, pleased with what he had been able to put into place so quickly. On hearing Tess enter their suite, he called out to her, 'Babe, I'm on the balcony. When you're ready, come and join me, bring a glass, I have a bottle.'

Watching as the sun had almost hit the horizon for the day, he sipped his wine, allowing his mind to wander to somewhere out there on the ocean. Realising that this must be what relaxation and indulgence were, a smile of total contentment formed softly on his face.

'What are you smiling at babe?' asked Tess as she stepped onto the balcony through the scrim curtain.

'Oh, gorgeous, just when I thought I couldn't be happier; you arrive and raise the bar another notch.' He smiled at her. 'Well, maybe there's one thing that would make it perfect!'

'Oh? Is there now?' Tess replied with a cheeky smile.

She took a mouthful of wine and placed the glass on the table. Looking into his eyes, she knelt between his legs and slowly undid his shorts, he quickly responded to her advances.

'Perfect now?' she asked as she teased him with her tongue.

'Perfect,' he said softly.

As she took him fully in her mouth, he laid his head back, enjoying her talent. She loved doing this to him as much as he loved receiving it. All inhibitions had escaped him at that moment. He didn't care that he was sitting on a first-floor balcony with only glass between them and the universe to see. Being outside in the open, Tess between his legs, and such an impromptu and unexpected pleasure was sheer bliss. He glanced up at the open sky and then looked down at this beautiful woman kneeling in front of him.

Touching her on the cheek, he said, 'I would love to take you from behind… here on the balcony.'

Without saying a word, she let him slip slowly from her mouth and looked up at him. She stood, lifted her skirt and place a finger each side into the lacy band of her knickers. She slowly slid them down her thighs till they fell around her bare feet. Her eyes looked upon him with a look of lustful desire. She reached for his hand to help him stand and pulled him toward her. She kissed him; her lips still moist from his initial pleasure. She turned, placing her forearms on the flat balcony railing. Greg lifted her tartan mini skirt and felt for her moist and swollen piece of paradise as she spread her legs a little wider, this had him immediately desperate to have her. His hands grabbed her hips and found her without any effort at all. From this angle he could give her his all and he did from the first stroke. She arched her back; her mouth fell open releasing a deep moan as that first stroke powered forcefully into her.

'Babe, can I be selfish?'

'Yes,' she replied still rocking from his deep thrusts.

She knew he was about to come with the increased tempo and then the throbbing as he held himself buried deep into her. As his breathing eased, he opened his eyes and slowly eased away from her. He fell back into his seat with his shorts still around his ankles, watching her bare bum disappear as she pulled down her skirt.

Greg let out a deep breath of satisfaction and reached for his wine. 'Now that's as good as it gets.'

At that moment, he looked out past the guard rail only to see a gardener looking straight at him.

'Shit! The gardener has been watching us.'

Tess turned to him with a beaming smile and said, 'He was watching us the whole time.'

Three nights before they were due to depart, Greg opened his laptop to check his emails. He had to prepare himself for the onslaught of work that would greet him on his return. It gave him the opportunity to check if there were new messages associated with his plans for the special April date for Tess. There were a few more messages confirming details, but no major work issues that couldn't wait, so he closed his mail.

Before shutting down, he casually clicked on a video, a clip from a porn site, an old favourite that used to be his company while on so many nights away alone in hotels.

Tess had walked in and plonked herself next to him on the bed and saw what he was watching. It was a soft swing scene with two couples enjoying making love to their partners, all four of them on the same bed, each watching the other. Tess was quiet, but Greg noticed she couldn't take her eyes off the screen.

He didn't dare ask, but as if she already knew the question, Tess said, 'I'm not sure, but that might be fun too.'

Greg put the laptop away. 'Yes, I think it would—with the right couple.'

While they had often had phone sex where the two of them were obviously aroused by imagining scenes involving other couples and even sometimes the fantasy of Tess touching another woman, Greg had never thought that Tess would be brave enough or want to experience anything even close to that in reality. Greg couldn't imagine the thought of someone else with his Tess, but the turn on of swinging with another woman or a couple was exhilarating. It was an experience that secretly fascinated him.

Was Tess sending messages that she may also want to explore a little more? He had a plan that could test taking her to the next level.

Chapter 14

Their magical escape was coming to an end. Their flight home was due to depart around 3.00 p.m. tomorrow. They'd already planned to dine out that evening in their now favourite restaurant and then enjoy their last naked reflective time on the beach before heading back to their room for the last time.

Greg wanted to make their last day delicious by adding a touch of surprise and spice to it. So, he decided on a special room service lunch. He chose a light pasta dish of spinach, sundried tomatoes, chicken, and bocconcini, a similar dish that he would often cook for her at home. He had visited the chef to provide the recipe and had ordered a bottle of a sparkling Tasmanian pinot noir, which she loved. The hotel staff had agreed to set the table for lunch on their balcony during the time Greg and Tess would be out of their room. He also arranged for their meal to be brought to them as soon as he called on their return around noon.

At 8.00 a.m., Greg was awake admiring the sleeping beauty that lay next to him with the deep blue water of the Pacific Ocean in the background. He heard the gentle knock on the door that he knew would be the two coffees he had ordered the night before. Greg slipped quietly out of the bed, covered his naked body with the hotel robe and answered the door. With a mimed 'Thank you' he took the much-needed beverages from the maid and closed the door with only a slight click. He placed the coffees next to the bed, disrobed and slid gently back into bed. With Tess facing away from him, he started to run his fingers down her back with the softest of touch. It was a little while before she acknowledged it with a soft shudder and a little purr of enjoyment. He lent over her and whispered, 'Your coffee is here gorgeous,' and kissed her neck. She turned towards him with a sleepy smile that was so beautiful, a wave of heat enveloped him nearly bringing a tear to his eye. Tess sat up against the bedhead as Greg handed her the mug.

As they sipped their coffees, Greg suggested that perhaps they dress and go for a walk and maybe a swim along the beach, before an early lunch instead of breakfast. Tess agreed. Greg's body was starting to react to the sight of Tess laying there naked and so relaxed, as she sipped her coffee. He looked at that mesmerizing body that had brought him so much pleasure. He had to draw on all his will power to not simply succumb and just make love to her again.

He hopped out of bed now a little aroused, he had to resist and keep to his plan.

They were soon walking through the lobby with towels in hand. Greg gave a nod to the smiling Polynesian concierge who nodded in return. The signal for the balcony table to be prepared. They placed their towels and shoes on one of the hotels plastic couches that adorned the beach, shaded by colourful striped umbrellas. Greg took her hand and they headed north along the pure white sand that surrounded this beautiful island.

They strolled in the shallow tempered water, just taking in the beauty and watching the local fishermen go about their daily business. 'I'm going to miss this place,' Tess said watching a mid-morning cocktail being delivered to a hotel guest who clearly hadn't just finished her yoga class.

They had walked a long way when Greg checked his watch. He turned Tess around and they headed back towards their hotel. As always, the return trip didn't seem to take as long. Greg checked his watch again and saw he still had ten minutes to spare. Once back in front of their hotel, Greg lifted the loose-fitting white linen shirt that Tess was wearing over her head, exposing the blue and white striped bikini top he had watched her remove most nights on this same beach. He took her hand and walked her into the waveless warm water. Tess tried to avoid getting her hair wet but once they started playing and splashing that was impossible. It was now time they headed back upstairs.

Having returned to their room, Greg suggested Tess grab a quick shower, so they could then make plans for a lunch. She didn't notice the dressed balcony table as the curtains were still half drawn. Once he heard the shower running, Greg opened the curtains, appreciating the elegance of the setting.

A knock on the door signalled the arrival of their lunch. All was served and in place just as the shower taps were turned off.

He'd collected an eye mask from a recent overnight flight and placed it along with two scarves on his bedside table. These were ready for her special dessert after their meal. He quickly changed into a pair of shorts and slipped on a white linen shirt, leaving it unbuttoned, casually exposing his now very tanned chest.

Tess emerged from the bathroom, dressed in a simple soft yellow sundress. The thin tied straps, mini length, and lemon hues allowed her smooth golden skin and sheer beauty to radiate. Greg drew in a breath, His heart never ceased to be enlightened at the sight of her.

He poured two glasses of wine and handed her one as he took her hand and directed her to the balcony.

'Wow, when did this happen?' You never cease to impress me, babe!' she exclaimed.

Greg, smiling, pulled back a seat for Tess to sit.

'Don't tell me you made this in the five minutes I was in the shower? This is the same as the first meal you ever cooked for me, isn't it?' she said.

'Yes, but I may have had a little help,' Greg said smiling.

They finished their meal, and after another glass of wine, Greg stood and reached out to her. He escorted her inside, closed the heavy drapes behind him and gently laid her on the bed. Without touching her he lay next to her. Looking into his eyes, she motioned to undress, but Greg reached out and stayed her hand.

'I want to do something new. Something we haven't done before,' he whispered in her ear.

'Okay,' she answered tentatively.

He opened the bedside drawer and pulled out the blindfold. 'I would like you to put this on, babe.'

A devilish smile appeared as she obliged, covering her eyes. Greg continued, 'Now, feel these.' He let the silken feel of the fabric glide over her fingers. 'I'm going to tie your hands with these scarves.'

'Okay.' She slipped her arms out of her dress straps, then brought her hands together, outstretched. Greg tied her wrists together gently, resting them above her head on the bed.

With a soft and seductive voice, he informed her, 'Tess, it will only be me touching you, but we are going to imagine we are having some same-room sex with that couple we met the other evening at the bar. I will talk you through what is happening, but I want you to imagine that it is Matt and Sarah sharing our bed.'

He kissed her cheek and neck before he continued in a hushed tone. 'Can you see them coming into our room? They're holding hands as they stand at the foot of our bed. We are naked and they're kissing as they begin to undress each other. Can you see them?'

'Yes,' was all she dared whisper in response.

Greg slid her dress down, revealing her breasts, as he whispered, 'Can you see they are both naked from the waist up?'

'Yes.' Her breathing a little faster.

'Can you see he has his hand up her skirt and she has dropped his shorts and underwear to the floor?'

'Yes.'

Greg pulled her dress down to below her waist and switched his kisses from her nipples to her neck as he continued his story. He could tell she was loving it.

'They're completely naked now babe, you can see hands all over their hot bodies. Are you ready for them to see you lying here, naked, wanting and wet?'

Tess nodded letting the vision fill her mind.

He removed her dress completely, not at all surprised that she wore no underwear. He seductively slid the dress over her hips and down her legs. At that point, he quickly removed his shirt and shorts. Lying beside her, with one leg over hers, he ran his tongue along her neck to her ear and said, 'There's one condition if we get involved with Matt and Sarah. Anything goes, except no penetration. Do you agree?'

'Yes,' she responded softly.

He found her lips and kissed her. He then whispered, 'Can you see and feel them next to us?'

'Yes, I can.'

'They are kissing and touching each other. Sarah is lying next to you. She's reaching out her hand. She wants to touch your breast. Is that okay?'

Tess's reply was instant. 'Yes.'

Greg tried to imagine how the soft touch of another woman would feel as he gently stroked the side of her breast and traced his fingertips around the base of her nipple. 'Do you like her touching you, babe?'

'Yes.'

Tess was soon lost in this fantasy world and could imagine and feel the sensation as if it really was Sarah's fingers drifting down her stomach, between her legs to eventually find her wetness.

'Do you like her touching you there?' Greg asked.

Tess replied faintly with a longer, 'Yes.' She was sure she heard Sarah say, 'I want to touch your pussy. Is that okay?'

'Yes,' Tess answered again.

As Greg continued caressing her bud, she moaned softly and rolled her hips, obviously lost in the delight of Greg's touch and the images in her mind. Greg reached up to caress her breast with his left hand as he said, 'Matt also loves your breasts.'

Tess arched, raising her chest higher, enjoying it.

Greg paused and then whispered, 'Tess, I am going to move over with Sarah but will be right here next to you.' He placed both his hands on her breasts and moved his body above her. 'Matt is over you now, admiring your beautiful body. He can't stop looking at you. He is hard from the sight of you. Can you see that?'

'Yes,' Tess said again.

'It's okay. I'm lying right here next to you with Sarah. I will be right here watching you and Matt.'

'Okay.'

'Matt is above you,' he said as he positioned himself there.

'Sarah has me in her mouth, and I'm loving it.'

'Mmm,' was Tess's only reply.

Greg saw she was there. She felt it. The sex was in her, next to her, and surrounding her. He moved as if he was Matt and slid down to kiss her feet, her ankles, her calves. As Greg laid the first kiss on her flesh above her knees, her legs fell further apart, and he progressed up her thighs as she physically beckoned for more.

'Are you enjoying Matt's touch, babe?'

'Yes, very much.'

Greg's mouth found her, and she gasped as he started licking her lips and scrolling his tongue around her clitoris. Her legs quivered, reminding him how much she loved that. His tongue and lips worked their way north, kissing her up her tummy and breast.

'Matt loves how you taste, babe. Can you see Sarah on top of me rubbing herself along me?' he whispered, so the image wasn't forgotten.

'Yes, I can, but don't do her, honey.'

Still acting as if he was Matt, Greg kissed her neck as he rubbed his rock-hard cock between her spread legs. 'Matt is right there and is desperate to enter you, babe,' he murmured as he pushed a little more pressure against her. He could feel how wet and swollen she was. 'He's so ready for you. You are so beautiful.'

'Oh,' Tess gasped.

'Sarah wants me inside her, babe. She's pushing against my knob, she wants to fuck me bad, just like Mike wants you.' He pushed his hardness against her again, this time almost parting her wet swollen flesh.

'Ye—err, no,' she managed to get out. 'Don't we have a deal?' Panting, she raised her hips towards him.

'I know, but Matt wants to be inside you. Do you want him?'

'I want you, Greg.' Tess was now almost breathless.

'I have my knob touching Sarah… Can I please just push inside her a little?' He pushed himself against her again, this time feeling her opening. He could see Tess's hips rising, feeling what Sarah wanted, what she so desperately wanted…

'No, you can't,' she murmured.

'Can Matt fuck you, babe?' He pushed so his knob was now a little inside her.

Unable to control herself, 'Oh God! Yes!' burst forth from her lips.

He pushed a little further inside her, just entering her a little more each time, teasing her, making her shake with anticipation. He continued to build on the moment. 'I want to fuck Sarah, babe. Please let me. Matt is fucking you. He wants to give it all to you. It's okay. I love you,' Greg said now almost panting.

In a heartbeat, Tess's reply was loud as she all but screamed out, 'Yes! Fuck her baby.'

Greg kept her thoughts right there. 'Can you see me pounding her, Tess? She is about to come for me.'

'Yes, I can see you with her, it's so hot.'

'Can you feel him too, feel Matt, he's right there inside you, babe?'

He slid deep inside her, he too now shuddering with each thrust. 'I want to see you come for Matt, babe, he is about to blow inside you.'

Within seconds, she was climaxing so hard, her whole body was nearly leaping from the bed as the waves of ecstasy pounded her body. He also exploded inside her as she came again. The pulsing of her vagina was more than it had ever been, like her body was trying to keep him there, milking ever drop of his love juices from him. This had been so intense and was much more than he'd ever expected.

Greg removed the blindfold and untied her hands. She hugged him tight, as if wanting to apologise for her indiscretion. She had just emotionally made love to another man.

Lying cradled in each other's arms, they continued to just hold each other without saying a word.

After a time, Tess whispered, 'That was such a turn on and so naughty. I felt a little guilty, but it's nice to have you back in my arms, babe.'

They spent their last afternoon cuddling in bed, dozing in and out of sleep and enjoying being together in the afterglow of such intense lovemaking. When they finally arose and started to get ready for their last night's dinner, Greg commented, 'You really enjoy that blindfold play.'

'Yes! I sure did. I would have thought you'd already know how much that turned me on,' she said with a laugh.

Greg smiled. 'Yes, I could tell. It was pretty hot for me too. I've always been aroused and fascinated by the thought of us having sex with others. I'm so happy to see your hidden naughtiness. Not only this afternoon but throughout our whole holiday. Tess, I loved how much you enjoyed it and how willing you are to share in these pleasures with me.'

Tess looked at Greg's face and could see his eyes were shining; he meant what he was saying. She drew in a breath, not knowing how to reply. Before he said another word, she just smiled gently, stepped forward, and kissed him. As the kiss deepened, she broke away and suggested, 'Perhaps we could have a late dinner?'

Those words triggered something, and Greg's mind flickered. He flinched ever so slightly in her lustful embrace and lifted his head from its nestled spot on her shoulder.

'What did you say?'

Tess smiled and squeezed him cheekily on the bum. 'I just said, perhaps we can have a late dinner?'

That simple statement transported Greg's thoughts back to the room in Sydney, recalling those first heightened, intimate moments with Kara. Out of nowhere, the words had hit him with a thud. The image of Kara removing her shirt and their first embrace vividly appeared in his mind's eye.

Kara, he hadn't thought of her the whole time. Greg stepped back and looked at Tess, then quickly refocused back into the moment. Tess was ready for more lovemaking.

Sensing his pause, a small frown appeared on her face.

'Or maybe we should get some dinner first,' he said hesitantly. Then with a big grin and a lighter tone, 'We don't want to wear ourselves out before our last night!'

Tess looked up. 'Yes, you're right as always. The holiday isn't over yet.' She headed to the bathroom to shower and got ready for dinner.

His reaction had surprised him. Sure, he had checked up on Kara on Facebook before they'd left Adelaide, but that was just innocent curiosity. She hadn't seriously entered his thoughts during the past few weeks, yet suddenly he was jolted back to a powerful memory and feelings for her by just that one sentence. Sure, that was the trigger of what was a poignant time with Kara and obviously an amazing, memorable time spent together.

'It's nothing to think about too deeply. It was just hearing the same words that Kara used that reminded you. No harm done,' he told himself.

Tess and Greg's evening together was glorious, and as expected, their last night spent on the islands matched the weather's steamy heat and sultry feel.

This holiday was much more than they both had expected in so many ways. However, like all fantastic holidays, it must come to an end.

They arrived back in Adelaide only days before Christmas. Before even thinking about gifts for each other, family, or friends, they first organised for Greg to move most of his belongings to Tess's apartment so he could base himself there most of the time, also signalling they were about to be a full-time couple. The relaxed, loving, and blissful holiday ensured no question about this move by the time they returned. Both Tess and Greg knew they felt connected and had expressed their love. This was the start of so much more.

Chapter 15

The silence was deafening. Greg had again disappeared from Kara's life, almost as quickly as he had appeared. She knew it was the right thing, but deep inside, her heart was breaking.

It was stupid to think that she could've been more than just a long-time curiosity that he had been keen to find. He had found her, kissed her, loved her and fucked her, and now for him that chapter of his life was closed.

She couldn't explain the inconsolable want that burned inside her. It was so much more than just that body, the mind-blowing sex, or those eyes—those alone could mesmerise any woman into a sense of irresistible connection. Even his 'Hello' immediately told a woman everything he could give her beyond that simple greeting, if you dared return a look or smile.

Despite all of his alluring qualities, what hurt the most was that she had so quickly found a loving friend and lost him again so fast. Tears started to well in her eyes.

He had been the only man in years she had trusted enough to open her heart to, and she did, and now after only two weeks he had gone, her heart was now in tatters. The tears were slowly following each other in a line down her cheeks.

Kara sat at her kitchen table, her elbows on her knees and her moist face in her hands.

'I love you Greg Sheppard,' she said into her hands and sobbed as the words burned through her.

Kara felt lost and meandered through the next few days that followed since their intense romance and sudden final messages. It had been a whirlwind, and she had landed with a massive thud back into the real world of being by herself once again. Only now she has had a taste of a drug she couldn't live without.

For the first time in her life, Kara didn't enjoy the solitude and peace of her own company. Her thoughts would always turn to him and the all-consuming warmth that would radiate from her heart as her mind's eye pictured him holding her, kissing her and loving her.

Then the slow deflation of realisation that would eat through her vision like an evil spirit changing the vibrant colours to a dark grey.

My God, get a grip of yourself Kara! You must forget about him. He's gone, and while he opened the door, you need to walk through it and start enjoying more of your one and only life. There are many more interesting, sexy men in this world to meet and enjoy.

It was now early December, and Kara had been so lost in Greg's spell that she was not in the least ready for Christmas. It was her favourite time of year when she could spoil her family and friends.

Kara got herself moving. She shopped, wrapped, decorated, planned, and hosted lots of pre-Christmas catchups with friends. She even accepted and went on a few dates, rekindling her happy self. So much more aware of her appearance and her renewed confidence and sexiness. She resumed her daily walks and gym work-outs, and by the time Christmas came around, she was looking and feeling good, really good!

She had almost put all thoughts of Greg to rest—or so she thought.

It was Christmas morning at her Aunt Sarah's house. Kara was helping prepare for the big family lunch when Sarah asked, 'Kara darling, have you heard anything from that Greg friend of yours? Kara, chopping a carrot, nearly cut herself with the knife at the mention of his name. Her heartbeat increased. She stopped slicing but didn't look up. 'No, he has his own life, that was just a bit of fun for us,' Kara said slowly as she glimpsed up to see if Sarah believed her. 'Okay, it was a fling, alright.' Kara smiled and started chopping again but the smile soon faded as her heart recalled the loss and that familiar stabbing pain. It was something Sarah noted.

'I see he liked one of your photos on Facebook,' Sarah said.

'Really, which one?' Kara placed the knife down and wiped her hands on her apron, then reached for her phone.

She opened Facebook, and there it was. A simple notification. 'Greg Sheppard liked a photo you are tagged in.'

Despite the outward frown, Kara smiled inside. *At least he hasn't forgotten me.*

She resisted her first reaction to send a 'Happy Christmas' message in reply. *You promised to let him be. Keep that promise you made to yourself… and to him.* With that, she turned her attention to the rest of Christmas lunch.

With their Cook Island holiday, Christmas, and the moving of Greg to Tess's unit now behind them, they had settled into blissful days, despite resuming their demanding work schedules and unpredictable timetables.

They awoke and ended each day happily with each other when work permitted. With Greg's interstate events and Tess's exhibitions and other work demands, they struggled to find many days together. Residing together certainly didn't dampen their desires or their sexual energy in any way, with both of them making as much time as possible to feel, enjoy, and pleasure each other.

By early February, Greg had almost all the plans in place for the 30th of April, except those that were left until the actual day. He had even arranged a secret meeting with three of Tess's girlfriends. With them sworn to secrecy, he had shown them the mock-up ring design and asked if they thought Tess would like it. He wanted it to be perfect the first time. It wouldn't be impossible to change the setting, just work and money.

The response from her friends was as he expected and hoped for, with possibly a little envy there as well.

Everything was going perfectly to plan till Paul called him to explain that he wasn't happy with the diamonds that had arrived from New York and he wanted to send them back. Greg's first thoughts were, *shit, I can't have this go wrong now*, but Paul reassured him, saying the ring would be ready well before the time. Nervous for the next response, Paul contacted him a week later to say that some beautiful, VSI, D-coloured stones had arrived at his shop and that the ring would be ready ahead of schedule. *That's great, because without the ring it wouldn't be much of an occasion,* he thought.

With little left to arrange now until the last week of March, Greg turned back to the earning money compartment of life. He had lots to get organised. An ICT software launch, a TV commercial, two trips interstate in the next two weeks, and a small promotional event towards the end of March for the launch of a Gourmet Weekend later in the year that he had his staff working on.

Kara Gilbert had called the team together for a meeting to discuss the gourmet food and wine festival that was looming closer each day. This was the biggest event by far for the area and her name was all over it. If it failed in any way it would be her head that rolled. She chaired the meeting and was impressed with the progress that each person had made.

'Now the media promotion, what's happening there, it should be going to air any day now?' she asked.

One of her team said that she had followed up on that but the person in charge of our project was on holidays in the pacific and would be completing it as soon as he arrives back.

'Well, can you follow up on that? We should've had a proof weeks ago. I believe we have the airtime booked for ten days' time.'

'Yes, Kara, I will call them straight after the meeting and express our concern.'

'No, I will call them,' Kara insisted. 'It's really not good enough. I know we are only small fry to them, but this is big to us.'

Kara soon closed the meeting and made the call her next priority. Once back at her desk she picked up the phone.

'Hi. I'm Kara Gilbert from the Clare Valley Regional Development office. Can you please put me through to your senior manager?' she asked.

She wasn't happy. A bit of fire had started to burn in her belly and she knew if she was left hanging on the phone, the next person she spoke to was going to get a serve. The receptionist had quickly transferred her to the executive director.

The director picked up the phone. 'Greg Sheppard,' he said in a bold, professional tone.

Kara was instantly in shock as if she had just been hit with a cricket bat.

'Hello, are you there?' Greg asked after the short pause.

'Greg?'

'Oh my God, Kara, is that you?

'Yes, it's me.'

'It's so lovely to hear from you.'

Kara quickly composed herself and said, 'Greg, actually, I am calling to complain.'

'Complain? What do you mean?'

Kara smiled realising how he must have taken what she said.

'Not about you lover boy, you were perfect,' Kara said with a smile. 'Your company is putting together our media production for the Clare Gourmet weekend and I feel a sample of what we could be getting is well overdue. We have TV airtime booked for ten days' time; I would've thought we would have seen a sample at least by now.'

There was an awkward silence between the two of them for a moment, before Greg eventually spoke.

'Okay, Ms Gilbert, leave it with me. I will personally get this sorted. I assure you it will all be done to your full satisfaction, and on time.'

'Thank you, Greg.'

'So how have you been?' he asked.

'I've been going well, keeping busy with Christmas and now this event. You know it takes us months to put it all together.'

'I'm sure it does,' he said feeling a little guilty.

'And what about you Greg, how are you going?'

'I'm going well... you know I think of you quite often, we had fun, didn't we?'

For the first time Kara felt the fine shell that was protecting her heart crack and she felt a burn start to seep through her fragile body.

'We did,' she said, her voice almost breaking.

'Are you seeing anyone?' he asked.

'Why ask me that?'

'Oh, I'm just curious, maybe a little jealous perhaps.'

Kara smiled. 'I refuse to answer. I don't have enough time to tell you all the delicious details of my many recent conquests!' she said finding her feet.

It was Greg's turn to laugh, not sure whether to believe her.

'How are you and Tess going?'

'We are going along nicely, I guess. We don't see enough of each other being so busy and all.'

Deep down that wasn't what Kara wanted to hear. Her heart's protective shell cracked open a little further.

'I am very happy for you both,' she managed to get out.

'Why don't we try and stay in touch Kara, you know you have a special place in my heart that no one else will ever have.'

The burn exploded through her body, and it took all of her might to not burst into tears and tell him how much she loved him.

'I better go,' she said softly.

'Okay, we will talk soon,' he managed to get out, but, with that, she was gone.

All the work Kara had done to build the protective barrier of her heart, destroyed in one phone call. That ache was back, the pain of Greg ripping that precious organ from her body. She couldn't breathe, her chest was in an invisible vice, crushing her. She lowered her head to the desk and let her tears spill.

During the next week, Greg had worked at pace to remedy the lag time that had impacted on Kara's event. *It bloody had to be her event that had slipped from my radar!* he thought. So, in his usual way, he powered into it. He had multiple demands, especially after so much time away enjoying his divine holiday and then moving to a new house and planning the secret event for Tess in April, but he was determined to deliver, especially for Kara.

Over the weeks following Kara's phone call, he'd messaged her every few days as promised, providing updates and to complete the details for the launch scheduled for the eighteenth of March. Everything was on track. He had quietly monitored his team to make sure that the Clare event was back on schedule.

While he always wanted to ensure his company offered no less than the best, he felt guilty about the initial slippage at the start of the Clare project. Since finding out that Kara was associated with it, somehow, he felt even more responsible. He involved himself far more than usual to make sure he had fulfilled each part of her project.

While the calls and messages between Kara and him were always centred around work, there was that 'thing' he felt. He sensed it in her too. The underlying sexual attraction was there, suggestive, and familiar, simmering gently below the surface at an arm's length of any real intimate conversation. Their conversations were no more than what you might consider how two professionals who had remained friends might engage, despite being former lovers. It was rarely more than a teasing comment, and largely their discussions focused on the project.

Greg didn't like to admit it, but he genuinely looked forward to speaking with her. He kept his thoughts and feelings in check. *There's nothing wrong about that. It's only affection for a former lover, and she is a long-lost school friend after all.*

The last item on the list for this week was to finalise a promotional brochure, and Greg asked his graphic designer to send the final copy to Kara's email for her approval before they sent it to the printers. He was heading to Queensland to oversee a tourism campaign launch, so he was about to board the flight when he received a text message from Kara.

> Hi, Greg. Are we on track with the brochure? I thought it might be ready by tonight?

> Haven't you got it yet? I arranged for it to be emailed to you before four o'clock today.

> Nope.

> Shit. Sorry, I'll get it back to you in ten.

Okay, thanks.

Kara's phone rang, and without even a 'Hi,' Greg said, 'Check your email it should be there.'

'Okay, opening it now,' Kara said with a smile in her voice.

There was a pause while Kara opened the email on her phone, clicked on the message from his designer, and downloaded the attachment. She couldn't believe what she saw. This was a brochure that was much more than what she had specified or could afford for that matter!

'Oh my God! Greg, what have you done?'

'What? Don't tell me you don't like it?' His voice was raised slightly, a bit worried.

'Oh no! Nothing is wrong. It's nearly too good. It's outstanding! Brilliant! But… I don't think we can afford this.'

With relief in his voice, he reassured her, 'Oh shit Kara, don't worry about that, just tell me the layout and wording are correct and I will get it sent for printing. As for the cost, it won't be any more than we quoted, to be honest, I'll admit that it was really my fault we fell behind on your job.'

'Why is that?'

Greg paused. 'Truth be told, when I raced off for a month on a holiday with Tess, I completely dropped the ball as far as work was concerned. This event got a little lost in that, and I am truly sorry.'

'Well, Greg, the brochure is perfect and the Clare Valley appreciates it. You don't have to do this though. I'm sure we can pay the full cost, and besides, everyone needs to fulfil their fantasies and escape when the opportunity arises.'

'It's my pleasure, Kara, the least I can do.' He waited a moment and then asked. 'Hey, Kara, so tell me, what's on your wish list, what do you dream or fantasise about?'

Greg's question came naturally enough, and he expected her to reply with her favourite travel destination and not what came next.

'Oh, yes, lots! To be honest, I've always wanted to be an actress, a director, or something to do with films.'

There was a hesitation as she fought with herself, and then said, 'Maybe kiss a girl and have a threesome. But as none of those will probably happen, my answer would be to visit the USA one day.'

Greg was taken aback. 'A threesome, kissing girls, really? Two boys or two girls?'

'Two girls, definitely!'

Kara realised she had just blurted her response to him without a thought of how this might sound. She quickly said, 'Oh! trust you to pick the threesome from my list.'

'Sorry, I'm surprised, but I guess I shouldn't be, that's up there on my list as well.'

'Okay, so, now you know one more of my secrets, surely you would know that most women wonder what it's like to kiss another woman or have a ménage à trois? Anyway, you opened the door and asked me about fantasies. Dangerous subject Mr. Sheppard!' Kara's heart was pounding.

Realising that Greg was obviously a little shocked by her response, Kara changed the subject. 'Sorry, enough silly stuff! How long are you going to be around Clare for the launch?'

Greg's mind was picturing Kara kissing Tess.

Having teased Tess with multiple partners during phone sex and after only recently seeing her increasing carefree attitude to being watched and then her reaction to his blindfold fantasy experience while on holiday, he was pretty sure she really felt okay with the possibility of doing it one day. But he hadn't actually asked the question.

During the years on his own, Greg had enjoyed several casual partners, and as great as that was, he was now at a time in his life where he felt more sexually aware than he had ever been and had been secretly searching to step his desires up to the next level. Tess had become the love of his life in every way, much more than their sexual connection alone. However, he had always been eager for her to travel this erotic journey with him.

Greg's event co-ordination mind was in top gear. This could be the opportunity for him to have Kara again, to feel those muscley legs wrap around him as he screwed her and not be unfaithful to his darling Tess. He felt a twinge in his groin as he remembered the amazing sex that he and Kara had on that first night. How her body pulsed and clamped him as she came over and over again and how powerful his orgasm was as he finally emptied himself deep inside her.

Greg composed his thoughts as he repositioned himself in his now tight pants and replied, 'Oh, yes, of course I'll be there. You should know, the TV crew can't be left to their own devices! So, let's make sure we catch up for a coffee or drink if the time allows.'

Kara hesitated. *What are you doing, woman? You know this is wrong.* If this was a game of snakes and ladders, she was being seduced by the snake and would end up back where she was, clinging to the rungs, desperately craving this man.

Whether in part embarrassment or part a suppressed desire, either way she said, 'Yes, coffee would be nice, but as you say, only if time permits. We'll both be busy.'

'That's great. Catch you soon. Anyway, I have to board my flight now. I'll try and call you later, Kara.'

He hung up without waiting for a reply.

Chapter 16

Greg arrived at his hotel in Brisbane, and made the calls to check on the plans for the morning, knowing it would be a frantic day tomorrow. He ordered room service since he didn't want to sit on his own in the restaurant tonight. He phoned Tess, and they chatted for ages. She sounded happy, but he detected that slight hint of melancholy, that she was missing him lots. He missed her too. These trips away were harder now since having spent so much time together alone on the islands.

After showering, he lay on the bed with a glass of wine and his book, intending to read until he was ready to sleep. Only half catching the words, his thoughts wandered back again to his call with Kara earlier that day. Truth be told, he had spent most of his flight thinking about what she had said. He checked the time; it was 10.00 p.m. He dialled Kara's number, half expecting she wouldn't answer.

'Hello, Greg.'

'How are you going, sexy?'

Kara smiled, she loved that he called her that. While she knew it was more of his natural affectionate greeting, than what he was actually thinking, but it always seduced her just the same.

'Well, I had a busy day, especially dealing with some random event company manager, so now I'm enjoying a glass of wine and reading till I fall asleep, and you?'

Greg smiled, still a little embarrassed that she brought that up.

'Yes, well, we know about those event managers,' he said not wanting to talk about that again. 'As a matter of fact, that's much the same for me—lots happening at work. Dealing with a most difficult client, travelling, and now I'm trying to relax. To tell you the truth, these hotel rooms are starting to get to me. What's your book about?'

'You know, typically girly romance, lust, sex and naughtiness, a bit of bed-hopping.'

'Sounds better than mine, just lust of other people's business success and desk-hopping! Are you in bed to stay or still got things to do?'

'I'm in for the night,' Kara said.

'Me too.'

They talked some more about the work ahead, the future events he was organising, and each touched on a little that had been happening in their lives since they last talked. Greg could feel Kara relaxing more into the conversation; her breathing was slower, softer, and the conversation more open. Greg was rapt that she was comfortable with him again after what had happened in the last few weeks. Kara's breathing became increasingly slower and deeper as she listened.

'Kara, are you touching yourself?'

There was a pause before she answered with a quiet,

'No! …Well maybe just a little, well, I'm lying here relaxed, naked, glass of red, lights dimmed, my soft music on, and the best lover I have ever had talking to me was too much, sorry, should I stop, does that put you off?'

Greg drew in a breath. The words suddenly just fell out of him. 'Kara, look, this is crazy I know, and I expect you think I'm behaving badly, and, yes, I might be and no, of course, please don't stop. My situation hasn't changed, you know. I'm now fully committed to Tess. You can tell me to go, but I have to say that I've really enjoyed being back in contact with you. You've been with me in my mind for years, you know that. When you told me today about your fantasy of enjoying some sexy play with others, it was such a turn on for me. I couldn't say it then, but… I must admit I have similar desires. I'm sorry. I should hang up now, please don't think badly of me.'

Kara listened to his rambling disclosure. This was not the usually composed Greg. Taking in every word, Kara thought hard. *He is feeling this. At face value, this is all so wrong, but why does it feel so right? You know you still have some feelings for him, but he has Tess. What do you really want here? That is the only question to ask yourself. You vowed to never succumb to the influence and coercion of anyone who wanted to control your life. Never again.*

Kara knew the answer. *You don't want marriage, a full-time partner, or anything apart from being surrounded by nice people and regular sex. Greg is a very dangerous drug and one I'm addicted to. My god I want him so badly right now.*

Her reply was hushed but clear. 'Greg, I am touching myself.'

He took a deep breath before replying.

'Are you really, sexy?'

'Yes,' she replied in a near whisper this time. There was a long pause. 'Kara, look, you don't have to—'

Kara stopped him. 'Greg… it's okay. I know what I'm doing. I know what we are doing.'

Greg now realised that Kara was also a drug he couldn't resist.

'Would you like me to tell you one of my stories?'

This was the moment. It was her turn for the intake of a breath, yet her response came easily. 'I would love that.'

'Okay, put your book down, lay back, and close your eyes, and I'll tell you a little fantasy of mine.'

Kara adjusted the pillows and turned out the bedside light. 'Okay, I'm ready.'

Greg began. 'You come up to Brisbane to share the weekend with me, all excited to have some fun. We haven't been together for a while. You meet me at the hotel where I'm staying. I'm having a few drinks with my work colleagues at the bar. We kiss and I hug you as you arrive. You know I'm thrilled to see you. I'll get you a champagne and introduce you to a few of the people around us. One girl who has had a few drinks already, pays you a bit of attention, asking are we an item or just friends… or friends with benefits, she sneaks out. "A bit of both," I say.

'I explain that you have come out of a long marriage and are busy exploring the new and exciting world of sex. "Well, that's a big world with many options," she says as she turns to grab another drink. She turns back after ordering, asking, "Have you ever had a threesome, Kara?" "No," you say. She tells you, "It can be amazing if it's done right," then turns back to collect her fifth glass of champagne.

'We look at each other and smile, and I ask you, "Would that interest you?" The smile on your face answers the question, so I say, "Well, she's pretty and keen. Shall I ask her? Let's see what she says." I'm now also on my fifth drink, so with confidence, I ask, "Have you had many threesomes?" With a naughty grin, she admits, "Just a few, why? Are you two interested?" "I think we might be," I say as I turn to you, and you smile with agreement. Before we finish our drinks, the three of us are heading upstairs to my room.

'As the hotel room door closes, I turn you to face her, holding your hands down behind your back, and start to kiss and bite your neck. I know how much you love that. She comes to you and kisses your mouth deeply, the way only another woman can. I hold you tight, and she unbuttons your top and pulls it over your shoulders, exposing your lacy white bra. She reaches behind you and between us to undo it. She lifts it over your breasts as she takes a nipple in her mouth. I release you to let your top and bra fall to the ground. I come around behind her and undress her. In no time you are both topless. You are enjoying feeling her tits as she sucks yours. Then she runs her hands up your legs and under your skirt to touch your now wet knickers. You can't see me, but you imagine I'm doing the same to her. You know I am. I slip her white lacy knickers to the floor, and you can hear her groaning from my touch as she sucks on your breasts. She turns and lays you on the bed, removing your skirt and knickers. You watch her and I strip, and we are all soon naked. I come to kiss your lips as she kisses your feet, ankles, knees, and thighs. She finds you wet with her tongue. Can you feel her, Kara?'

'Yes, I can, mmm,' Kara murmurs.

Greg continues. 'I kiss you hard as I feel you getting off from the oral attention she is giving to you in every fold between your legs. I don't want you to come yet, though. There's more to come. She's working her way up your tummy to find your lips. You can taste yourself on her tongue as she lies on top of you. I'm looking at you both—two hot women joined. It's such a turn on for me. You see me standing back, watching you both and stroking myself. I know that you seeing me do it turns you on. I straddle her from behind. Her legs spread over yours, I tease her with my erection. You can feel her getting excited as she kisses you harder. You can tell when I enter her; you can feel her body tense against yours as I thrust harder and harder inside her. She lets out a cry and grips you tight. You know I've made her squirt; you feel it run between your legs.

'I roll over onto my back and pull you onto me, so you are lying face up. I take your hands in mine and squeeze them tight as I slide inside you from beneath you. She kneels between your legs, our lovemaking on full display for her to see. She takes a moment to watch, but then you feel her fingers caressing you. I hold you tight to me, as we are both going to have our way with you. I pump you gently, and she works your button with her tongue. Let me hear you. Let it all go, babe.'

Kara barely said a word as Greg spoke. She was there, in that fantasy, feeling it all. Lying across her bed, she arched her back as she imagined that her own fingers, which were moving and thrusting into herself frantically, were that of another woman. That vision was all she needed as that beautiful heat erupted sending sparks to every inch of her body. She felt her body clamp around the two fingers as she imagined Greg filling her.

Greg listened to Kara's orgasm build, picturing the pretty girl from his work naked between her legs, licking and sucking her. He wanked himself faster as the story progressed. The sound of Kara's release was all Greg needed. His groan was too much for her, sending Kara spiralling into a second climax.

It was minutes before either of them could speak. Greg broke the silence first. 'Are you okay?' he asked softly.

'I'm more than okay. That was bloody amazing. Oh my God, that blew me away... literally.' She laughed. 'I so want to do that again!'

Greg chuckled. 'Well, I've blown here as well, so that makes two of us. Kara, I'd love to do that for real one day.'

'So how would you go about finding a lady?' Kara asked.

Greg thought for a moment before saying hesitantly,

'Well, I could ask a couple of ladies I know to see if one of them might join us... but... are you serious?'

'I find the idea very exciting. I'm truly fascinated!'

Greg couldn't quite believe it.

'Well, Kara, you completely astound me sometimes, but, yes, I know what you mean,' he chuckled. 'Okay, let's think about this some more. Hey, Kara, thank you for tonight.'

'Thank you, Greg, for all of your talents today. Sleep well,' Kara said before hanging up the phone.

Greg lay there, his thoughts turning over. He couldn't find the right box for these feelings to rest. It seemed like every time he encountered Kara Gilbert, there was something unexpected that emerged. She was like no one he had ever met before. He thought of Tess, he knew full well that he didn't love her any less because of the phone call with Kara. He tried to analyse the situation. There was no clear answer. She was becoming more of a force and an attraction than either of them knew.

Chapter 17

*B*ack at home, the Clare event was looming, and Greg knew he would be travelling away again much to Tess's dismay. She'd not said anything, but he felt the twinge of sadness each time he left with his overnight bag. He too, had felt some actual guilt about having enjoyed his contact with Kara, and he'd tried to stop thinking about her as any more than that of a special, but only casual friend.

Maybe her talk of threesomes was just a fantasy, the same as it was for Tess? He tried to convince himself so he would stop entertaining thoughts about his own secret desires or any possibility of these ever being realised—especially with Kara. *Sure, she is lovely, and I really like her, but it can only end in pain.*

He wanted to make Tess his one and only woman now. He had to.

Greg turned his sights to finalising the plans for his special night with Tess. He had the major things in place, but it was time for the finer details. Some were now getting urgent. The ring design and stones were all set, but he needed to get hold of the ring that Tess wore on her ring finger to get the size. This was all important, as it had to fit perfectly when he gave it to her. But she never seemed to take it off!

He had to somehow get this ring measured and the details back to the jeweller post haste. Greg needed a plan.

Time for a weekend treat and little escape, he thought. *It will be good for both of us anyway.*

Greg checked all the nearby beach locations, far enough away for a pleasant escape but a location with a professional jeweller in close proximity. He settled on Middleton Beach. He made a call to the jeweller, explaining he would likely have only a brief window of opportunity while he brought his lady down for the weekend and asked if he would be available to measure her ring? The jeweller was most obliging, saying he would be more than happy to help.

Greg was grateful, especially as the jeweller wasn't being asked to make the ring. Greg said he would like to purchase a large solitaire pearl necklace from him as well to match Tess's dress ring as a nice way to compensate the jeweller with at least some sale and also a bit of a backup. In the event Tess became wise to his plan. He could always explain he wanted to match her ring with something special. So, he followed up the call with a quick email to confirm the order for the necklace and a picture of Tess showing the ring on her finger.

That step organised, he booked accommodation on the beachfront, not too far from the shopping precinct where the jewellery shop was situated, for three nights and two full days of sun and beach. It was set. They could let loose, ride down together on his motorbike, and it would hopefully show her that the memories of their trip and his feelings for her had not waned in the least.

March, being so hot still, was perfect as they set off Friday afternoon, both having left work early, so eager for this escape.

Greg had only two possible windows of time to grab her ring and get it to the jeweller while the shop was open. That afternoon or Saturday morning. Knowing he wouldn't rest until he had the ring measurement, he wanted to try for Friday afternoon. So, after checking in to the hotel and a leisurely late lunch, he suggested they take a swim before exploring the beach. They returned to their room and changed before strolling down to the beach.

They chatted for ages and lay soaking up the sun. Greg read and appeared a little distracted, in the hope she would decide to go for a swim. He had discreetly kept checking his watch, mindful of how little time he had. With the sun streaming down and Greg reading his book, Tess eventually said she would hit the water.

Greg looked up at her and said, 'Hey, you'd better take your jewellery off, hon. If you lose anything in that swell, you'd never find it.'

She looked at him, a little perplexed, but he had turned back to his book. *He's never said that before, but he's probably right*, she thought. She removed her necklace and rings, shoved them in the pocket of her shorts, and headed to the water. At the first opportunity, Greg grabbed the ring he needed and hid it in his own pocket, hoping like hell she would forget to put it back on when she left the water.

As she returned, he stood up with her towel and wrapped it around her before pulling her close. 'God, you are breathtaking to watch walk from the water.'

She didn't give her jewellery a thought.

They made their way back to the hotel, and while she showered, Greg slipped out of the room and jumped on his bike, hoping the jeweller could honour his promise and measure the ring as soon as he arrived. He rode like hell, trying to be back before she left the shower. It all worked like clockwork. The jeweller knew instantly who Greg was as he burst into the shop, his motorbike left parked on the footpath right outside of the door. The jeweller had the pearl on a fine gold chain, ready for Greg to inspect in a box on the counter.

While Greg checked the necklace, the jeweller measured the ring. He paid for the necklace, thanked him warmly, and was back on the bike and soon at the hotel.

He raced into the room, breathless. He had made it. Tess was still in the bathroom, music blaring, and thankfully had no idea. Greg found her discarded shorts on the floor, slipped her ring back into the pocket, and poured a wine. He quickly emailed Paul with the ring size. Another box ticked, and he could now relax, sit on the balcony, and enjoy his lady and the view of the ocean.

The weekend was perfect. They had cruised down the coast on his Kawasaki the next morning, checking out the beaches and little spots along the way. They filled their weekend, just like their holiday, enjoying meals, good wine, walks, and many intimate moments. It was what they both needed. Late Sunday evening, they ventured to the beach. Lying side by side, they watched the sun fade, having spent the previous hours making love, showering, dining, and chatting endlessly. Neither wanted Monday morning and their return to work to come.

As darkness consumed the evening light and with people leaving the beach to head home, Tess sat up, looked at Greg, and smiled. Slowly, she removed her top and undid her bra, letting them fall away.

'Remember this?' she said with a grin.

Moving to sit close behind her, Greg wrapped his arms around her and stroked her breasts as he nestled his head into the side of her neck, kissing her from her shoulder to her ears and cheek. 'I will never forget this or anything about our amazing holiday.'

Her body pressed back into him as she raised her head, lengthening her neck to soak up every touch of his lips. He smiled as his lips touched the chain of the pearl necklace which he'd given to her the previous night at dinner.

'I love you, Greg Sheppard.'

'You might never know how much you mean to me. I love you too, Teresa Merchant.'

With her still wrapped in his arms, Greg thought about their holiday again and asked Tess what she loved the most.

'Oh, everything really. Just being with you the whole time was the best part.'

'Nothing else? Not even our island tour?' he asked with a laugh.

'Oh, you mean those highlights; Well, all the sexy moments we shared will be forever imprinted in my memory. We should never stop that, you know,' she said. 'When you are away, perhaps we need more phone sex, like the blindfold experience you gave me. That was amazing.'

The mention of phone sex and that scene reminded Greg of the words Kara had mentioned only days ago. 'Surely you would know that most women wonder what it's like to be with another woman or have ménage à trois.'

Greg responded softly, 'Hey, Tess, that was one of my highlights too. I loved how you responded to the story about us with another couple.' Pausing again, he swallowed hard then asked, 'Babe, would you ever really do the blindfold scene for real?'

Tess drew in a breath before turning herself around to face him, looking him in the eye. 'Honey, I have thought about this quite a bit. I get how much of a turn on that would be. To me, fantasy is one thing, but having someone other than you touch me is something I can't even imagine possible. Besides, honestly, if you think for one minute, I could watch you screw someone in front of me, you're dreaming! You mean too much to me to share you with anyone. I'd just be so jealous. So, while I will forever love these stories to heighten our fabulous lovemaking, I really couldn't. I hope you aren't disappointed.'

'Of course not. I understand completely, I really do. I just needed to ask, so I know, that's all. Come on, we're already late for our date in our room,' he said with a laugh. As she stood, she slipped her top over her head and her bra in her pocket. They then strolled back to the hotel hand in hand.

Truthfully, he was a little disappointed. He had wanted Tess to be a willing partner in his unearthed kinky desires, but he also knew that she based her reaction on her true feelings. She adored him, deeply. Greg had been so blessed in finding and having her in his life, and anyway, he wasn't sure if he could really watch another man touching his Tess either.

God, another woman I could, though, that's for sure, he thought.

Chapter 18

This little weekend break had done Tess and Greg a world of good, especially recharging them both for the weeks ahead, where Greg would be away for nearly a month with barely a night at home. It had also guaranteed that the April night with Tess was a step closer to perfection.

The Clare event was next on the calendar, and so a week later, it was not unexpected that his phone pinged with a message from Kara.

> Hi, Greg. I'm hoping you received the run sheets for the launch next Saturday. They have been finalised now. Parade start time has been moved to a bit earlier. Mayor's official opening is still at noon. Let me know if you see any problems. Otherwise, catch you next week. Kara

He smiled. She was back to business, on track, and organised. He had not heard from her since their heated phone-sex call, and he wondered how she would handle their working relationship after that time.

He gave her a quick call.

'Hello, Kara! Organising me and the world as usual, I see.'

'You should expect nothing less, Mr Sheppard. So, when do you land in Clare?'

'I'm hoping to arrive Friday evening, so I can get an early start Saturday morning. Now that your parade time is earlier, I don't want to risk the news crew missing the start.'

'Hey, would you like to grab dinner Friday night? Might be good to catch up, to check all the details before the morning. I'm sure it will be crazy.'

'Great idea. I have a few things to check before, only minor. It will be nice to see you too.'

'Okay then. You tell me the best time, and I'll try to book somewhere.'

Greg was about to say goodbye but paused. He thought for a second and then mumbled, 'By the way, I followed up on a couple of possible contacts for a… threesome.' He paused, cautiously awaiting her response.

'Really, how did that go?'

Greg heard her tone change and imagined her looking around at who may be listening.

'Sadly, not too well. Both of the ladies I thought may be keen are now in relationships and declined for now.' He knew he shouldn't be doing it, but that lustful drug had a good hold of him now.

'But there are other options, he said.'

'Oh, that's disappointing, but what options?' Her body now tingling with desire.

'Why don't we talk about it on Friday?'

'Of course! Hey, why not come to my place for dinner? We can speak more privately and, you're most welcome to stay, but no pressure.'

He paused again. 'Are you sure about that?'

'Sure, why not, don't you want to?'

'You know I do.'

'Done then!' Kara said with finality.

'Are you sure?'

'Greg, this may sound bad, and this is so unusual for me too, but I know about your life and everyone in it. I'm not a part of that, and I don't want to be. All I know, in response to your question, is that I'm sure that I would love you to come over, eat with me, and stay the night. I would really like that. I know I'm a bad influence, sorry, but goddammit, you created this monster!'

'Yes, you are a very bad influence all right, shall we make it your place at around six, is that okay?'

'That sounds perfect.'

'Text me your address. Until Friday then. We have work to do.'

'I'll send it now.'

Kara sent him her address and knew she would be smiling for the rest of the week.

As soon as the call ended, Greg's mind was racing, and the excitement of anticipation flowed through his body. He couldn't believe how he had agreed so easily to meet and be with her again. He'd always been able to walk away from brief encounters in the past—until now. Greg found himself excited at the thought of spending another night with Kara.

Having been up since 5.00 a.m., Kara had been on the run all day, checking and double-checking every detail for the event. She'd chaired the final meeting with the planning committee, met and welcomed the mayor, taken him through the details of the entire program and a full rehearsal of the launch ceremony. With as much as possible done before the next day, she stole away around 3.00 p.m. to get herself and the food ready for her private rendezvous at her home. This was the event from this weekend's program that she was looking forward to most.

It was close to 6.00 p.m. As the anticipation built, she had paced around, checking her watch every few minutes, and looking out the window. She finally resolved to open the wine and pour herself a drink before turning up her music and focusing on the final preparation for their dinner.

As soon as he opened his car door, he could hear the music booming from the house. He smiled on hearing Starboy's 'I feel it coming' playing. Kara was signalling her anticipation of his arrival. He called out, 'Hello,' but there was no response. Looking through the screen door, he could see her, her body moving to the music. He opened the door.

She was standing at the sink and hadn't heard him as he entered the kitchen from the carport. Startled by the sudden feel of his hands around her waist from behind, she turned.

It took only seconds for him to find her lips. He caressed and gently bit her bottom lip, while his fingers explored her body, lifting her dress to squeeze her behind, finding with little surprise that she was without underwear. She was instantly aroused and welcomed his touch. It was at this point that their eyes connected, and he uttered a soft, 'Hello.'

His hands continued caressing her body, quickly reacting to the moment. His fingers now searched with hunger, finding her warm and wet. She started to grind against his touch, slowly at first, then harder and harder, as if she were trying to feel every part of him through his fingers.

She moaned as her hands grasped his chest, desperately clenching his shirt. He could feel her muscles twitch and pulse against his fingers in orgasmic shivers.

Kara's mouth explored his neck, kissing and sucking him. Pulling back, she looked into his eyes momentarily and uttered her first words. 'God, I've missed you.'

Wrapping his arms around her, Greg pulled her whole body to him. Before she knew it, her dress was on the floor, and somehow Greg had unbuttoned, unzipped, and removed his shorts and jocks leaving only a sliver of fabric between them. Kara reached out and grabbed his shirt, lifting it up over his head. They stood in her kitchen, naked, breathing hard, their mouths kissing and tasting each other's bodies.

He turned her, bending her over the kitchen bench. With his hands grasping her breasts and his lips kissing her neck, his penis found her, slipping firmly inside her. Kara loved this position; this is how he could penetrate her to the deepest point. With each thrust it was much more than just his rock-hard flesh inside her, it was him, it was the man she adored like no other, inside her body, her mind and her soul. Having him again, after all this time, was nearly more than she could take. She could not contain her pleasure much longer. She gasped and cried out as he thrust into her with each stroke, more powerful than the last.

Greg loved how tight Kara was from her lifetime of dancing and how her muscles would clench and squeeze him, with and without intention. Looking up, he could see the street through the window which meant a passer-by could easily see them.

'We're pretty exposed to the street, babe,' he whispered.

'I don't care.'

His hold on her tightened at her reply, and he drove into her again, deeper and deeper until he felt her body tighten, quiver, and finally yield to the sensational rush of her orgasm.

His arrival had been profound. This was so much more than she could imagine as a first time to host a man in her home since her divorce. This was the start of something incredible.

Kara finally found her voice as her breathing calmed. 'Well, welcome to my home, Mr Sheppard. I can tell you're pleased to be here,' she said with a cheeky grin.

'You bet, Ms Gilbert. These are just the work meetings I enjoy the most.'

She took him by the hand. 'Time to see my place. You can't escape the tour.'

Still both naked and Greg still somewhat erect, Kara led him through her home room by room, describing the work she had done and her next plans.

As they entered her office, Greg stopped and pulled Kara into a close embrace. 'You have a lovely home.' He kissed her lightly on the lips before skimming his mouth down her throat to kiss her neck. His teeth sank into her neck, gently at first and then harder.

'Oh my God,' was the only response Kara could give as she nearly melted in his arms.

Greg lifted her onto the edge of her desk and asked, 'Have you ever been fucked on your desk?'

'No,' she said and he was again inside her. 'You are the first man in this house in the four years since I've been here on my own,' she whispered in his ear, between gasps. He thrust into her harder, frantically kissing her, making her come in what only felt like seconds.

Afterward, she was in a haze of complete delight. So, when he asked, 'So, what's for dinner, you hot thing?' all Kara could say was 'You're thinking about food? I'm not sure I can walk!'

That made him chuckle. 'A man needs to keep up his stamina. The night has only just started, sexy.'

Kara grinned. 'I see. Well, don't break me, Superman. I'm still quite new to this, remember?'

They walked back to the kitchen, finding their clothes scattered where they had been shed on his arrival. Kara slid back into her dress and finished preparing their meal, her breathing almost back to normal. He slipped on his jocks and poured a glass of wine for them both.

'Ahh…' He took a sip before raising his glass to hers. 'Thanks for having me, Kara.'

'Ha, ha, hilarious!' replied Kara drolly, noting his intended double meaning. She eventually made a salad and served their dinner before she dared get too close to him again. Of course, she had expected they would have sex, but this was already far beyond her imagination, and they hadn't even reached the bedroom yet.

They talked over dinner about her life, her daughter and her plans for the future, while enjoying the lovely Clare Valley red wine. Kara finally stood up and started to clear the table. As she reached out to take Greg's dinner plate, he grasped her and softly said, 'That dinner was just amazing, delicious. Thank you.'

She kissed him on the forehead. 'Thank you, it was my absolute pleasure.'

'You are my pleasure tonight,' he replied.

He motioned for her to sit on his lap. She lifted her dress and swung her right leg to straddle him, facing him with her arms around his neck. As she kissed his neck and cheek, he lifted her by the waist, adjusted his jocks, and lowered her onto him. Divinely mounted, she rode him from tip to base. moving from standing to a deep grind into his lap. Greg's hold on her waist grew firmer as he moved her fast and faster upon him. As she felt the pressure rising and every inch of his shaft throbbing inside her, she pushed herself down hard onto him. He felt her orgasm erupt from deep inside her, her head falling back as she cried out to the ceiling.

When the shuddering subsided, they looked at each other and grinned.

'Well, dessert was amazing too, Kara,' Greg smirked.

'I think we might need to wait a while for coffee and after-dinner liqueurs,' Kara replied cheekily as she moved to stand up. 'You'd better come and help me clear the dishes, so I can keep those hands occupied with something other than my body.'

As they cleared the table, they chatted. Kara was a little surprised to learn that Greg enjoyed cooking and, like her, loved creating his own dishes. He was genuinely interested in getting the recipe of the dish she had prepared for him.

As Kara finished putting away the last few items in the kitchen, Greg walked through her place again, looking at the photos and getting the feel of her past life. Each room had quite a distinct and different style and décor, yet somehow it all blended tastefully. The home emulated the unique character that was Kara Gilbert—both predictable yet random and surprising, all mixed into one.

'I've found it. Come here, Kara. I've found my favourite place,' Greg called out.

Kara walked into the lounge room to find Greg lying on his back, still naked, in front of the fireplace. She had left the blankets from the lounges and a few cushions there, being the place where she loved to lay and read or just curl up.

He had stretched out, his arms behind his head, and he grinned as he said, 'Want to come and join me?'

Kara knew this was the perfect time for her little surprise. 'Okay, I'll be a minute. I'll get us something special to drink.' She returned to the kitchen, grabbed some glasses, and poured the drinks.

She arrived back to the lounge room with two glasses and placed them on the coffee table before kneeling to the side of Greg at his knees.

'What do we have here?'

'I thought this might be nice for dessert,' she said with a smile. 'You said once that you would like to enjoy the phone sex fantasy story that I told you for real... so I think it's time for a taste of liqueur.'

Kara's imagined story took a leap into reality as she let a mouthful of the coffee liqueur martini, which had been swilled to warm in her mouth, drizzle over Greg's groin and trickle between his legs to his bum. Kara sucked and licked the cocktail from his body, savouring every inch of him and losing herself in the taste as she went. She explored every part of him with her tongue, her lips, and her hands.

After she had tasted and savoured him, he wanted to reciprocate. Laying her on her back and positioning himself on top of her, he kissed her delicate flesh as he let his hard-on rub over her, tantalising her, before finally entering her. This time, so heightened by her stimulation, it was powerful, turbulent, and forceful. The exultant passion and aggression took Kara to a place she had never known or even imagined. Again, she succumbed to her body's uncontrollable, explosive reaction.

They changed positions many times over the next hour, each time finding a new part of their bodies to stroke, excite, and penetrate. It was when Greg was once again lying on his back with Kara pushing herself onto him that she lost herself in the sensation. She was sex.

She had never been so intimately aroused in her life. This was the first time she'd had sex in her home since her husband left. This place had become her sanctuary, where she felt most at ease and safe. She had no idea how the combination of the multiple orgasms with the man she adored more than anything, could have such a profound effect. It had stimulated every nerve in her body. He had not only penetrated her body but her soul; he was no longer in her, but was a part of her.

She had lost control. She didn't care or have any conscious realisation of what was about to happen. She rode Greg hard with him so deep inside her, her mindless needs controlling her actions. He purely radiated throughout her body. With her eyes closed, she was nearly hallucinating, seeing herself in a colourful world of ecstasy, of total euphoria. This was to be an orgasm like no other.

The heat rose in her, stronger and hotter than she ever thought possible, as if her body was about to burst open and her insides lay all over the lover below her. Her heart pounded and her body shook as the heat reached boiling point, rising to her throat, almost choking her. Kara exploded. A strangled scream tried to escape her, but she had no breath. Her body arched and her head back as her juices erupted from deep inside her, gushing all over him.

The warm juices flooded across his groin and ran down both sides of his hips. The waves of her orgasm were so powerful, Greg could still see and feel her body twitch and shudder for a long time afterwards, as she lay on his chest completely spent. This was her seventh orgasm for the evening.

Greg then asked softly, 'Are you okay?' She just nodded in reply.

Her body was still blissfully trembling, so much so, that she could barely breathe and certainly couldn't speak.

After a time, they headed to her bedroom. The remaining hours until morning flowed in waves of words, caresses, sleep, and orgasmic pleasure. By the time they emerged for the start of the next day, Kara had come at least four more times. Greg had never had a night like this before. They were both totally spent.

Neither could believe what they had experienced and that it would ignite an insatiable appetite for more.

Chapter 19

Over breakfast, Greg and Kara still buzzing from their enormous night of passion were now keen for more, to push the limits further, to find a woman to join them. It would be their first threesome.

Greg told her that there were sites where you could post ads for casual encounters and see other people's ads. Greg asked if she might be interested in soft swing?

Kara looked at him in a confused way and then with a smile said, 'I don't know what that is.'

Greg smiled back, 'I didn't either, until not long ago. It's when you meet with another couple, and you have sex usually on the same bed. It's also known as 'same room sex.'

'My God that sounds hot, so no touching the other couple?'

'Sometimes, if you are resting or finished you may lay next to them and caress them as they make love, it is very hot. Sometimes the girls might get a little adventurous.'

'Oh my god, I could do that,' Kara offered, starting to feel her body react as she pictured herself there. 'Shall we start with a threesome?' offered Kara.

'No, I tell you what. You write an ad for another girl, and I will do one looking for a soft swing with another couple,' suggested Greg.

'But I have no idea what to write,' she said.

'Just write from your heart and what you feel. Another woman will appreciate that. Plus, an ad from a woman will feel more genuine.'

During the next few nights, she searched the web for things like sexy talk, casual meetings, threesomes, and swinging.

She was astounded at the number of sites there were with ads for women looking for men, men looking for women, men looking for men, threesomes, and couples seeking soft or full swap swinging—basically any combination you desire.

It surprised her to discover that most of these people were also her age or older.

She drafted an ad from the perspective that she never thought she would be prepared to share her man with someone, but was curious about touching and playing with a woman and how she was excited at having the chance to watch her man enjoy the pleasure of another. After all, he wasn't really her man anyway! Greg also drafted an ad seeking couples, promoting their interest in same-room sex. They found a popular dating site for these casual encounters and registered.

When Kara signed up for the site, she felt rather self-conscious and naughty, but naughty is what she wanted.

The responses were many, phenomenal, in fact, for both ads. There were messages every day and throughout the night, every night. Kara was astonished. Replies came from all sorts of people: single people wanting to join them for fun and couples of all ages. From those in their twenties, through to others in their sixties. There were hundreds of hits to view their ads within only a few days.

Excited at the response, Kara enthusiastically replied to them all. It soon became clear that most were trolls, sleazebags, and weirdos. Often men getting a chance to talk about sex with someone, largely for their own instant gratification and pleasure. They would ask about explicit details of sex the couple was interested in and pictures of the bodies they might see. There were also lots of single men pretending to be a woman in the lame attempt to elicit attention or just chat to enhance their right-hand self-pleasure.

Kara quickly learned to be cautious with her replies, being clear about what to say, how much to offer, and holding back from sending any photos until she could establish a clear dialogue and communicate with the female to meet before any more interaction.

Filtering through messages and checking profiles of others was time consuming. Kara was nearly despairing at how few suitable people she could really find who felt and looked okay. Then she found one.

With a mix of trepidation and excitement, Kara read the message. This lady needed an outlet and desperately wanted to have sex but had never before considered a threesome. This was intriguing but daunting too.

What if I just end up watching Greg have sex? Could I do that? she wondered.

Despite her initial hesitation, Kara replied. They chatted and it wasn't long before Kara was convinced this lady was genuine. She was aroused by the curious fascination that led this lady to contact a couple.

After they exchanged a few messages, they had a date to meet for coffee. Kara messaged Greg and, thankfully, his schedule found him being able to grab an hour to meet. They settled on a coffee shop in a shopping centre, making it a public, innocent, and casual meeting. It also facilitated an easy escape if things got weird.

It was the strangest of meetings. The woman named 'Pip' told them how she desperately loved sex and how her partner could no longer physically perform for her. Consequently, she had spent years seeking alternatives for casual encounters, but the supply was lean. Then she saw the ad Kara had posted and thought, *To hell with it. They look decent, and… why not?* Pip shared how this wasn't her preferred option. She insisted she had no bi tendencies or curiosity about experiencing a woman; however, the chance to share and engage with a man, as had been described, was worth a meeting. She set out her terms of contact and expectations and a desire to confirm a 'play' date.

Perhaps not the sexiest form of offers, but this was a person genuine to explore a threesome. Like Greg and Kara, it would be a first time for all of them, so it was probably a great opportunity. Greg and Kara discussed it, noting the rather sad and clinical approach to accessing a sexual partner which perhaps was increasingly a reality for the more mature. It was possibly the only way to satisfy the real desires, that for many women, increased as they got older.

Greg and Kara were still nonetheless, excited. While they both thought she wasn't super attractive—she was plain, slim—and a willing partner. Besides, it was to be their first attempt at this.

They set a date in a week's time with contact details should circumstances change. That was it. They had a threesome booked.

Kara knew that she had to play this low key, especially knowing that intimate contact and sex with any woman was not Pip's preference. She really only wanted Greg, so Kara would need to ensure she afforded Pip as much play with Greg as possible, while maintaining some sort of connection to get her aroused and open to possibilities. So, Kara told Greg she would maintain contact via messages beforehand and try to inspire an appetite in Pip for the two of them to get involved.

Kara sent a series of friendly messages to her and described that the aim was sexy fun, reassuring her she hadn't considered herself to be bisexual, rather more curious to know how and what a woman felt like to touch and learn more about her own body by exploring another. They would only do as much or as little as she felt comfortable with.

Pip's responses were indicating that she was getting more excited and had seemed to have lost a little of her rather clinical or business-style manner that Greg and Kara had encountered at their first meeting. They were to meet at Greg's apartment. He hadn't looked to sell the place yet, and there was still much of his furniture there, given Tess had a fully furnished apartment. It was, therefore, an ideal spot for their little encounter. Greg had a meeting that morning for work, so he gave Kara details of where to find the spare key. She arrived early with an assortment of drinks and other things to host their little gathering.

Kara hadn't checked with Pip what she liked to drink, so she settled on champagne. As the bottle chilled, she prepared a simple platter of food with strawberries, grapes, assorted cheeses, and pâte. She also arranged an assortment of body oils and some lube discreetly on the bedside table, just in case.

Kara had selected her clothes thoughtfully that morning, choosing a simple white lace dress that zipped down the back for easy undressing. Her underwear was only a bra, white lace but not fancy, and no knickers. *Let's be a little bit more daring*, she thought.

As she walked around Greg's apartment, setting out the glasses and checking the blinds and the bedroom to make sure everything looked welcoming and ready for fun, she realised she had been walking on tippy toes—such was the mix of excitement and nervousness that had permeated throughout her body. She was possibly about to touch a woman intimately for the first time, and she would watch Greg being touched by another woman and screw them in front of her. It was both thrilling and frightening, and it poised her on her toes like a precipice. Anything could happen. She knew she would settle, though, as soon as he arrived.

Greg made sure he got to the apartment before Pip, knowing Kara would need him close before their guest arrived. They also needed time to talk a little first. This was a whole new experience for them. Kara poured them a drink as they spoke about how this might go. 'Are you still sure about this, Kara?'

'I'm excited, but I'm hoping I won't disappoint you or Pip.'

Greg smiled. 'As I thought. You always put others first. What about you, though?'

'Well, it's strange, perhaps. I know I want to see you have fun and that she doesn't really want a woman to touch her. I won't really know how I feel about sharing you until it happens, but it feels naughty, and that's exciting, isn't it?'

Greg was privately full of admiration and relief. Kara's first thoughts were not about herself, but of him and the other, and she was still willing. 'You are amazing, Kara. It's sort of like how I feel. Right now, I'm looking forward to the whole experience. I'm not sure how to feel, given that I've never had sex with anyone I didn't have some sort of feeling or connection with, and I don't want you to experience anything but sexy fun. Just know, I'm not attracted to her. This will only be like live porn and play, not serious. Anytime you want, just tell me and it will all stop.'

Kara kissed him, then raised her glass to his. 'Let the fun begin.'

Greg was quietly amused when Pip arrived and found her still as regimented as she was at their first meeting. So serious and proper. Kara was the perfect hostess, greeting her warmly at the door with a hug and offering Pip a drink and something to eat while they all settled on the couch to chat. Their initial conversation was yet still rather stilted and reserved, with Pip asking formal-type questions. Greg felt he was being interviewed for a job that he didn't care whether he got. He knew he had to lighten this up, so he turned to Pip, rested his hand on her knee, and said, 'So, tell me, lovely lady, are you the type that can come over and over or just enjoy a big one and need a rest?'

Pip smiled and replied, 'As many times as you like, Greg.'

As Greg stood up to get the champagne bottle to top up their drinks, Kara turned to Pip and asked, 'Would you like to help me undress our man then?' Beckoning for Pip to stand, Kara took her by the hand and led her to stand in front of him. 'I'm sure he would love your help.'

Without hesitation, Pip reached out and undid the button on his jeans and unzipped his fly. Kara smiled at Greg as she moved behind him and pulled his polo shirt up over his body. With his upper body exposed, Pip's hands roamed his chest. Kara pulled his jeans to the floor, leaving him standing in his jocks alone. Kara moved around behind Pip and whispered in her ear, 'Would you like me to undress you?'

'Yes— sure.'

Without hesitation, Kara reached for the zip at the back of Pip's dress, letting it fall to the floor. As she removed her bra and slid her knickers down Pip's legs, Kara's fingers had the first touch of another woman's flesh in such a sensual way. Pip's skin was alabaster white, smooth, and soft. Kara asked her quietly, 'Are you feeling okay with this?'

Pip nodded and whispered, 'Yes, it's nice.'

Pip was still relishing in letting her fingers explore Greg's flesh.

'Would you like to taste him?' Kara whispered into Pip's ear again, this time loud enough for Greg to hear.

'Yes, if it's, okay?'

'Of course,' Kara assured her.

Greg sat down on the couch as Pip knelt in front of him, leaving Kara to stand behind her.

At that moment, Greg looked at Kara with a hint of disbelief. She had started the transition from awkward into sexy play in an instant, where minutes ago, he thought he would need to be the one to take the lead here.

After quietly unzipping and removing her own dress, Kara knelt naked behind Pip. She remained still, just watching as Pip slipped off Greg's jocks and started to lick, suck, and roll her tongue over his growing erection. It was then that Kara felt the full sensation of the moment.

Looking over Pip's shoulder, Kara's eyes locked with his. They were shining, vibrant, and wide with a hint of trepidation mixed with excitement. In that moment, he reminded her of a little boy who had just sneaked a third cookie from the plate—guilt and indulgence melded together. His eyes were searching for hers, looking for assurance that she was okay. She smiled and nodded before leaning forward over Pip to kiss him. She whispered, 'Enjoy,' then slipped back into her previous position caressing Pip. Greg let his head fall back a little, relaxing into the sensation of Pip's oral stimulation.

As she knelt behind her, she drew in a breath. Kara knew it was time. This was to be her first sexually intimate touch of a woman. With a featherlike flicker at first, she reached out and let her hands caress up and down Pip's back. Kara trailed her fingers down her spine, around her peach shaped cheeks, and then up the side of her body. She felt Pip's body fully relax and melt back into her touch.

It was permission granted. Kara continued to explore, allowing her hands to reach around Pip's waist and cup her breasts in each hand. All the while, Pip continued to suck and relish in Greg's hard body. After a few minutes, Pip reached her arm around to feel for Kara, letting her hand stroke her skin.

Sensing it was the right moment, Greg said, 'Let's go upstairs ladies.'

As soon as they entered the bedroom, they laid Pip in the middle of the bed, Greg on one side and Kara on the other, letting their hands caress all over her body. As they each sucked a nipple, Greg's fingers worked their way down between her legs, finding her very wet. He stroked her into a frenzy before kneeling between her spread legs and teasing her with his rock-hard flesh.

Shooting a glance at Kara, he silently asked, Okay? At Kara's nod, he entered Pip, gradually, inch by inch. Pip drew her legs higher, wanting all of him. With Kara lying beside her, kissing her and rubbing both of her breasts, and Greg deep inside her, Pip wasn't far from her first of many orgasms.

Greg's right hand reached between Kara's legs. He rubbed her just the way she loved, gliding up and down between her lips and then sliding inside her, his fingers rhythmically beckoning on her G-spot. Kara's sexual voice built with her impending orgasm. Both women, aroused by each other's building orgasms, almost on cue, came together in unison. Greg feeling the clenching of each of their bodies.

As they settled from their high, he caressed the inside of Kara's thighs and slowed his movements inside Pip before sliding out of her and lay again to her side, his fingers caressing the soft skin of her chest. He felt exhilarated, knowing that this was an experience most men could only dream about.

Then a phone rang, interrupting the moment.

It was Kara's work phone. Now? Of all times! She grabbed the phone from the bedside table and raced downstairs to take the call. After ending the call, she rushed back upstairs to the bedroom. Entering the room, she was rendered motionless, fixed-on-the-spot standing in the doorway, as if momentarily stunned at what she saw.

They were on the bed where she had left them, except Greg was between Pip's raised legs. His firm butt cheeks rhythmically clenched and releasing as he thrust into Pip again and again. Kara hesitated as a flicker of jealousy threatened to take her over, but then she stopped and reminded herself… this is your party too.

Overcome with the desire to feel the two of them, Kara quietly climbed onto the end of the bed behind Greg, kneeling between his legs. She reached down, sliding her hand beneath him, and wrapping her fingers around the base of him. His cock was warm, hard, and wet from Pip's juices. He throbbed in her hand as he pushed in and out of Pip's body. Kara's fingers slipped further down his shaft until she felt the smoothness of Pip's lips, her juices coating her fingers.

Kara pressed her body close behind him, her breasts on his back, while keeping her thumb and index finger wrapped around him and letting her other fingers slide over Pip's delicate flesh. Kara had never felt a sensation like this.

My God! How divine. Greg is doing her, through my fingertips. Kara's body moved in perfect time with him, both riding her. Pip's eyes were closed, and her cheeks flushed as her head moved gently from side to side. Her fingers clung to Greg's shoulders, clawing deeply with each thrust. Her breathing changed from deep and slow, to a hard, fast series of gasps and moans. She was about to come again.

Kara kept her fingers resting on her, waiting to see if she could feel anything that matched the obvious oblivion Pip was feeling. Pip's pelvis lifted to meet him at every thrust. Kara removed her fingers to allow Greg and Pip's tender skin to rub each other as close as they could. Shuddering, Pip let out an enormous cry, and Kara watched her body melt into the sheets and pause. Her orgasm was charged and all-consuming.

Kara was breathing as hard and fast as Pip. It electrified her body. *I'm feeling what it's like for a guy when they are screwing a woman.* Watching and feeling firsthand, every second and stroke of intercourse was mind-blowing. As if they had both fucked her, her own body had absorbed their pleasure as her fingers played her favourite tune. Kara's orgasm was euphoric. She had caught their desire in every resounding breath.

When Greg moved to lie across the end of the bed, Kara motioned for Pip to lay on top of Greg facing upwards. He was still hard. As Pip climbed on him, Kara reached between her legs to grab hold of him. Stroking him with her right hand, Kara carefully parted Pip's swollen lips and guided him inside her.

Kara's sensations and thoughts kept leaping. *What a thing to do? Who helps their man to enter another woman? And what a sensation it is! Being right here, between the millimetres of flesh, touching a woman's most intimate part of her body and holding your man's penis at the same time?*

In this position, Kara could see Greg's face and looked into his eyes. Then she let her fingers, tongue, and mouth taste and tantalise Pip's body while Greg penetrated her from beneath. Pip had lost any apprehension about sex with a woman by this point, so lost in being pleasured inside and out by them both. Her next orgasm was explosive and fast, resonating through them.

So intense was this session of play, they had to stop for a brief pause. They all lay on the bed, resting as their breath subsided to a gentle pace, the three of them silent for a moment. The two women were lying next to each other, side to side on their backs, Greg to the right of Kara.

Pip broke the silence. 'Kara, you have beautiful nipples.'

It was such an unexpected statement; Kara was momentarily lost for words.

Greg responded, saying, 'Yes, she does.'

Kara rolled onto her side, facing Pip. 'Thank you.' After a brief hesitation, she asked, 'Hey, Pip, would you mind showing me how you touch yourself? How you masturbate?'

'I like to rub and finger myself firmly… like this.' Pip demonstrated, rubbing the outer side of her lips in a circular motion with two fingers. 'Oh, and I love oral.'

That was all Kara needed to hear. 'Well, I know something Greg would love to see.'

As promised to Kara, Greg, despite his mounting desire, had not yet come. That moment was reserved for the joy of seeing his fantasy for this threesome. When discussing preferences, Kara's only request was that he release his seed into her so she could get to feel that intimate penetration and that guttural and delicious cry that escaped him every time he exploded. The pulse and throb she could feel was the ultimate for her.

She knew what he wanted. She'd planned to make sure it happened. Greg had shared how he would love to be fucking Kara from behind while he watched her lick and finger another woman. But not yet.

'Can I kiss these lips? Are you okay if it's just me alone touching you?' asked Kara as she reached out and placed her fingers over Pip's, joining in with the rhythm as Pip pleasured herself, before sliding her fingers down further. She allowed the tip of a finger to rim just inside her. Nodding, Pip closed her eyes and opened her legs a little farther apart.

Kara knelt between her legs and leaned forward, kissing the inner flesh of Pip's thighs before tracing her tongue through Pip's lower lips, tasting the moisture that was building and spreading from inside her. The blended scent and flavour of Greg having just penetrated her, mixed with her juices, was exhilarating. Kara slipped her middle and index finger into her vagina, loving how soft and warm this felt. Kara pushed her fingers deeper, exploring further. Turning her fingers upwards, she found the little mound of gently ridged flesh.

It is so much easier to find a G-spot in another woman than trying to find my own, thought Kara as she moved her fingers in a steady beckoning motion inside Pip, feeling her get wetter and wetter. Kara glanced up at Pip, seeing she still had her eyes closed and was gripping her breast with her free hand, her head tilting back in pleasure. *I must be doing alright*, she thought.

She didn't stop. Luxuriating in the feel of the soft, juicy warmth, Kara increased the depth and speed each time she thrust her fingers. Adding the sensation of her mouth, Kara licked and sucked her, every now and then flicking her bead with her tongue, drawing out each nerve towards her next orgasm. Kara glanced towards the side of the bed where Greg had been lying, but he'd disappeared. She knew where he would be. This was what he wanted to see and feel.

As Greg approached her from behind, she could feel the intensity of his arousal before he even touched her. Taking a firm hold of her hip with one hand, he leaned forward and rubbed up the full length of her spine from her arse to between her shoulders and down again with the other hand. He pressed himself against her as he stared over Kara's shoulder, watching her lips and fingers working Pip, thrusting in and out.

Kara could feel his knob and hard thick flesh between her cheeks, searching for her. Sensing the heightened power in him, she knew every vein was bulging, and the second he entered her, it would be resounding. It was sheer magic.

Just then, Pip let out a small cry of pleasure, heralding she was poised to erupt. Kara felt her legs shiver beneath her. Kara increased her effort, feeding off the two people surrounding her, both of whom were going to blow. Greg's force was so deep, it instantly brought Kara to the edge. He exploded into Kara as Pip let out a groan and Kara's body spasmed into orgasmic delight. That moment was the absolute highlight. Kara and Greg's fantasy had been realised in the most pleasurable way.

They had little energy to speak after that. Their time together wound up gently, yet quickly. Kara and Greg thanked Pip and bid her farewell. Kara also knew it was also time for Greg to head home. After a swift kiss goodbye, he swiftly paced towards his car, turning to give Kara a last glance and wave. They shared a look, and by the smiles on their faces, they both knew. They each had loved this whole experience. It was a new high.

With no question, Greg and Kara had just become swingers.

The drive home gave Kara much time for reflection on the afternoon.

My God, Kara! What just happened? You are no longer the innocent country-living woman, are you now? A bisexual sex goddess now perhaps? She laughed to herself. *That was amazing… I think I like the new me!* The experience was surreal, but also so vivid. Being touched, touching, watching, feeling another woman and Greg at the same time, unimaginable. Kara had been both shocked at herself and transported to a new plane of ecstasy, especially seeing Greg so aroused and feeling him so powerfully during his ultimate moment.

This was a whole new phenomenon. They had experienced a threesome and it was amazing! Later that evening, Kara received a message from Greg.

Are you free if I call around eight?

For sure. I've been bursting to speak with you.

Me too. Until later then.

Chapter 20

*R*ight on 8.00 p.m., Kara's phone rang. Punctual and precise as usual, Kara thought with a smile.

'Hello, sexy. Well, that was a whole new experience today, wasn't it? How are you feeling?'

'I can't believe it, really! I'm so surprised and secretly proud of us. We had a threesome! I'm still quite surprised at myself. How did you feel with the two of us women?'

'It was amazing. She wasn't someone I could ever imagine wanting to sleep with, so it started out feeling strange, but it was so good. Just watching you and seeing you with her was so hot and arousing.'

'I know. I felt it in you.'

They continued to recount the various poignant moments and their feelings. They'd both been watching each other throughout the whole time. It was seeing and sharing in each other's pleasure that had been the biggest turn on, taking their feelings and physical reactions to a whole new, heightened level. In fact, they both admitted they'd felt more connected than ever, despite another person sharing in their sexual play.

'This must be the reason so many people like playing with others,' said Kara. 'And how about you, Mr Sheppard? What a legend! You made the two of us come at the same time.'

Greg chuckled. 'That felt pretty special, I must admit. That's not something many guys can say they've done.'

'See, you are a Superman!' Kara laughed.

Greg laughed which suddenly faded to silence.

'Hey, are you still there, Greg? You've gone quiet on me.'

Greg had been in a state of torment from the beginning of this rekindled relationship. It had started as a genuine but purely idle curiosity about the lost girl from his childhood years. But now, the many feelings that had developed since they'd met, had truly surpassed it being the once in a lifetime chance to make love to your childhood sweetheart. It wasn't only getting to know the many faces and talents of this intriguing woman; his own feelings and attraction to her had taken him aback. She was unique and strangely addictive, like no other he'd met.

It was as if she thought and saw life through a different lens, unlike other women he knew, worked with, or had relations with. Such a mix of contrasts, she was worldly, intelligent, and a high achiever like him. Since their time together, he'd seen a different Kara—vulnerable and innocent, but open to explore and take risks. He knew he had guided and helped her to emerge sensuously and sexually, yet all the while, she'd also been leading and teaching him too. She could see him. All of him. She adored him but challenged him too. She had dared him to open up his hidden desires.

Added to the fact that Kara shared in realising some of his fantasies and had responded so naturally within today's encounter, had astounded him. But he felt so guilty. He loved Tess. She was beautiful, bold, sexy, and was passionately devoted to him. Yet he was drawn to Kara and wanted her in his life too. When he first made love to Kara, he and Tess were in a relationship where they both knew each of them had occasional outside interests, but that was then, and this is now.

This had to stop. He was now committed to Tess, but Kara had somehow made her way into his heart and his head too. She offered him the opportunity for all of his fantasies to be realized.

But he was about to ask Tess to marry him?

Surely, I can't love them both, can I?

Overwhelmed by these thoughts, he almost forgotten Kara was still on the phone.

'Sorry, Kara, my thoughts drifted off. This has generated a whole new state of mind for me. I love how you and I share in these same secret desires and how brave we've been to try this together. I must admit, I never thought I'd find anyone who would dare share in this, especially a girl from my grade seven class!'

'So, you didn't think I'd be the sexy, adventurous type, hey?'

Greg was quick to reply. 'No, I didn't. Never saw that sign at primary school, or even twelve months ago, but I certainly know differently now.'

'I know. I was such an innocent when we met, wasn't I?' She giggled. 'To tell you the truth, I didn't think I was this daring or horny either! Somehow, you've brought out a naughty, insatiable appetite in me that I didn't appreciate or even dare to reveal. Thank you, Greg.'

'Oh, it's my pleasure. Thank you too, Ms Gilbert.' His tone became deeper and a little more serious. 'You are a very special woman. You are my "first and forever," you know.'

Then he paused again. This silence was longer, and just as Kara was about to ask what was wrong, she heard Greg take a huge breath.

'Kara, look, I need to tell you something. I need to apologise for not telling you this before.'

Panic rose in Kara.

He was about to tell her about the engagement plans, but once again, something made him hold back. He needed to get this right in his head first. No, not now. Not after today, he told himself.

Greg quickly responded. 'It's just that I'm off to Sydney soon, and then I head to New Zealand. I've got others travelling with me, so I won't be able to talk or message much until I return. Thanks so much for today. You did an amazing job getting it all organised. You made it happen. You thought of everything. It meant a lot. I enjoyed our amazing time together.'

In response, Kara thanked Greg for his willingness and encouragement to share in the day. She told him not to be concerned about not being able to contact her while he was away and reaffirmed how much she had enjoyed the afternoon as well. The call ended with a promise of a catch-up sometime soon.

But each of them felt uneasy when they hung up, and the realisation of what they had experienced hit them.

Later that afternoon, when Kara's Aunt Sarah casually asked her if she enjoyed her afternoon off, Kara felt a twinge of guilt and confusion.

Oh my God, if she only knew what I really did this afternoon! She would never understand. I am such a deviant. Oh, God! Am I a wicked woman? Kara had a few soul-searching moments, but she secretly admitted that it had felt so bloody amazing. She could not believe how much she enjoyed swinging and now desperately wanted more, a lot more. *Is there something wrong with me? And what kind of awkward place does this put Greg in?* That little pain kept scrolling through her mind.

She felt a bit relieved that Greg had to fly to Sydney and New Zealand for a few weeks. It put a space between them both and the intense experience they had shared. There would be time to consider the situation more after he returned.

On the plane to Sydney, Kara was all Greg could think about. He tried to consider the situation from all sides. He mustn't keep stringing Kara along. He must let her go; it was the right thing to do. If he was ready to commit to Tess, he had to do this 100 percent. He couldn't hurt Kara with false hopes of more, or devastate Tess if she caught them out. Tess was his woman and everything he could ever want. She was beautiful, fun, intelligent, and sexy. But, all the while, Kara had introduced him to a new drug, a very addictive drug that he couldn't get enough of. He wanted more—more of Kara and the fantasies that she offered.

A warmth of excitement and fear raced through him. God, I'm officially a sex addict. I have the best and just want more. A man could search a lifetime to find a woman who matched his own insatiable sex drive, and he had found that in Kara. He wondered how far would she actually go? Could we tick the box of every sexual fantasy he could imagine?

Damn it! Why can't this be simpler? Why can't I have them both— the best of both worlds? Have my cake and eat it too. Why can't I have a Mercedes and a Ferrari in my garage? he lamented. That thought made him smile. He and Kara were so akin in their approach to life and their thoughts, and they had the same massive sex drive. They held the same kinky desires, and he was sure she would try almost anything his heart desired. Without Kara in his life, there would be a massive hole. Greg was torn between doing the right thing and feeding this uncontrollable, kinky addiction. He had an indescribable attraction to a woman who he'd witnessed transform from a single divorcee who hadn't had a man since her husband four years before, to an irresistible, insatiable sexy woman.

What is it about Kara? he wondered, and then answered himself. She's intoxicating with a lovely soul, and I know she adores me, even though she tries to hide it. She is the only one I can share my dreams, passion, and kinky desires with. She's become a confidante—like a mate, but then again, just maybe I got caught up in the fantasy? What is it about this kinky stuff I enjoy? Is this really the only reason I'm so attracted to Kara? Maybe I've satisfied this itch? It could all stop now, couldn't it?

He sat back in the seat of the 737 and decided he would call Kara once he arrived in Sydney and tell her about the engagement to Tess and that he shouldn't see her anymore.

But it took Greg the whole week and then the next before he worked up the courage to call her. He sent her a message first.

Hi, Kara, okay to call?

When Kara heard her phone signal a text message, she was a bit surprised but pleased. Instead of waiting for him, she just dialled his number. He answered straight away.

'Hello sexy.'

'Hi, Greg. This is a lovely surprise. So, what can I do for you? Work or pleasure?' she asked in a light-hearted tone, not expecting his next words at all.

Greg just blurted it out. 'I need to tell you that I'm going to ask Tess to marry me. I should have told you before. I'm really sorry. I was caught up in our playing. You are so addictive. I thought I could just have it all, and have you both, but I can't. I can't do it anymore. It's killing me.'

His speech stunned Kara into silence. It wasn't the engagement itself. She wasn't surprised that Greg was proposing and planning his life ahead with Tess; he had always been open with her about that from the start. But Kara didn't want to hear it. She knew this would happen one day; she just didn't want it to. Her thoughts somersaulted.

Why am I so surprised? Greg was never mine. He was always Tess's man. Did I just use him for my own selfish desires and lustful pleasure? But Kara knew, deep down, that to her, Greg had become her man. They made passionate love, over and over— on the phone, and in her house, and with others. She allowed him to consume her and had given herself to him completely and willingly.

Did I ever mean anything more than a casual friend to him? Was it just the sex? Did I only hear and feel what I wanted to, or was he only telling me what he knew I wanted to hear? No, he wouldn't deliberately want to hurt me like this.

Kara was fighting hard not to feel discarded and betrayed.

With the thoughts and questions whirling through her mind, she couldn't find the words.

Panic flared inside Greg at the silence on the other end of the phone. 'Kara, are you okay? Say something…please.'

Desperately trying to process her thoughts and hold back her tears, Kara didn't know how long it took for her to reply. Eventually, the words escaped her, fighting to keep a steady tone. 'Thank you for telling me.'

'I'm so sorry. I planned to tell you from the first moment we spoke after I returned from my overseas trip with Tess. Before the trip, I wanted to celebrate having spent two years with her, but while on holiday, my feelings for her deepened, and I sort of decided then.'

Kara's voice raised an octave as she said, 'I see. Tell me, how is it you can spend all this time with me and share in a most intimate swing fantasy, *since* you've been back from your holiday, and all the while, you are in love with her enough to want to marry her? You even told me that you love me! I'm finding this too hard to comprehend at the moment. Before I begin to feel even more of a fool, I think I'd better go.'

'Kara, no, please wait. Let's talk. Let me try to explain,' he called out desperately. 'I do love you!' But before he could finish his sentence, Kara hung up.

Kara barely slept that night. Her phone had pinged repeatedly for an hour after she ended the call with Greg. There were more messages throughout the night, but she ignored them all. She knew it was him.

Vivid memories of intimate, sensual moments with Greg kept appearing in her broken dreams, jumbled with images of engagement rings, and wedding scenes. The random flashes didn't stop. The two of them touching and screwing Pip, the ads they had posted, the scene when they first met and made love, his face, and the feel of him screwing her in every room of her home. Recollections of the words they had spoken and the gentle look of his eyes upon her.

These images kept cycling through her brain, jolting her back to a state of wakefulness each time she dared to drift into sleep. It was as if her thoughts were trying to protect her from drowning into an abyss and turmoil of feelings and thoughts about Greg. How could she possibly survive without him? He'd burst into her life, penetrating her to the bottom of her inner being, and now with one phone call, he was gone.

By six in the morning, she couldn't lie in bed any longer. She had done this once before. This time she knew she had to be firmly resolved, accepting and understanding her own feelings about him and herself. She had indulged and encouraged this connection with him again, just as he had with her. They had both behaved badly.

She had known how devoted he was to Tess, and yet she did nothing to stop any of this recent contact or sexual play. Somehow, she'd justified to herself that her secret times with Greg were okay, as if he wasn't married or in a committed relationship with Tess. Besides, that was his problem to deal with, anyway. But, in reality, that should have mattered. It could cause the same amount of pain—for all three of them. The blame was not all on Greg.

She was equally selfish, wanting, and desperate. The news of the engagement was the key to close and lock that door—for his sake even more than hers. However, she knew this goodbye would be much harder than the first. So rather than by text, she took a long time and composed an email.

When Kara had ended their phone call, Greg was overcome with the worst feelings. It was as if he had swallowed a cocktail of nails and pure alcohol. His head spun, his chest hurt, and he was sweating profusely. It was like a close friend had died and he had killed her.

How the hell can I live without her? She's always been there to take my calls, share my fantasies, and act them out willingly. What about her? I've just dumped her like a toy I was sick of playing with. I didn't think about what this might do to her. She must be so upset! God, I miss her already.

He knew he couldn't leave her like this. He kept dialling and messaging, going crazy, wishing he could take it all back. But she didn't respond. Greg paced his room for what seemed like hours. In that time, he drank a full bottle of wine and hardly slept. He sent messages on the hour, every hour that night.

It wasn't until early the next morning that he heard the familiar sound of Kara's tone on his phone. Oh God! Finally, she had messaged back.

Greg, I've sent you a message. Please check your email.

He opened his email app and saw her message. He hesitated. Wanting to read her words yet fearing what they might say. He clicked it open. He could immediately see that this was a long message. He drew in a breath and read. A tear crept down his cheek.

From: Kara Gilbert <karaG@bmail.com>
To: Greg Sheppard <Greg@PrecisionEvents.com.au>
Subject: I understand. Congratulations. Thank you and farewell

Dear Greg,
Sorry about hanging up so abruptly. Thank you for telling me about your plans. While I was shocked, hurt, and upset by the timing of your news, I sort of understand why this was hard for you to tell me until now. At first, I did consider that you had used me for a last fling or fantasy. But, knowing you, I sense it was more than that. Like me, you don't like to deliberately hurt people. You may have withheld information from me, but you have never lied to me. Tess, as you described, has always been your "leading

lady" in your life. I was always intended to be an unexpected distraction, isn't that what you called it? I suspect that when I shared my hidden sexual fantasies, this obviously sparked a new, arousing fascination and attraction. I also encouraged us to spend time together, to fulfil my own secret pleasures. So I'm also responsible and a willing part of this entanglement. In my heart though, I also know that people can and do love more than one person in their lives, often intimately and deeply, each in different ways. That's more common than we think, as I believe not any one person can ever fulfil all our needs and wants at any one time. So please never think for a second, that my feelings for you are not genuine.

For now, you need to know that it's time for me to become the 'leading lady' in my own life. I can't be a supporting actress in your life story anymore. I need to be the "Tess" in someone else's life. I do hope, given time, that she will appreciate and fulfil all your secret desires, and that you will now remain true to only her. She deserves and needs to be the centre of your attention and life. There is no place for me in that.

So please know I will never forget you, or what you have given me. You ignited and inspired me and helped me find my true inner self. There has always been a piece missing, and I didn't know it until you came along. So, you've made me whole again. I will forever be in your debt. You were my missing piece all along. My only regret is that I didn't find you again or realise this about you, or me, decades before now.

I truly wish you and Tess a wonderful life together. Sure, this will hurt for a while, as it did the first time when we said goodbye, maybe even longer. But this time I am a little happier knowing you are following and filling your heart. It's time for me to look beyond and find someone to fill mine.

With much love,

Kara x

Tears were rolling by the time he finished reading her message. *How can she be so understanding, considering my circumstances and her own? God, I burned her. Again. Yet her first thoughts are of what's best for me. Could I love this woman any more than I do now?*

His initial response was to send a message back. He started to compose a reply. Until that moment, he hadn't realized how strong his feelings for her were. There was a huge hole in his heart, a place only she would ever fill.

However, partway through his reply, he stopped and re-read her message. Kara had stated the facts. She meant this. She understood better than he had. She already knew what he hadn't been brave enough to admit.

This was really goodbye. What a bitter pill to swallow.

Kara had been so understanding and thoughtful. *Why couldn't she just yell and scream and make it easy for me?* But he knew that wasn't the person she was. He took another deep breath and then slowly released it.

Suddenly, a different feeling overtook him—not panic, not fear, but acceptance. In a moment of clarity, he knew the right thing to do. He needed to respect her words and really let her go… even if this would hurt him for a long time too.

He sent her a simple message, a YouTube link to the Whitney Houston song 'I will always love you.'

She'd never heard the words from his lips. There was nothing else he needed to say.

Chapter 21

Unsure what Greg's reaction might be to her message, Kara had been hesitant to open Greg's emailed response. She didn't want to speak with him again. It would just reopen the wound and drag out their inevitable goodbye.

Now mourning the loss of more than just a casual friend with whom she enjoyed some sexual pleasures, she had become way too attached to him, and not only because of their shared sexual desires.

From the first instant they had reconnected, she had been lying to herself about her blossoming feelings. Now it was too late. She truly loved Greg and always would. When she saw his reply, she knew he felt it too, but it would only hurt all of them if they stayed in contact.

It took Kara a couple of weeks to compose herself before she was strong enough to decide that was enough. As tough as it would be, it was time to move on.

Kara was lost and left in a void for another reason too. Her sexual desires had been unleashed, and now she had no outlet for them.

During this time, she was still receiving messages from the ads she and Greg had placed for threesomes or couples for soft swing, most of which were from frustrated, lonely single guys who wanted to engage in sexually suggestive messages. Few had any real intention of meeting or enacting their expressed desires.

Once past the initial sexy dialogue and banter, she would tell them she was really a researcher and wanted to understand more about why they might be on the sites. The stories were contrasting and fascinating. One young man was so besotted with the idea of an older woman that he had dismissed ever dating anyone closer to his own age until he had slept with a woman at least thirty years older than him. He had sent Kara pictures of his face and body. He was gorgeous, but genuinely believed no girl would ever want him because he was so inexperienced. This poor guy was convinced he needed a mature, experienced woman to take his virginity.

After a few nights of messages, Kara had to sternly set him straight. 'Look, please stop wanting me. You really don't want to be with someone so much older than you. You are too young, too lovely, and exactly what many young women hope to find. Delete your ad. Don't message me again. Go out on a real date. Be brave and only come back to here in twenty years if you're unhappy or want something beyond the usual that most couples enjoy.'

Some months later, he messaged her out of the blue and said, 'I just wanted to say thank you. I met a girl. I've been dating her for a while, and she and I are really in love. You were right. I needed to be brave and grow up and into a relationship. It is scary, but not so bad. We are teaching each other.'

There were a few other responses that were interesting and seemed like possibilities, especially the couples; however, most were located interstate. Kara would still reply to acknowledge their messages and confirm interest but would indicate that she and her partner travelled lots, so it would take planning and quite some time before they might be available.

She spent lonely nights messaging back couples and talking about what they might do when they caught up, sometimes sending sexy pictures. Often, she would get aroused imagining her and Greg with them and take the thoughts to bed with her. She kept details of some couples as some sounded genuinely decent.

She wasn't ready to shut down the ads, although she couldn't contemplate swinging without Greg.

Eventually, she stopped trolling online, accepting the reality that she needed to create a new life for herself.

So, a new Kara—the social animal—emerged. Likened to the tales of a young vampire on the hunt for first blood, she took to exploring new possibilities with a vengeance. She worked hard by day, diving headfirst into every project or task, starting her days early, writing submissions, holding meetings, generating sponsorship for projects and initiatives, and nearly overwhelmed her board and staff. Now with the same determination, she attacked her social life outside work.

Kara posted more ads on sites as a mature single woman looking for a date. She changed her clothes and her look, emerging even more sophisticated, even a little sexier than before. The new look woman started heading out; often to bars, dance clubs, shows, and sporting events. She accepted all invitations from friends and work connections with the sole purpose to meet new people and have as much fun as she could find. Later, she realised this was tainted with rebounding behaviour, which was full of a poor attempt to say, 'Fuck you, Greg!'

She was ever cautious about what her family might think about her active social life, especially her daughter and Aunt Sarah. At home and at work, people still saw Kara as the lovely lady who deserved to find someone special and hadn't had the chance to find anyone who deserved her. But in the private life of Kara, she was a woman who was searching. She now held a glance longer with people to elicit a conversation and reaction, and allowed herself to stand out. She would talk to anyone she met. This was a bold Kara who was open to the world and afraid no more.

She wasn't blatantly flirting or trawling for sex or men, but she was finally projecting her real self. She didn't have any crazed desire to jump into bed with just anyone who offered. She wanted to let her fun, open, and refreshed personality shine. There was a part of her that wanted to have sex with someone new just to put a bigger distance between her and Greg.

As the bolder, more confident Kara emerged, she suddenly started noticing people who were interested in her, whereas before she hadn't realized. Perhaps it was because she now allowed her sexual self to reflect in her walk, her look, and overall demeanour.

It took her a while before she could respond. It had been months since she had said goodbye to Greg, but she hadn't really let him go. Finally, she realized it was time. Yet, subconsciously, as she would later find, he remained the yardstick by which she measured every other man.

As is usually the case, when least expected, she found a man who snagged her interest. She was lined up outside a nightclub, finding herself in two minds about even trying to enter.

A guy behind her tapped her on the shoulder and asked, 'Excuse me, but is it even worth the wait to get in here?'

Kara turned and smiled, noting a tall man wearing a dusky blue suit. She surmised that he was probably ten years her junior, obviously on an 'after work boys' night out,' as behind him, stood three similarly dressed guys, with matching carefree bravado expressions.

'Well, that depends entirely on what you hope to find inside, I expect,' she replied with a laugh.

He chuckled at her response. 'I expect you're right. So, I take it you are waiting to meet someone inside?'

Kara smirked. 'I suppose I am, sort of. I recently met the manager and the DJ. I'm here to say hi and enjoy a drink and the music.'

'So, you're not here to meet someone in particular. Like on a date?'

Kara's smile widened. Now that was subtle—not! 'No, I'm not on a date. Just here to see and enjoy my friend's club.' She turned around again, facing the door.

Hearing the guys mumbling between themselves, she could just about predict the next approach, and she smiled to herself.

'Excuse me. I'm sorry I was rude. My name is Jake, and this is Mike, Stephen, and Dom. We all work for the same company and these guys are over from Canberra for work, and I 'm taking them out. Our conference ended today.'

'It's a pleasure to meet you, Jake. My name's Kara, and I sort of live here in Adelaide.' She extended her arm, shaking hands with him and his colleagues. 'So, what are you looking for inside this club?'

Jake was surprised but coolly impressed by her casual yet formal response and firm handshake.

'I'm not sure, probably just want somewhere to drink and hopefully meet some nice local people. Get the feel of this place while we're here.'

Kara ignored all references to meeting people. 'So, what do you know about our fine city?'

'There are obviously some very nice, polite women who live here,' Jake grinned and continued, 'Actually, I live here, but don't get out that much.'

Kara didn't take the bait. 'That's nice to hear. If you'll excuse me, I don't do line-ups, but I hope you enjoy the club.' She turned and walked out of the line and headed off. Despite her initial casual interest in this guy, she suddenly found the small, suggestive talk all too silly, predictable, and uncomfortable.

With a brisk pace, she headed for the next street to a wine bar where another of her friends, Daniel, worked. It was time to have one quiet drink and then head home.

Daniel was there behind the bar. They said hi and she ordered a wine. After about ten minutes, someone tapped her on the shoulder. 'Hey, I wanted to apologise about all that before,' the voice said. Kara turned and recognised Jake.

'You don't think following a woman to a bar is being too forward and weird?' She knew she was being rather rude, but tonight, she didn't care. Kara was no longer into games, and she was not at all interested in meeting anyone anymore. Inside, she was back with Greg, laughing and touching each other, her thoughts savouring the love and passion they shared.

She realised why she had connected so easily with Greg. He knew and accepted her for who and what she was. She wanted to forget him, but every man she'd subsequently encountered had only reminded her of how easy their relationship had been and how awkward, self-indulged, and stereotypical other 'suitable' men had become. Greg had faults, as she did too, but both of them were determined, focused, and could see solutions quickly, which caused them to become impatient and frustrated by others.

Yet, such was their sensitivity to people that they had each learned to suppress the desire to outwardly express their exasperation as best they could. Kara knew if she and Greg would have spent all their time together, they might have butted heads, but he had offered her the relationship she had needed. 'Let's be friends and have great sex. We'll indulge our fantasies and watch each other's backs. We'll love one another for who we are, enjoying only the best of us without fanfare or crap. We own or owe nothing more.'

Kara still craved that relationship, where she could love, feel loved, and give herself completely, but not feel obligated to give any more than she was willing to give. Nor would she expect more than what they freely offered. She knew what she wanted—a cool, caring friend, a lover, and someone who just accepted her. That was it. She didn't want to become predictable, responsible, or controlled, nor for him to feel any of those things about her. She wanted someone who was basically 'free of her,' but, remained closely connected because they were enhanced by her, and she with them.

'That's ridiculous,' she told herself. 'No man could ever get this thinking, and you cannot describe or show this in a way that anyone might understand.'

Perhaps you're only lying to yourself, wanting everything intimate and genuine but without any of the challenges that come with a full-time, everyday relationship. You really don't want to live with another man again. You're probably just damaged goods. Even Greg would never really understand your current way of thinking. How do you describe a love that doesn't follow the traditional beliefs, wants, and desires?

These thoughts raced through her mind as she feigned interest in the monologue that Jake was relating to her.

'Kara are you with me?' asked Jake.

'Damn... yeah, sorry!'

I've ignored this poor beggar, and he's trying so hard. Time to park Greg right now. He's not here anymore. This guy is.

Kara turned to Jake and smiled widely. 'Sorry, Jake, you were saying?'

She later discovered, once she gave him some airtime, that Jake was a lovely, decent man. He was more interesting than Kara had expected. He took care of his appearance, was a hard worker, and had a sharp eye for detail. She had been surprised when he'd noticed Kara's shoes and even recognised the brand. As the evening moved on, he talked about his travels, work, and love of music. Their light banter turned into an easy, genuine conversation. So, after about an hour, when Jake invited her to re-join him and his mates for a late supper, Kara found it simple to accept.

She had been instantly welcomed into Jake's group of workmates. The conversations flowed and didn't isolate her to have merely identified her only as a potential 'hook-up.' Kara relaxed and let the night flow around her. This wasn't so bad. In fact, it was fun.

Now and then, mid-conversation with his mates, Jake would steal a glance at her and mouth, 'You okay?' as if to check in that she didn't feel uncomfortable. She smiled and nodding back to confirm she was fine and enjoying herself.

At one point, she caught herself thinking. *That's the sort of thing my Greg would do.* She then scolded herself. *Oh, you're doing it again, measuring every guy against your Sheppard checklist, aren't you? Stop it now!*

At the end of the evening, as Jake's mates stood to leave, Jake took Kara by the hand and turned to the rest. 'Well, it's probably time we left too.' He leaned over and picked up her coat from the back of her chair. It was as if he'd done this for her a hundred times before. 'Goodnight, guys.' They walked hand in hand from the club, and Jake hailed a cab.

When it pulled up at the kerb, he opened the door and turned to her. 'I've had a great night, and I won't be offended if you want to get into this cab and go straight home on your own. Honestly, I've got your number, and I will definitely call you, don't worry about that. I just hope you've had a nice evening.'

He motioned for her to get into the car, and Kara was just about to climb into the cab, but she hesitated. 'Jake, thank you so much for everything this evening. It's been a long time since I've been out where I've been so warmly welcomed, like I was one of a group of long-term mates. I had fun. Hey,' she paused and smiled, 'do you feel like grabbing a last drink or a coffee before I head home?'

Jake took her by the hand and helped her back to stand next to him. After he apologised to the cab driver, they turned and walked into the first wine bar they came to.

Kara and Jake chatted on for another couple of hours, Kara learning more about his role as an electrical engineer and being responsible for managing design projects for new buildings and a consultant for other companies. He'd shared how he'd not had more than a couple of dates with anyone during the past three years, after the end of a nearly ten-year de facto relationship. He declared he was now basically a workaholic who only gave up work time these days to enjoy the gym, beach or an occasional night out with mates.

Kara shared lots about her professional role, country life, and her past married life. She said little about her intimate and unusual relationship with Greg. She knew that needed to remain private for now for both their sakes, and besides, she wasn't ready to talk about something she was still struggling with herself. They soon realised that they had become the last patrons in the bar.

'Oh, my goodness,' exclaimed Kara. 'I think it's time to go!'

They both laughed as they walked out into what was now the early hours of the morning.

'Now I really do need to get home!'

Jake smiled and nodded as he took her by the hand and led her to the nearest taxi rank. Opening the door to the taxi, he asked, 'Which direction?'

'East, I'm staying in Norwood.'

'Now that is a shame. I'm heading to Henley Beach, so we can't even share more time on our way home,' he said.

'That's okay.'

Jake squeezed Kara's hand, leaned forward, and kissed her gently on the cheek. 'It's been an absolute pleasure, Kara. Thank you for a most enjoyable night, and I will call you.' He then handed the cabbie fifty dollars, saying, 'Get this lady home safely, please.'

With that, Kara smiled and climbed into the cab. Jake closed the door and watched as the taxi pulled away from the kerb. Those last couple of hours were the first time in the past four months that Kara had not thought desperately about Greg. Before the cab had even arrived at her aunt's unit, she had received a message from Jake.

> Kara, I meant it. It was a superb evening. Hopefully, more fun times to come. Jake.

Chapter 22

The next morning, as Kara stretched, luxuriating in the fact it was Saturday at last and she had no need to race out of bed, her phone pinged.

> Good morning, Kara. I hope your phone is on silent and I haven't woken you. I just wanted to be in your first thoughts this morning and to let you know that mine have been of you and to say thank you again for our fun and lovely night. Jake x.

Kara read and reread the message. Now that was sweet—a bit too much, but sweet, nonetheless.

A warm glow came over her as she recalled the events of the night before. She had stumbled across a quite interesting guy, and while she had first considered him to be yet another wolf in sheep's clothing, she had discovered him to be a genuinely sincere man. Rather than try to seduce her into his bed, the two of them just had fun and got to talk. All night. She messaged him back.

> Good morning to you too, Jake. I'm just awake, but don't worry, your message was a nice way to start the day.

The next series of messages resulted in Kara accepting an invitation for lunch at a Greek restaurant at Henley Beach. She politely declined his offer to come and collect her from her aunt's place. It seemed crazy as he lived at Henley Beach, but she wasn't ready for him to know exactly where she stayed when visiting the city. She caught a cab to the beach, despite it being a long way. It allowed her to enjoy a wine if she felt like it, and added to the feel of an easy Sunday by not needing to drive.

They had a relaxed, lovely meal, and their conversation easily picked up from the night before. After lunch, they walked along the esplanade, stopping at Joe's Place. As they left the café, both with coffees in hand, Kara headed north back towards the direction of the restaurant, but Jake touched her arm and asked, 'Would you like to see my house? It's just up the road near here, I'd like you to see where I live.'

Kara hesitated and took a sip of her coffee before answering, not looking at him. She didn't want to assume that there was anything behind the seemingly innocent offer. She took a deep breath before answering. 'Sure. It seems silly not to see your place, if it's nearby.'

Jake took her by the hand and led her across the street. He stopped in front of an impressive two storey house. 'See, I wasn't joking. It is close by.'

Kara laughed. 'You so weren't joking!'

She relaxed and let him lead her into his home.

'I bought this place when things fell apart with Lou. It was in pretty bad shape— a bit like I was.'

Kara caught his words, for the first time Jake was revealing how hard the breakup had been for him.

'Lou? Is she the lady you were with for ten years?'

'Yes.'

'The place looks amazing. Did you do the work on it yourself?'

'I did all the redesign and did some of the building work, but not all of it. My brother is in the building trade, so he managed most of the major work. It took a couple of years, but I enjoyed it. It did me good.'

'It sounds like fixing up this place was a bit of a healing project, a lot like mine. It's funny how home renovations help to change you on the inside too,' said Kara.

Jake nodded and smiled before he replied. 'Very true. So how long did it take you?'

'The house or me?' she asked.

'Both.'

'I redid the whole house and garden which took about three years to create my little sanctuary. My emotional restoration, took a little longer. But all the changes have been a big improvement. I'm happy with everything. Come on Jake, give me the full tour!' she laughed, wanting to change the subject.

'Sure, come on through.'

When they reached the upstairs balcony, Kara breathed in the vista and allure of the seaside. The esplanade was alive with people against the backdrop of the beach and sea, which seemed to extend forever. 'Just look at that view. I can see why you love living here.'

Jake stood close to her, watching her taking in the panorama spanning before her. They didn't speak, but each was conscious of their body's proximity. Without a word, Jake clasped Kara's hand, raised it to his mouth, and kissed each of her fingertips. As he got to the last, he turned her to face him. Pulling her close, he leaned down and kissed her from the nape of her neck, moving upward to under her chin, and then finally reaching her lips.

Kara accepted his kiss willingly. His tongue penetrated her mouth as if it were warm, melting chocolate. She moved in closer to him as his hands explored her back and shoulders as they kissed. Slipping his hands under her blouse, he caressed her bare skin as he traced the outline of her bra. His fingers followed along the top of her bra before gently uncovering her breasts. He cupped and fondled each one, teasing her nipples, all the while still kissing her deeply, never letting their lips part.

Now getting aroused, Kara's grip on his body tightened. She started to not only accept his kiss but join him, pushing herself firmly into his hold on her body and mouth.

Her right arm wrapped around him as her left hand explored his body, stopping only to grip his butt as their kissing intensified.

She moved her hand from his behind, sliding it to the front of his body and taking a firm grip of his inner thigh.

Jake nearly exploded at that point. He had not been this excited about touching a woman in a long time. Work had been his consummate passion for so long, and casual dates and sex were more of a pleasant distraction as opportunities arose... until now. This woman was different from anyone else he had dated. Since they had first met, he'd been struggling not to reach out and touch her hair, feel her body, or kiss her, and he'd been undressing her in his mind since they parted ways until she arrived at the restaurant today.

She had him fascinated by her unique, sexy aura, rendering him uncharacteristically unsure whether to make any advances before now. He sensed a forcefield that seemed to suspend her within an arm's length. It was as if this lady had a trespasser warning sign or something inside and around her that signalled the need for permission and care before daring to get too close. Yet she had a strange and enticing flavour. Her understanding and views of people and the world were insightful, genuine, and obscure all at the same time.

He wanted to know and experience more of her.

Now she was here, so close to him, responding to his touch, her hand between his legs, and he was now so hard and ready for her. Breaking their kiss, he slid his hands from her body and took her by the hand, leading her from the balcony doorway to the centre of the living room.

Once again standing in front of each other, they pressed their bodies together, their hands exploring everywhere. Kara gripped his inner thighs and rubbed over his bulging crotch. Jake's hands moved to her jeans, and as he undid the button and slid down the zipper, her hand froze, and she broke away from the kiss, paused, and drew in a breath, ever so slightly.

Kara's mind had hit full throttle the moment Jake had kissed her fingertips. She knew so little about this guy really, but his interest in her and his touch all seemed genuine.

'So why the apprehension, Kara?' She asked herself. She stopped at that point. She knew why. *But Greg is no longer a part of your world. This man is here and wants you. It's time to move on.*

It had felt nice to be kissed and touched again, having been so long since she had felt Greg's touch.

She jolted herself back into the present and reached for Jake's jeans to unbutton them with near urgency. They undressed each other, still kissing and touching their bodies as they exposed each new piece of flesh.

Once Kara was fully naked in front of him, Jake whispered, 'You are beautiful.'

She didn't say a word. She couldn't look him directly in his eyes. She didn't realise it, but instinctively she knew that eyes were the portal to a person's soul. She'd entered Greg's. She wasn't ready for another. Reaching out, she drew him closer to her body, feeling his hardness pressed urgently against her. Jake trembled as she slightly raised her hips and ground herself against him, letting out a small moan. Jake needed no further invitation.

He gently lifted her by the waist and moved her in one motion, seating her on the lounge and kneeling on the floor in front of her. His hands roamed her body from her breasts, over her stomach and to her thighs as he randomly trailed kisses over her, stopping only to suck on her nipples and breasts. As his lips glided closer to savour the delicate folds of skin between her legs, she started to breathe faster.

'Taste me,' she gasped, allowing her legs to fall open wider.

Jake wanted nothing more than to let his tongue feel the warmth of her wetness and to taste those lips, now visibly glistening with her growing arousal. With a firm grip, he held her legs apart and buried his head between them. He slid his tongue under the hooded skin to expose her clitoris, rolling and circling around it, savouring how tight it had become. He wrapped his lips over her, sucking her bead gently, drawing her sex into his mouth. His fingers adeptly glided between her lips, deftly feeling inside her.

Kara had finally let go, allowing herself to be lost in the sheer pleasure of her body being enjoyed and stimulated again. When her inner muscles contracted as the pressure built, she could no longer bear even the tip of his tongue on her.

'I want you inside me!' She pulled his body up, halting the intensity he created with his tongue's attention. Her muscles flexed and pulsed against his fingers.

His hard body aligned with hers. She instinctively wrapped her legs around his waist. His lips finding hers, he held her tight and entered her with a forceful uncontrollable thrust.

All he needed was permission, she thought as she took every inch of him. The first occasion she and Jake had been intimate was more about self-protection than what she felt for Jake alone, and Kara knew it. No matter how nice, wonderful, or exciting any man might be, her first sexual encounter with another man after Greg was all about creating space and an insurance policy for her heart and soul.

But now, in this moment, it was about servicing a raw desire, she desperately needed this. She wrapped her legs around his body as Jake lay on top of her—hot, groaning, and delivering his thickness with every thrust. Her body had relished in being aroused, touched, and stimulated again. She loved sex, and this was a man who wanted with eagerness to pleasure her.

As they lay on the couch together afterwards, Jake dozed next to her. She let out a huge, contented sigh. See, you can enjoy another man. She closed her eyes, relaxing back against his body.

In the weeks that followed, Jake and Kara spent many nights and weekends together whenever she was back in the city. Jake messaged her every evening to check in on her and chat about the events of their respective workdays. Kara enjoyed this aspect of their relationship most of all, as she still found that it was often on her nights alone when she felt the pangs of missing Greg, which would creep up on her unexpectedly, the withdrawals of that drug.

When she was in Adelaide, which was most weekends, Kara and Jake would enjoy their time together, wine tasting, dining at different restaurants, going to concerts, and spending days just talking for hours as they strolled along the beach. Kara genuinely enjoyed his company and appreciated his caring and sensitive attention to her and others. He was truly a lovely man.

Their lovemaking had gradually become bolder, but it was in this space, that Kara had still been left somewhat unfulfilled. Jake was a confident and sensitive lover who wanted to satisfy her, yet her underlying taste for the slightly kinkier and more erotic pleasure that swinging with Greg had introduced into her life, had resulted in her being left somewhat unfulfilled.

Kara wondered if Jake would be willing to be more adventurous, and if the suggestion of sex with others might stimulate him even more.

One evening, when she was home in bed in Clare, Jake had called her after having hosted a dinner with the staff from Canberra again. Kara had declined the invitation to join them that night, given she had a load on her plate with work and really couldn't face the thought of driving to and from the city on a Thursday night. Jake had had a few wines and was in a horny mood. After the usual catch-up about their day, Kara asked Jake if he would like her to tell him a 'sexy bedtime story.'

Intrigued, he responded, 'Yes, absolutely.'

Kara instructed him to hang up, get undressed, get into bed naked, and be ready for his 'phone date' with her in about ten minutes' time.

Jake was already getting aroused at the thought of Kara's call.

Kara phoned and asked, 'Are you in bed?'

'Yes, I'm all settled in, and I'm all yours.'

'Well, I thought, it may be time now to move up to the next level.'

'What do you mean?'

'You'll see. Now, are you all ready, lights out?'

Jake leaned over and clicked the switch on the bedside lamp. 'I'm ready.'

Kara drew in a breath, releasing it slowly before beginning. Her voice was slow and hushed as she set the scene.

'We're on a big ocean liner, cruising the Pacific. It caters to people our age, and we're going for seven nights. It's a relaxing escape with lots of food, drinks, and me. On the first few evenings, we have dinner at the typical twelve-person dining tables and become acquainted with quite a few of the many different people on board, enjoying their company. There's one couple we've really connected with from the outset, and on the third evening, they invite us to join them for after-dinner drinks at one of the bars. The conversation flows easily with these two until late into the night. It's great to just relax and engage with some fresh, easy-going people.

'The next day is a "go ashore" day. Almost everyone opts for the full touristy island tour, but after quite a late night the evening before, we remain on the ship, enjoying a late breakfast in our cabin. We head ashore and wander along the pristine beach. You ask if we should perhaps grab a towel, in case we take a swim. "Probably not," I say but throw one in my bag just in case. After a short walk, we lose sight of the ship and find ourselves on a secluded beach; not one footprint marks the virgin sand. It's as if we are the first and only people to ever walk there.

'We stroll to the far end of the cove, grab the towel, and sit and luxuriate in a place that feels like it was made for us alone.

'Having the beach to ourselves, it's too tempting to get naked and enjoy the water. It's such a turn on to watch each other strip out of our clothes in the open and then stroll down into the crystal-clear tempered water. We swim for a distance then stop, enjoy a kiss or two and the feel of the warm water of this tropical island on our naked bodies.

'We notice a couple coming towards us. We soon realise it's the couple from last night. She is wearing a little bikini, white with dark blue polka dots and he's just in a pair of swim shorts. They recognise us and wave. He calls out, "Hey, do you mind if we join you?"

'"Absolutely," I say, "but we aren't wearing any clothes!" They both grin as he replies, "We can do that!" He helps his lady out of her top, and they remove their bottoms. We both watch as they approach; they are much like us, fit and trim.

'As they get closer, you pull me towards you. I'm in front of you facing them, and they take up the same pose. We talk for a while as you and I admire her breasts, as you catch him often looking at mine. I can feel you getting a little aroused behind me, and I know your mind is racing, trying to keep from getting hard, but you can't help it. You tease me from behind. I hear you sigh and now you've given up worrying about the erection you can no longer hide.'

'They seem to be caught in the thrill of their exposed nakedness and knowing we are watching them. He runs his hands over her tits. She laps it up, her head tilting back and arms widening as if to entice us to watch. You slide your hand between my legs, and even in the water, you can feel my silky juices. I reach behind my back, without turning around, and grip you. We're both so turned on. I loosen my grip and keep chatting to the couple about how we found the cove in such pristine condition, giving you time to get your erection somewhat under control, before saying, "Shall we go back to the beach?"'

'We leave the water, both of you men still semi-aroused. You really don't care that she is noticing you. We lay on our only towel. They do the same, positioning themselves right next to us, closer than you would normally expect. Both of us girls are laying on our sides, looking at each other, and you guys lay on your sides facing in. You caress my body and I let my hand reach behind me to run up and down your thigh.

'He does the same, boldly letting his hands roll over her breasts, up and down her stomach and thighs. You can see her nipples becoming erect in front of us. Feeling brave, you slide your hand between my legs, and I spread them willingly. Both of you guys are hard again; there is no hiding that now. I turn to you, nuzzling you to lie on your back, and you pull me on top of you, finding me without effort, and I let an audible groan escape, as you slip deep inside me.

'We almost forget we aren't on our own, but then we see they're doing the same. We girls look at each other, smile, and reach out to touch and hold each other's hands. I am so getting off on watching both of us enjoying our men as we rock back and forth. She runs her hand up my arm onto my breast, and I reach out for hers. She whispers to her man, "Do me from behind," as she repositions herself to kneel up close, her face in front of me. As she passionately kisses me, she slides her hand down between us, her fingers caressing me with a gentle, circular motion as you continue to slide in and out of me, your cock now sliding between her fingers.

'By now, she is kissing my breasts and working her way south, indicating to you to let her have more of me. You edge me off you, allowing her full access to my body, and she slips between my legs and finds me with her tongue. Now standing and watching the two of us girls lost in each other, you glance at her man. He just smiles and nods towards her. Understanding his silent consent, you move behind his lady and start teasing her from behind with your cock. He has moved to kiss me, and just as he does, I see you take her.

'I take him in my hand and stroke him a couple of times before pulling him towards my lips. I take him in my mouth and can taste her juices that cover him. I can feel you thrusting into her as she continues to pleasure me faster and faster with her tongue and fingers. He asks me, "Can I blow in your mouth?" I give him a nod and I look you in the eye and say, "Fill her, babe."'

Kara paused in her storytelling voice to ask Jake, 'Are you ready to blow, babe, 'cause I'm about to.'

As Kara moaned through the phone, Jake uttered his first words. 'I'm going to fill her! I'm doing her hard. Can you feel me pounding her?' Kara couldn't get any words out as her orgasm exploded. The groaning sounds of Jake coming, heightened and extended her own gushing climax. Kara could hear Jake panting, struggling to steady his breathing.

After a few moments, he blurted, 'Oh my God, I really got off on that!'

'I could hear,' Kara said, laughing gently. In a hushed tone, she added, 'So, you like the idea of enjoying the other couple, Jake?'

'That was an incredible story. I've never had phone sex like that before,' he muttered.

'Well, I don't need to say sweet dreams then, I suppose!' Kara giggled.

Jake just let out a simple 'Goodnight, Kara,' in a groggy, hushed tone.

The next morning Jake rang. They had tentatively planned to have lunch together the following day, as Kara had a meeting in the city.

After confirming that Kara should be finished by twelve thirty and could meet him at his office in Waymouth Street around 1.00 p.m., Jake paused and then asked in a tone that was rather cautious, yet his words were clearly attempting to be casual, 'Kara, I love your imagination. I haven't stopped thinking about your story from last night.'

'Well, thank you, Jake.'

'That sort of thing turns me on,' he added quietly.

'I'm so pleased you enjoyed it.'

His next question puzzled Kara a bit. 'It was only a story… wasn't it? I mean, what prompted you to think of a story like that?'

'Oh, I just find the idea of some kinky play a bit of a turn on, I suppose. By your reaction, you enjoy it too.'

'Well, I can't say no, now, can I?'

When they met for lunch, the phone sex experience had noticeably been all-consuming for Jake. In every conversation, he kept returning to the subject.

Kara was becoming totally confused. Jake seemed to be excited and had definitely been aroused and interested, yet his questions were probing, and she sensed a strange tone in the way he spoke to her about the phone sex, such as: 'Where did you think of the story?' and 'would you ever want to do that for real?'

She first thought his questions were leading him to a place where he was entertaining group sex. She casually told him they could post an ad if he wanted to find out more and see how many other people enjoyed that experience for real. Jake went silent at that suggestion, but then the questions continued. Kara avoided answering many of them, no longer sure if he was fascinated with a desire for more, or if he was fearful.

After that day, most of their catch-ups started with a barrage of questions, to which Kara would remain silent until he realised, he was making her feel uncomfortable. Then he would stop, look at her, and smile. But she noticed that he would go silent again.

She could nearly feel his lust and interest in her build and then withdraw sharply every time he spoke about it. After each time they made love, he always asked, 'Am I enough for you? Should I be doing more?' It was like he needed constant reassurance.

He was obviously fascinated, aroused, and intrigued by kinkier sex, but there was fear and a growing abhorrence in his feelings too.

Jake was confused. He was smart enough to recognise he was somewhat tarnished with the dilemma of the social morals and expectations of living a monogamous lifestyle which in today's society no longer held true for so many. But for him, any thought of the real experience of swinging or sex with someone beyond one woman, was something that shocked him. His own reaction to the concept, in contrast to Kara's inclusive attitude and seeming acceptance of this lifestyle, had surprised and disturbed him.

In the following weeks after the phone sex, Kara suspected that Jake no longer trusted his feelings about her. She doubted that he could entertain anything beyond suggestive talk as a fantasy and, ultimately, he would be turned off, rather than turned on, by the idea of actually engaging in any sexual play beyond with one woman.

Kara understood this; however, she also knew she was far more honest with herself and accepted what others might describe as being too 'out there' or liberal in her thinking, pleasures, and desires.

She and Greg were not deviants; nor were they extraordinary, unsavoury, or undesirable people. It was quite the opposite. They had both become self-aware, trusting, understanding true inclusivity, and had openly dared to express their own sexual desires in a way that was natural to them. While it may fly in the face of the socially accepted by the majority, it still felt right, not only for them but for the growing number of people who were enjoying swing clubs, bars, and posting ads on so many sites dedicated to soft and full swing.

Kara could not judge Jake and understood his dilemma, but she also knew that having become so self-aware and having experienced the pleasure of this form of sexual play, that she could not sustain a relationship with someone who found her behaviour, her desires, or her views as somewhat promiscuous or perverted. Deep down, Kara knew he was not that man.

Kara now thought the relationship with Jake was doomed. She continued to hear his questions and gave him time to process his thoughts and feelings. His advances towards her now see-sawed from avid intimate attention to her, to sudden withdrawal and silence, as if she was repulsive.

This was his values and attitudes to deal with and not hers. She understood that, so Kara waited for his next round of questions, and she answered him honestly with clarity and explicit detail, so he understood that she was, in fact, a swinger. That she had engaged in little play and only with one partner, but surprisingly had found it to be arousing and stimulating. It extended her desire and confidence. She told him that ultimately it had been this experience that had allowed her inner self to glow and had brought her to a point where she became attractive to him. She explained that she understood he may not accept or understand her attitude or forgive the fact that she sexually enjoyed being watched and touched by others in the company of a trusted partner. Kara also told him the story she had told him was one that her former partner had shared with her during phone sex and had further ignited her desire to enjoy that lifestyle for real.

When she finished recounting her experiences and how it made her feel, Jake just looked at her. He hadn't spoken a word. She knew the instant he looked into her eyes he'd already left her. The next day, Jake sent her a text message.

I'm sorry, Kara. I didn't realise you were THAT kind of woman. I so wanted us to work, but I can't deal with this. Jake. x

Kara did not reply.

Chapter 23

$\mathcal{G}$reg had struggled through those first days after his call to Kara, but he knew he had to put her out of his mind—for her sake even more than his. He had finally accepted that although he loved both of these women, the archaic custom of today's society forbade it.

'You can only have one in your life, apparently. Kara needs to have someone with her, beside her, whenever she needs or wants them. She needs more than I can give her,' he told himself.

While accepting this, Greg found himself at a loss for the next couple of days. He experienced the turbulent mixed feelings of sorrow, guilt, confusion and most of all loss, and yet being blessed all at the same time. He knew he still had so much love in his life with Tess and also that he had the rare chance to have found a friend and love with Kara. This played heavily on his heart.

Dealing with emotions was something Greg tried hard to avoid, as this was something he couldn't fully plan or control. Greg knew he had to be open and talk more with Tess about Kara. He just had to find the space and words that could convey some sense to his feelings, in a way she might understand. He was still trying to decipher it himself.

It was some simple words from Tess that unknowingly helped him to find the peace and the distance he needed to focus and settle once again. Greg was scheduled to fly home the next day, and she wanted to let him know her work plans had changed and could now meet him at the airport.

Greg answered with an unusually quiet 'Hi there' and not the usual 'Hello, babe' or 'Hello, sexy.' As she spoke, he was just listening saying nothing more than a word or two. She knew instantly something was wrong.

'Hey, hon, are you okay?'

'I'm okay. I'm just a bit distracted. I've had a few things on my mind. Nothing for your sweet self to worry about though.'

'Want to talk about it? Anything I can do?' Tess asked, always so loving and supportive.

'Nah, I've just been trying to work through an issue that cropped up here, but I don't think I can come up with any solutions. Anything I can think of will probably just make it worse, so it just feels unfinished.'

'Don't be too hard on yourself. You can't fix everything, you know. Sometimes the best thing you can do is step back and do nothing. Time and space can sometimes make problems disappear. Besides,' she said with a laugh, 'I have a problem here that only you can fix. I'm missing you and your body terribly!'

Greg smiled to himself and replied, 'That's no good. I will definitely have to do something about that. Thanks for calling, babe. Hey…' his voice lowered an octave, 'I can't wait to see you tomorrow.'

Tess was right. The best thing was to do no more than allow time and space between him and Kara now. So that night, before he went to sleep, he reread every message from Kara, allowed a tear or two to shed, and then deleted them all from his phone.

'Let her go. She deserves more than I can give,' he said. 'Enough now.'

He awoke feeling much calmer and knew he could return to focus his attention on home, Tess, and his plans for April 30th.

Now only a couple of weeks out, he had to make sure he had the finer details on track. Greg knew he was working in the morning on the special day he had planned for Tess, making the timing critical but not impossible. By this time, having all the major components in place, it was now time to join all the pieces together.

Finally, the ring was ready with only five days to spare. Greg was flying to New Zealand after his event in Sydney. So before departing for Auckland, he arranged for Paul, the jeweller, to fly down from Brisbane to Sydney and meet him at the airport.

Greg's first sight of the ring was a mixture of shock, relief, and joy; he came close to shedding a tear. It was exquisite and exactly as he had hoped. After a beer and transfer of the balance in cash, Paul boarded a plane back to Brisbane. Greg then had to travel overseas with this priceless ring and not lose it. The little velvet box didn't leave his sight.

The ring was in place; now to the last and finer plans of the event.

For the next few days, Greg went over each element, trying to think if he could have missed anything. It was the end of April in Australia, and while only Autumn, the weather should still be mild. But in typical Sheppard style, he left nothing to chance and had a table reserved in the restaurant just in case the weather turned to crap.

The day had finally arrived. The weather forecast predicted a sunny day and warm evening with a fifteen-knot onshore wind from the southwest and a one metre swell. Greg's forty-eight-foot Riviera was a big boat with two powerful turbocharged diesel engines, so in these conditions, that baby would make it down to Glenelg easily.

Tess was welcomed into the morning with Greg's loving attention showered all over her body. Reluctantly dragging themselves from bed they showered, dressed for work, and Greg made breakfast, keen for her to be spoilt all day. As she stood to leave, Greg came up close.

'Happy anniversary, babe,' he said pulling her into his arms.

'Happy anniversary to you too, darling,' she responded, before kissing him passionately.

They held there in a deep embrace, before Greg eased back. 'Hey you don't want to be late. I'll see you at dinner tonight.'

'So where are we going?' she asked.

'You'll find out tonight,' he said cheekily.

'Alright then, sir! See you tonight!' she laughed as she headed out the door.

Tess glowed all the way to the office. She was always so touched that he never forgot this date and had created this as their special day to commemorate the announcement to him that she was now free and wanted to be with him. Throughout her workday, she kept thinking back to the amazing surprise escape to Sydney those couple of years ago, the dress, and the smoking passion in the taxi back to the hotel. She smiled as she tried to imagine what he was planning. Knowing this was now their sort of two-year anniversary. She guessed he would plan something more than just dinner for that night. This would be a happy day.

Because they were to spend the night on the boat at the marina, Greg knew he would need to take clothes, toiletries, makeup, and a hairdryer to the boat for her to have for the next day. Not too hard.

As soon as Tess drove off, he ran around gathering all the gear they needed for the night away. He then left for work and found it difficult to stay focused, especially as he noticed the breeze starting to pick up as the day went on. He kept assuring himself it would be fine.

Greg finished work about 2.30 p.m.—about an hour later than he would have liked. He raced home and grabbed his dinner clothes and headed for North Haven Marina.

Arriving at the marina, he noticed the wind had picked up to what seemed like at least twenty-five knots. After several trips back to the car, he'd loaded everything on board. He untied the boat and headed out of the shelter of the breakwater into the open ocean. A one-and-a-half-metre swell confronted him on a ten-degree angle off the nose. Shit!

He had no choice but to push on through. He had originally pictured himself cruising at seventeen knots with a beer in hand, admiring the scenery. Now, it was a case of having to drive it the whole way, up and down every wave, at a speed of only nine knots. Spray covered him and the entire topside of the vessel. He would not make up any time at all at this pace—or worse, be even late.

It would now take over an hour to get to Glenelg, and he could miss his mooring in front of the restaurant that the attendant had promised to save for him. Greg was feeling the pressure. Not only was he late, but now he would need to clean and dry the deck of the boat before anything could be set up.

His thoughts were racing. All his precise plans were unravelling before his eyes. He was getting anxious. He didn't settle for anything less than perfection for any event. This was his job, putting together million-dollar corporate events. Surely, he couldn't fail at this little two-person dinner. He was madly reviewing his plans and the 'what-ifs' as he continued to push on through the swell.

The marina attendant only worked till 4.30 p.m., so he knew if he arrived any later than that, he couldn't be assured the prime mooring position next to the restaurant would still be free. To top it off, sea spray had drenched him from head to toe, his only pair of shoes were full of water, and he couldn't have been any wetter if he had fallen overboard! Thankfully, he'd grabbed a change of clothes.

He had lost well over an hour by the time he arrived at Holdfast Shores marina and had so much extra work to do, but the wind had eased, the mooring was free, and the sun was still out. He heaved a sigh of relief. However, he still had a very large boat to clean and himself to get changed.

Greg quickly tied the boat to the mooring, making sure the rear transom door had clear access for the restaurant staff and they wouldn't be tripping over ropes. As fast as he could, he ran upstairs to the restaurant, told the manager he was there, and said he needed fifteen minutes to dry the rear deck area. Greg worked frantically to get things dried. The restaurant manager soon arrived and started setting the table with glasses, cutlery, plates, candles, and an ice bucket for the champagne.

'Phew!' Greg said. Everything was nearly back on track.

He checked the time. It was 5.30 p.m., and Tess would finish work any minute. Then he realised what he'd forgotten. 'Oh shit!' With the distraction of the delay and everything having been soaked, he had forgotten that Tess didn't know the limousine would be there at her work to pick her up.

Greg sent a text message with instructions she was to leave her car at work and that a driver would be outside to pick her up. Tess replied with an 'Okay' and a love heart.

Done and back on track! The boat was dry, Greg was dry, they'd set the table, Tess should be on her way, and the weather was now much better. He grabbed a beer, sat back on the padded rear deck seat, and breathed a sigh of relief. He checked his watch and headed towards the drop-off point of the marina. Time to meet the star guest.

Within a minute or two, a black S Class Mercedes Benz arrived. It stopped, and Tess stepped out, looking like a movie star. *Maybe he should have gotten a red carpet?* he thought.

Why was it that every first sight of her made his heart miss a beat? Greg greeted her with a cheeky smile and kissed her tenderly on the lips. With only a 'hello' and another gentle smile, he took her by the hand and led her down towards the boat.

Tess saw his boat, which was no real surprise to her, given she was at the marina, but as she approached, the magical setting that Greg created came into view. The manager, dressed in a black suit with a white shirt and a bow tie, stood onboard with a silver tray and two glasses of champagne. It looked like a setting for royalty or an A-list Hollywood couple. So much so, that people passing by were stopping, pointing, and taking pictures. It took Tess's breath away. 'Wow,' she whispered to Greg.

Greg guided her onto the boat, giving her a wink, and she just beamed back at him. She took the glass of Veuve Clicquot champagne offered by their maître d' and thanked him.

Greg had remembered to buy two bottles of the Petersburg French champagne that he knew she loved, purchasing them duty-free on his way back from New Zealand. She nodded approvingly as she took her first sips. The manager left and soon arrived back with the hors d'oeuvres. Greg and Tess ate, sipped their champagne, and chatted about their day. They ignored the onlookers, who continued to stare and take photographs.

A bottle of Cabernet and a bottle of crisp Chardonnay arrived that Greg had pre-selected at the planning session. They were now getting a lot more attention from the wharf above. Tess was enjoying the whole ambience of the evening—the surprise, the weather, the wine, the food, and the elegance of the setting. To Greg it was more the relief that it was all back on track and going charmingly.

Entrees arrived, this time delivered by the head chef himself, dressed in white and a chef's hat. He explained he had prepared a sample of every entrée on the menu, and with a smile, he returned to the kitchen.

After such a big day, Greg felt the effects of the wine and needed to make an attempt to slow down a bit. He needed to be sure he didn't relax too much until each part of tonight's plan was complete.

He had decided to 'do it' between the entrée and the main course. It would still be daylight and he really wanted her to appreciate the ring to its fullest. When they finished the entrée and the waiters cleared the table, Greg looked towards the dock. There were still many people in the marina—eating, drinking, or just having a stroll to watch the setting sun disappear in the west. Greg knew the time had come.

He reached in his jacket pocket and then his pants. His fingers kept feeling around and fumbling for the box. The ring was gone. Greg's heart almost stopped at that moment as he pictured it sitting on the bottom of the ocean somewhere between here and North Haven.

Tess noticed a pained expression on his face. 'Are you all right, babe, lost something?'

'No probs. Just excuse me for a sec.' Appearing almost calm, he went downstairs to search for it, all the while the panic rising and his heart racing through his chest. He suddenly remembered. Of course! He had changed clothes after the wet trip up the coast. The ring was quickly located where it had been since the morning. In the pocket of his now wet work pants. After a couple of deep breaths to calm himself, he climbed the steps and returned to the table.

He stood in front of Tess and looked into her beautiful blue eyes before dropping to one knee and holding out the sparkling diamond engagement ring. Tess covered her mouth to suppress a scream as he said,

'Teresa Merchant, will you be my wife?'

Tess froze in shock. This was not what she was expecting at all. Only her eyes moved as she glanced from Greg to the ring and back again.

They were both unaware that all the background noise from the people in the marina and restaurants had faded to almost silence. It was as if the world had stopped, not just for Greg, but for the hundreds waiting in anticipation of her reply.

Tess was speechless. She had not given the slightest thought to marrying again. Although she knew the answer. Her heart, head, and mouth were all bursting to say yes, but being so overwhelmed by the moment, she couldn't find her voice.

'Yes.' The word finally escaped her lips. She stood to hug him but wobbled on her feet. Greg reached for her left hand and placed the ring on her finger; it fitted perfectly. She could only just hear the cheering and clapping from the marina as the tears welled in her eyes and rolled down her cheeks. She let out a small giggle as the cheers continued. Tess held him tight, her head nestled on his shoulder, and she whispered, 'Yes, yes, yes,' in his ear before stepping back to study her new beautiful ring.

The main course arrived at this point and signalled to the on-lookers it was time to disperse and leave the couple to enjoy their intimate evening.

The main course was divine—a rosemary-infused rack of lamb to share. Neither of them was hungry now, but they devoured most of it. When the table was eventually cleared, Greg sat back and relaxed, wine in hand, feeling so relieved it had all gone perfectly to plan.

He surprised her in so many ways, and she had said yes. He was sure tonight had truly surpassed their first special occasion night in Sydney those couple of years ago.

The wind had completely dropped and left them with the most beautiful evening. Greg went up to the restaurant, paid, tipped, and thanked the manager and staff for doing such an amazing job.

It was late by then and most people had gone from the marina and the beach. Greg suggested they go for a walk along the beach in the moonlight for a little change of scenery. It was a warm balmy night, and the stars were out. As Greg walked, holding her hand, he thought about how the last three months had built towards this moment. So many things could have gone wrong, but thankfully it all fell into place; it couldn't have been more perfect.

As the two of them reached the quiet end of the beach, they stopped and lay together on the sand. There were few words spoken but their touch said it all. They kissed and cuddled and eventually made love there on the sand under the stars.

The next morning, Tess woke to the smell of coffee that Greg had just purchased from a café on the marina.

'Good morning, my gorgeous future wife,' he said as he handed her the coffee. He sat back on his heels at the end of the bed to just take in the beautiful specimen in his bed. With no make-up and her silky blonde hair everywhere, she was still breathtaking.

As Tess looked at Greg, her eyes sparkled and an enormous smile appeared, the events of the beautiful night before coming to mind. Then her expression changed as she moved to scramble out of bed.

'No rush, babe,' he assured her. 'You've got the day off. I spoke to your boss. It's all sorted, but we'll set sail shortly.'

'You spoke to her?'

'Yes, we have all the time we need.'

'You are simply amazing. It's no wonder I love you so much.'

He smiled and left to prepare for their departure. He fired up the two big diesels, letting them warm up before untying from the mooring. Tess joined him on deck, coffee in hand, bare feet, denim shorts and a white T-shirt.

'Can I help?' she called out, knowing full well that he liked to do it all himself.

'All good.'

They set sail for North Haven. Greg steered the boat to head north, and about a mile offshore, the water was calm. With only the background hum of the engines and the occasional seagull to be heard, Tess wrapped her arms around him and rested her head on his shoulder. 'You've made me the happiest woman in the world.'

In the days that followed, Greg and Tess visited their family and friends to share the news of their engagement, and with such a magnificent ring on her finger, it took no time for Tess's work colleagues to instantly realise she was now engaged. The engagement delighted everyone.

Chapter 24

Against her better judgement, Kara looked at Greg's Facebook page. She convinced herself it was just to see his face and to remind her of the times they had together and what could have been. The first thing she noticed was his Status was 'Engaged.'

Kara's reaction to the discovery was bittersweet. She was pleased Greg had followed his heart and his love, as he had said he would. It was easy to see how happy Tess made him. Understandably, Kara was also tinged with a touch of sadness and pain, as this also announced to her that their friendship and any intimate moments with him were now completely a thing of the past.

Kara took a day before sending a message to Greg.

> Congratulations! I hope you know that all I want is for you to be happy. Both of you. May each moment of your lives together be very special. Kara.

She watched tentatively for the next few days, but thankfully he didn't reply. She just wanted to say it. She meant it. Somehow it made it real and helped the space between them become even greater despite knowing that their connection and special kind of love would always remain.

The afterglow of the amazing and unexpected extravagance of the dinner, proposal, and night on the boat with Greg enveloped Tess. The emotion and magnitude of the moment had completely overcome her. She had been so openly and publicly adored by Greg; it was nearly too much to believe that it was real.

The attention to detail, the setting, menu… and, my God, the ring! The whole night was resounding and made her heart burst. She had found a special man in Greg, and she could barely believe he was hers, to love and be loved by.

Tess had never felt this happy in her life. She had Greg to thank for that. She knew he wasn't perfect by any means. He was driven and had unwavering determination, which often resulted in him being impatient, opinionated, and sometimes agitated. He focused on one thing at a time only, so he found transitions from work to home sometimes difficult. She was sure this was what contributed to those times when she could feel him being distracted and distanced from her. But she accepted this to be the nature of his character and knew that when his attention was on her, it was all consuming, devoted, and complete.

She was his fiancée. The thought of marriage to someone again had not even entered her mind. However, she was here. Again.

In love, engaged, and ecstatic about it! Regarding the wedding, Greg had told her, 'This is a time for you to shine. I would prefer a low-key, more intimate and casual event, as it's only about you and me. But it's even more about how and what you want to enjoy on our wedding day. No matter how large or small, babe! I know you will make and do whatever you feel is right for us both.'

They'd talked about there being no rush and taking their time to make it exactly right. Greg had also indicated that it would probably suit him best after the first part of next year. He had prospects of heading to the United States in late December or January, having been approached to manage a major launch event for a US company who was looking to start a new retail chain across Australia. 'It would be good to have that trip well behind me, so I focus my attention on us. That's probably the only thing I would ask.'

Tess loved how Greg was so keen to make it theirs and how he'd listened, suggested, and accompanied her to so many places to research the options and ideas for their special day whenever he could during the following couple of weeks.

'A man who loves to shop as well as your other talents!' she exclaimed to him as she pinched him on the bum as they entered another store to get ideas for gifts for their two friends who had accepted their request to be witnesses on their wedding day.

As time passed, Tess got absorbed in the plans for the wedding. There was so much she wanted to do to make it special. Her first wedding had not been what she wanted. She'd allowed much of the event to be dictated by her bridesmaids, her mother-in-law, her ex and everyone else. This time she wanted this to be perfect. It would be exactly how she had always imagined her wedding day to be. Her perfect day.

Greg would be busy by the end of June with another major event in Brisbane in August, which would take him away for a few weeks, so Tess had the next couple of months when Greg would still be in Adelaide to involve him in plans as much as possible. They had so many ideas initially about where to hold their wedding, but eventually settled on a winery. Tess had wanted to check everything with Greg, so she had a clear idea of what he preferred to wear, food he would like on the menu, the style and format for the ceremony, favourite music, and the people he wanted most to invite as guests.

Greg had thought hard, choosing about a dozen close and loved family and friends with whom he knew had a connection to both him and Tess. This was a second wedding for them, so it wasn't like it would be a cast of thousands. As he scrolled through his contacts on his phone, he stopped at Kara Gilbert. With a sigh, he allowed himself only a split second to recall the memory of her face and the passion they had shared, the look on her face as she came as he filled her body with his, but that was then and this now. He straightened and took a deep breath. He knew there would always be a little hole in his heart only she could fill.

As Greg was preparing dinner one evening, he glanced over at Tess seated at the end of the dining table, surrounded by what was a sea of brochures, fabric swatches, paper, magazines, and madly checking emails on her laptop. Greg smiled. The wedding planner at work. He realised this had become a regular scene in the past month where Tess would arrive home, change, pour a glass of wine, and get comfortable at the dining table to shape their special day.

Greg loved that she was so excited and wanted to lead the plans. He had originally worried that she might be reluctant to suggest things she wanted, because of him being a professional event manager. So, one night, while cradled in each other's arms, he whispered, 'As you know, my job is about planning and promoting events, but my life is about being with you. I will do anything and be as involved as much or as little as you like, but I know, whatever, it will be the most beautiful day for us. Besides,' he said jokingly, 'maybe it's your turn to surprise me!'

They both laughed, and Tess snuggled in closer to him. 'I will surprise you, Mr Sheppard.'

So, with the major focus of surprise in mind, Tess had got to work. Creating a unique wedding was now her main project. Securing a venue was a priority, but she needed to know how many guests.

She had Greg's list, which was small. Already she had so many more, given her larger family, girlfriends and their partners. She thought of key people associated with Greg's work, many so influential clients, that it could be strategic to invite some of them as guests too. That could not only balance some numbers but could benefit Greg and her professionally at the same time.

Originally, she had suggested they hold the ceremony on their 'anniversary date' of April 30th next year, which remained their special day and was far enough away to avoid Greg's trip and commitments early next year. Greg had said this was perfect, and the weather could still be fine for a gathering at a boutique winery. After finally settling on a guest list that now included family, friends, and a lot more, the first chosen location of Paulette's Winery in the Clare Valley would be far too small.

Tess searched and decided upon Seppeltsfield Heritage Winery in the Barossa Valley, as it was renowned for hosting grand functions for up to five hundred guests, and as one of the oldest wineries, it boasted magnificent views and a dining hall that could surely impress. She contacted their functions manager and was delighted at the possibilities, menu choice, and options to host a most spectacular wedding.

The date, however, was the problem, with so many weddings booked through April and nearly every weekend until the end of the following year. Tess didn't want to wait until summer next year for the next date. She was heartbroken until the manager suggested that there was a date open on January 12th. Tess knew Greg had said he might be in the US during December/January, but she was sure his work should be finished by the 12th. Anyway, he can just fly back. It's his wedding, after all. So, she accepted the booking and sent the deposit post-haste to secure the date. She was so excited.

That evening when Greg arrived home, she was nearly bursting. 'Greg, I think it's time to catch you up on the plans,' she said. 'I've been busy and made such progress with everything. I'm sure it's time for your first part of the surprise that I promised you. I know we wanted our wedding to be on our anniversary date in April, but I've secured the perfect place for us to host our special day. I know you can't wait, like me, so we can now be married January 12th at Seppeltsfield.'

Greg was surprised. He hadn't considered that Tess might want to hold the wedding so soon. Taken aback and not wishing to dampen Tess's excitement, he said, 'You have been busy.' After a minute, he softly asked, 'Hey, Tess, so there wasn't a winery that could host us on our special anniversary day?'

'I had thought that might be the perfect time too. Paulette's in Clare could host us in April, but they couldn't quite manage all the guests.'

'I see. How many guests are we having?'

'Well, I've kept it to about a hundred and eighty,' she replied.' I have so many friends and family, and we both have so many work colleagues and connections that it was hard to keep it to any less.'

Greg didn't say a word for a moment. He honestly hadn't thought they would have anything much beyond thirty guests, with only close family and friends.

Since being together, they had often talked about enjoying intimate events and dinner parties, rather than larger events. The proposed date was around the time of his US trip, and this was a major deal, for which the planning was all-consuming. He was sure he had mentioned this to Tess. He wanted this job to be far behind him, so he and Tess could relax to enjoy their special day and escape for a holiday too. Tess had caught him by surprise alright—he was in fact rather shocked.

He breathed in. Finally, he found his voice, holding it to a whisper, to quell his rising dismay. 'Hey, babe, that's a lot of people. You know this is about being special for you and me most of all. January will be tricky. I may not have mentioned that this is when I am likely to be in the US and—'

Before he could say another word, Tess blurted out, 'But this is the only date they have free, and it's the perfect location! I can't do anything right, can I? I knew it. You really didn't think I could do this!' Tess was hurt, and the words just burst out of her. She had hoped Greg would be as excited as she was, but he had simply asked questions.

'Hey, Tess, hold on a moment here. I want this to be special for you, I do, but it's just—'

Tess cut him off again. 'Yes, sure you do! You want special only according to you. As always, just fit it around your work. It's just another function to you! What about me and my business? This is my chance to shine like you do. I'm so pissed off with you right now, I don't want to talk about it anymore. I'm so over this whole wedding.'

With that, she sobbed and turned to head off outside.

Greg just stood there. This was so uncharacteristic of Tess.

But he had five sisters, two daughters and been with countless women to know this is a natural phenomenon in the female make up, and not something to be taken personally. Greg drew in a deep breath and walked to the kitchen. He grabbed a couple of glasses, and a bottle of wine. He searched through his phone, finding the song he had sent to Tess after their first date. He turned on his speaker and slowly raised the volume. After he filled the glasses, he strolled out to the back deck where he knew she would be. He walked up to her as she sat, curled up in the little swing seat near the roses.

After handing her the glass, he leaned down and kissed her on the cheek. Her cheeks were still burning red and wet with tears. She looked up at him. Her eyes had softened, and the Tess he knew and loved had returned. Her glass shaking a little in her trembling hand, she took a sip of the wine and then let out a sigh. She stood up, faced him, and placed her free hand on his cheek. 'I'm never going to find enough words to say how sorry I am, Greg.'

'Shh now, it's okay. We'll make this work. I know you've put so much time into this.'

Tess wiped a tear away and said, 'Please let me say this. I really did only make this all about me. I didn't think about "us" at all. I allowed myself to get caught up in the occasion and forgot what it really was all about. I want it to be big and wonderful for us and nothing like what I had with you-know-who. I hope you'll let me start again?'

'Of course, babe. I probably expected something smaller, my life is always about big events. But this is a big event for us. So, whatever you want is what we will have, and I truly mean that. I think the January date hit me, as I will be busy and won't be here to help. Plus, I had secretly hoped you would pick our anniversary date, so we could even grab a holiday too.'

Tess just nodded. Greg took the glass from her hand, set both glasses down on the ground, and as she stood, he drew her into a firm embrace.

'Whatever you want, but let's not talk about it anymore tonight.'

Tess stepped back briefly to look at him, then nodded and smiled. She nestled back into his arms, and they just stood there for a while.

Later that night in bed, Greg looked at Tess as she lay drifting in and out of sleep next to him. She had worried him. She had never erupted about anything like she had tonight. It was a side of her he had never witnessed before. He felt guilty for having left her with the plans in recent weeks and was soon to be travelling away again, so he wasn't able to lend a hand. He felt even worse, as he was still yet to find time alone with her, when he could talk with her about Kara. He had to tell Tess everything. He let his thoughts drift back to the guilt he had also felt when he told Kara about his plans with Tess. This time, it was more about his reflections on himself.

I never intend to hurt anyone, but perhaps I'm not the easiest person to be with? He let all these thoughts go, as he suddenly felt Tess's hand reach out to feel the warmth of him next to her.

Chapter 25

*T*he rain was endless. Winter had arrived in early June and stayed for keeps, still depressingly wet, windy, dark, and miserable. August was no better. Kara was sick of it.

She was over the damp clothes resulting from the countless number of dashes from the car to the office, the heavy drone of unproductive, serious meetings, starting and ending each day in darkness. She tired of the way this endless winter dragged on, pulling down everybody's energy, and sense of fun.

Since the Jake experience, despite going out on a few odd dates and spending time with friends, she'd met no guy who she could consider having a relationship with or even just a one-night stand. Life was boring. *I've just got to get out of here for a while*, she thought. She was feeling miserable and craved sunshine and an escape. To anywhere but here.

'Do something about it, Kara,' she said to herself. 'But what?'

And then, without notice, she had two separate messages from friends, which reminded her she did, in fact, have choices. She didn't have to stay here! Two dear friends, Jessica and Andrew, had a seasonal apartment in Darwin and had often invited her to visit. She'd recently received an invitation from them to come up. 'There's a music festival on here next week, Kara. It's beautiful here now; you're most welcome to stay for as long as you like.'

Later that day, Kara was checking out the newsfeed on Facebook and the many posts from other friends. The post from Rebecca and Michael, in Brisbane really caught her eye. 'And you wonder why we moved to Brisbane?' The image of her friends in shorts and T-shirts, all smiles, against a backdrop of blue sky and a tropical garden was the trigger she needed. *You've not been to Queensland since you were a kid, so why not?* she thought.

Kara started checking out places to stay and things to do. Yes, she would spend time with her friends, but she should also make the most of her time to explore Brisbane and check out any fun events and places. Who knows who I might meet? Kara had a newly formed, insatiable sex drive that needed feeding. God, I could do with a man right now!

After booking a flight and accommodation in what looked to be a great motel in Fortitude Valley, she was so pleased she could be situated in the best spot for markets, couture boutiques, and yet still be close to the CBD, galleries, and nightlife. As she scrolled through the page on the 'What's On' in Brisbane website, she looked at the festivals, shows, and food events. There was so much happening there. Then she saw it.

'Oh seriously… this can't be?'

But it was. The Festival of Film Production was being held at the Museum and Art Gallery precinct. Kara loved these sorts of festivals, which had such a variety of things on show, static displays, food, entertainment, music, and a chance to meet people from behind the scenes in some of her favourite films. But it wasn't the festival program that surprised her: Greg Sheppard was listed on the site as a contact for exhibitors. It couldn't be possible. Of all the places I choose, Greg is there.

She stopped and thought, *maybe I'll just cancel… Don't be silly. Chances are you won't see him, anyway. But you want to go to the exhibition. Okay, well, if anything happens, you can be a grown-up about this, and if you see him, surely you can just say hello? Anyhow, you know he is engaged. You can be just friends. Not so long ago, he was your best friend.*

Eventually, Kara decided not to change her plans. She decided to simply send Greg a message to say hi, let him know she was likely to be in proximity, and check his reaction. She waited until twenty-four hours before she departed for Brisbane. Then she sent a brief message.

> Hi, Greg. Hey, any chance you might be interested in a coffee if I happened to be nearby in the next couple of days?

> Kara! Hey, it's so nice to hear from you. Sure, I'd love to catch up, but nearby where were you thinking?

> Brisbane. I need to escape this weather. I booked a holiday and bought tickets to the event at the Convention Centre. I accidentally found your name amongst the 'What's On' listings, so I thought I'd better find out if you were actually an attraction too, lol.

> Are you kidding? I would love to catch up. Call me when you arrive.

> Great. I'll message you when I land. For sure. See you soon.

Kara travelled to Brisbane. It was beautiful. As soon as she alighted the plane, collected her bag, and walked outside, she looked up and there was nothing but a pristine blue sky, warmth of a bright sunny day, and such a sense of relief to leave the grey and dank feeling of South Australia's miserable winter behind her. She was also feeling good about the chance to see her friend again.

Kara realised the minute she heard his voice that she had missed him even more than she wanted to admit.

She had booked a hotel in the Valley as she wanted to visit the home décor and designer boutiques on James Street that she'd heard about. This spot also looked to be within an easy walking distance to the city centre. She had spent too much time sitting around for work and at home lately, hiding from the cold.

After checking in and unpacking in her room, she sent Greg a text.

> Hi there, I've arrived. God, this sunshine is glorious. Let me know if and when you feel like a coffee break. Cheers, Kara

It was only minutes before he responded to her message.

They met for coffee at a little café near her hotel. Greg shared all about his holiday with Tess, and Kara shared about her work and life in the previous months, with neither holding back much about all their experiences.

Kara felt twinges of jealously about Tess being able to enjoy Greg all to herself and then their plans for a wedding in the early stages of next year. Equally, Greg felt a tinge of jealousy at hearing about the younger Jake taking his place in Kara's life in recent months. The coffee catch-up turned into a long lunch enjoyed at a little alfresco Italian restaurant with their sense of fun and pleasure in spending time together having so easily rekindled.

'You'd better get back to work, Greg!' Kara said, noting it was now close to 3.00 p.m. 'I'm still around for a few days yet, so if you feel the need to escape, call me. Besides, I'll probably see you when I get to the exhibition tomorrow.'

'Oh, hell, I forgot, I organised a ticket for you to get into the exhibition and join me for the sponsors' lunch. No obligation, but it might be fun.'

'Fantastic, thanks Greg. You really didn't need to do that. That would be lovely.' She stood up and signalled for the waitress to bring the bill. 'Before you say anything, Mr Sheppard, this is my shout this time. I'm the one who's taken you away from work today, and it really has been so great to see you.'

Greg grinned. 'Far be it from me to argue with you, Ms Gilbert. I already know you are a force to reckon with!' Once she'd paid, he stood up and gave her a hug goodbye, kissing her lightly on the cheek and taking in her smell, a fragrance that immediately had his mind flooding with memories. 'Thanks, sexy,' he said as he turned and walked away.

Kara smiled. She loved it when he called her that. She headed off to walk the city and take advantage of having time to just wander, shop, and reflect on her lovely time spent with Greg again. But her thoughts became a little more uneasy as the afternoon wore on. She knew that the end of the year would come in a flash, meaning their wedding was not that far away.

To have had contact with Greg again and spend time with him, despite being only for a coffee and lunch, was so wrong. This was just tempting fate for both. She couldn't believe the lie about 'ex-lovers being able to meet casually' that she had been telling herself in the vain attempt to justify this. By the time she returned to the hotel, she decided she couldn't keep perpetuating casual contact with Greg, even though this time, it had been genuinely unintentional. As she was about to send a message to say maybe she shouldn't go tomorrow, she received his message.

> Kara, I would love to have dinner with you tonight if you are free. We had such a great day, and truth be told, I may have missed you a little.

Kara hesitated, as butterflies ravaged her stomach. She had been so sure she could say 'No more,' yet with only one message, he had drawn her to him. She could taste that drug that was Greg Sheppard. She dialled his number.

Greg answered within the first two rings, saying, 'Hello, so did you get my message?'

'How can I resist an invitation like that? I'd love to join you. What time did you have in mind?'

'Well, I'm close by and ready to go anytime now. I'll come over to meet you if you like, as the restaurant I have in mind is just near your hotel in the Valley.'

'Sounds good, but hey, do you mind giving me time for a cool-down and a shower? I've just walked back from the city.'

'Sure. Want to meet me in the bar?' said Greg casually.

'Okay, sure. I'll try not to take too long.'

'Okay but don't make me have to come up and get you.'

Kara was tingling at the thought, her legs almost failing her. A rush of heat radiated up through her body almost taking her breath away, she could hardly hold the phone. She had just received a massive dose of that drug and her heart pounded. She had to swallow before she could speak. The pause was drawn out but she finally said softly, 'If you decide to come and get me, my room is 502. I'll tell reception.' That was all she could say, her heart was about to explode, and her body was already reacting to what could be.

'Okay, thanks. 'See you soon,' he said.

Chapter 26

$\mathcal{K}$ara was still shaking uncontrollably when she dialled reception and arranged for a key to be ready for him, and then poured herself a wine. She fell into the couch and put her head in her hands. 'What are you doing?' she said through her shaking fingers. She was now totally overwhelmed with lust and desire and now with the possibility that she could have the best lover she had every known make love to her again had taken her beyond any sense of reason.

She grabbed the new top she bought in the city and set up the ironing board, realising that she'd better get organised and try to be ready before he arrived. She quickly ironed her jeans and top and was about to race into the shower when she stopped for a moment.

She walked out onto the balcony with her glass of wine and just stood there, looking out across the city. She took in a deep breath. She had only had one sip but she was drunk, intoxicated by the drug she knew she would never be clean of. She looked at her watch, she was not going to be ready in time, and she didn't want to be. A twinge of hurt pinged her heart at the thought of his lovely fiancée Tess.

Kara was caught somewhere between guilt and the first genuine sense of belonging in her life. She'd always considered herself a nice, caring, and responsible person. Now here she was doing something that could cause others' pain. She took a large sip of her wine, let out a sigh, then turned and walked towards the bathroom.

She turned up the music, undressed as if for him, and headed for the shower.

Greg arrived at the hotel on time. He sat at the bar sipping his beer contemplating the consequences of this relatively innocent catchup. By the time he was halfway through his beer he had remembered the many times he had made love to this beautiful woman. It wasn't long before he finished the second beer that the thoughts of her naked up in her room had consumed him. He went to the reception, collected the key, and headed up to Kara's room. As he entered the suite, he heard the music. He saw the bottle of Shiraz on the dining table with a glass next to it. As he walked over to pour himself a drink, he called out, 'I'm here,' but Kara didn't hear him.

As he headed towards the balcony to sit and wait, he glanced in the full-length robe mirrors and noticed that the bathroom door was wide open. He turned and walked to stand near the door to again attempt to let Kara know he was there.

As he approached the door, he couldn't help but see her in the shower, her back to him, obviously lost in singing and moving to the sound of the music as she washed her hair. Enjoying the sight of her naked body swaying and rolling to the beat of the music, he realised then that she had no intention of being at the bar to meet him. He stood there, sipping on the wine, watching. His mouth was dry, a thirst the wine wouldn't quench. He recalled the many times he'd pleasured that body inside and out. His heart was now racing and his groin reacting to the delicious sight.

My God, I shouldn't be doing this. He turned and looked away but without moving looked back at her again. Kara turned slowly towards him, her hand slowly running the bar of soap across her breasts. With his eyes not leaving hers he placed his glass on the vanity and despite the guilt he felt, he couldn't fight back what he desperately wanted to do. His heart was pounding as he removed his clothes and stepped into the shower behind her.

'I loved seeing the water run down your body,' he whispered in her ear. He took the soap from her hand and rolled it firmly over her breasts, stopping only for a moment to gently let her nipples flick between each finger. As the intensity of his movements over her flesh rose, so did he.

Now fully hard, he pressed against her. He ran the soap between her legs and her head fell back onto his shoulder.

Kara could feel every nerve in her body twitching. The desperate desire for him to be inside her once again was uncontrollable as he slowly traced around the edges of her labia. It was electrifying. Unable to hold it in any longer, she let a moan escape as she luxuriated in the warmth of his body so close and hard.

Greg's needs now matched hers but he waited and whispering in her ear, 'God, I want you so badly but are you sure you want this?' he already knew the answer but he wanted to hear her say it, thinking that somehow it made it right.

Kara breathed in hard. She could barely find her voice, all the while bending her torso even farther forward tempting him to take her, 'Oh, please, yes.'

Greg turned her around to face him. He lifted her and she instinctively wrapped her legs around him. He lowered her onto him. She took him all, as her head fell back and her mouth open wide as she rode him. The scream of her orgasm filled the apartment and his mind. As the final wave of ecstasy left her, he lifted her from him and stepped from the shower. He reached for a towel and took her hand as she turned off the water. He kissed her as he dried her, the water that still ran down her face made it all the more delicious. He led her to the bed and set her gently down. He lay next to her and ran his fingers along her chest. 'Is this how it's going to be every time we run into each other?' he asked. Her head was back and her eyes closed.

She turned to him. 'Would you like it to be?'

'Yes, of course I would, But… Jeezuz I'm getting married.' He paused and softened. 'You know I love you and always will. You give me something no one else can, you know I can't resist you.'

'Well don't,' she said as she climbed on top of him. She rubbed her swollen sex along him as he had softened slightly. It was no time till he was again ready for her. Without any hands or effort, she had him inside her. As she rocked back and forth, she whispered, 'Tell me what it would be like if we had found another couple to join us.'

'Damn you,' he said with a smile, as Kara still rocked slowly above him. He told her to close her eyes as his fingers slowly slid down her body.

'Okay, so once we have met and felt happy with the other couple, we would invite them to our bedroom. I would offer for him to undress you and we would watch. Then I would do the same to her. She would then undress me, and you do the same to him. You may feel the need to touch him as you remove his pants. I would then take your hand and guide you to sit above me. They would watch me fill you as you positioned yourself on me. As you rock above me, as you are now, he would lay his naked woman down and with her legs spread, kneeling between them. You would see him hard and her wet pussy aching for him to fill her. You watch as his knob disappears inside her and you see her face reflect the welcome to his initial thrust. He runs his hand down your back as you continue to ride me and then he touches your breasts giving your nipples a pinch. You return the touch and run your hand over his back and bum cheeks feeling them clench and loosen with each thrust.'

Greg then asked Kara to lay on her side and he entered her again from behind.

'You can see them clearly now, your private live porn show. He takes your hand and slides it between their bodies, you feel his hard shaft sliding in and out of her wet pussy, your finger finds her clit and you can't help but stroke it. You can feel her push against your fingers and you know you are going to make her come. Her hand finds your arm and she starts to squeeze it as her climax builds. You can feel how wet she has become and can see he is pounding her hard and also about to explode. Her first groan sends him off as he pounds the last few thrusts into her. She also comes and you feed her fire with your fingers.'

Greg was pumping Kara hard now as the story also had him completely aroused. Kara's orgasm exploded as did he, from behind he had her deep and felt the clenching pulse through his full length as she milked him of every drop.

As their breathing settled, he lay cuddling her, his softened erection still inside her. He felt the first sign that she was crying. She rolled over to face him. 'I am so sorry, Greg. Really, I am. I'm such a bad person, and I've tried so hard not to be.'

Her eyes again welled with tears. 'I feel so guilty. It's so wrong of me to keep wanting you and putting you in a position that risks your relationship with Tess. Greg you are a drug that I am helplessly addicted to. I want you and the naughtiness we fantasize about. The threesomes, foursomes and orgies, I want them all, but I want them with you, only you. You're the only person who understands me and whom I trust. But you're getting married soon, for God's sake!'

Greg raised a finger to her lips. 'Shh now.' As he wiped away the tears from her cheeks, he looked at her and said, 'Kara, you are not alone in those feelings. I've struggled constantly with this since we first met. You were the one who told me that people can and often need to love more than one person, and we can't help where our hearts and feelings land sometimes, no matter how hard we try. I feel guilty of course. I love you and I love Tess. I want what you want, to enjoy swinging with you and others. I want you to be happy, and yet I also can't deny that I feel hurt and jealous when you have someone else in your life. So, for now, let's help each other deal with our unique situation, and maybe let's just acknowledge that we have a groovy kind of love and naughty, kinky desires and accept it. I really don't know what else to say or do.'

Kara smiled meekly. 'Okay. There is no denying it. We are naughty in so many ways. Maybe that's the thing? Maybe we shouldn't try to solve this right now or get too serious about it this minute and just accept where we are. Just here. I've tried so hard to walk away, and I just can't. I don't know what we should or shouldn't do anymore.'

Greg's furrowed brow dissolved. He smiled and then suddenly broke into a laugh. 'Well, we probably should get ourselves dressed to enjoy some dinner!'

Kara laughed too and headed back to the bathroom to finish getting ready.

That night over dinner, they both steered away from talking any more about the entanglement of their unique relationship or feelings about each other, choosing instead to share in a light-hearted and fun evening. As Greg topped up her glass, Kara decided it was time to tell him more about her time spent with Jake. She asked, 'Do you want to know the real reason Jake and I didn't work out?'

'Only if you want to tell me,' he replied.

'To be honest, things were good and hotting up. I started to gently suggest the fantasies about watching each other with others when sexting while he was working away. One night we had a phone sex date. I told him the story about having sex and playing with a couple on the beach. You remember, it was a story you told me once.'

Greg nodded with a smile 'I know it well.'

'Well, he got so turned on, and that was some of the best phone sex we'd ever had together. That night he said how much he loved it and that it felt so good, and I thought he might want more of it.

'I thought it was the right time to ask him if he would enjoy being with another couple. He thought I was joking at first, but then I think he realised I was genuine, and I sensed a bit of confusion in him. I didn't elaborate more than that initially. He didn't say, but I wondered if I'd shocked him, but I wasn't sure. Over the next couple of weeks, he kept raising the subject and asking me questions like, "How did you think up that story?", "Would you seriously be willing to have group sex?" and "How much and what would you be willing to do?"

'Then he got to asking me if I had ever done it before, with whom, and how I came to the idea of playing around with others. Then he asked if he was satisfying me. He couldn't let it go. At first, I stupidly thought he was asking me because he was warming up to the idea, so I just opened up and told him I had experienced a threesome before, that I enjoyed kinky sex, and about how exciting it can be and how it adds to the bond between a couple. I told him that I wouldn't want him to share in this if he didn't want to, but if he did, it might be a bit of fun and we could check some sites for a casual encounter with another lady or a couple.

'I'd read him so wrong. He was horrified. That was it for him. The next day he sent me a message to apologise and say he didn't think I was *that* kind of woman and thanks, but no thanks, to both swinging and me.'

Greg listened intently to Kara's account of the breakup, and his thoughts immediately went to the conversations he'd had with Tess about the same thing, and all the while noting how she'd been so much more considerate of his desire to play out his fantasies. 'Kara, I'm sorry to hear that, but that lifestyle is not for everybody.'

'There is nothing you need to be sorry about,' she responded. 'It was his attitudes and values that led to this. I was so upset at the time—really not as much about breaking up, but more that he'd so instantly labelled me as some sexual deviant, judging and dismissing all of me because of having done something, in fact, that turned him on. It felt like it's okay for a guy to do this, but never okay for a woman to feel the same.'

'I think you're probably right. You know, I raised the idea with Tess.' Greg explained to Kara about what had happened during their trip to the Cook Islands, how he had seen Tess display so many signs that signalled she was keen for kinky play, but she'd been honest enough to say she could understand his desires but couldn't bring herself to share herself, or him in reality.

'It shows she is understanding and honest and didn't judge you. That is really something.'

Greg nodded. 'Well, sexy, looks like it's just you and me who are the kinky ones. I don't think you're a bad woman at all; naughty for sure, but not bad!'

Chapter 27

$\mathcal{G}$reg said nothing for a few moments. Then he said in a most pensive tone, 'Hey, seriously, Kara, I know you told me about all the singles and strange ones who responded to our ads, but did you get any responses that sounded promising?'

'Actually, there were a few couples that sounded okay. Most weren't from South Australia, though.'

'Any from Brisbane or around here?'

Kara grabbed her phone, and after scrolling through some text messages, she said, 'Yeah, there is. I thought I'd kept it.'

She held out her phone for Greg to see. The message was from a couple named John and Anna who replied to their 'Same Room Sex' ad. They indicated they'd been involved in the swing scene for some years, were interested in same-room sex, mutual massage, no full swapping but willing to do only as little or as much as another couple wanted. They had sent pictures, contact details, and the address of their seaside Gold Coast home to host for an evening.

Immediately after he finished reading the message, Greg started dialling their number. 'Is this, okay?' he asked Kara quickly. 'Ready to see if they are still keen to meet?'

Kara just grinned and nodded. Of course, she thought. Let's do it. Greg spoke to John at length and then spoke to Anna briefly. The conversation sounded positive. Kara heard Greg say, 'Well, I'll speak with Kara and see if she's free Monday night and I'll call you back to confirm the details. That sounds great. Thanks.'

Greg told her the details of the call. 'They sounded genuine and were open and keen. They had explained that we should approach it like a night with friends. We go for a drink to simply get to know each other, and if we don't feel okay or it doesn't feel like fun, there's no obligation.'

Kara agreed it sounded great. As she wasn't leaving until Wednesday, this worked out well. Greg would be finished with the exhibition late Monday morning and wasn't scheduled to fly out until Tuesday lunchtime, so it could work. They had to get to the Gold Coast, but as it was only about an hour's drive, that wasn't too much of a problem. Kara suggested that they book a hotel close to where the host couple lived, just in case, so they could make an escape if needed. Greg agreed. No matter what eventuated, they would have fun, either with another couple or on their own. Greg called John back and arranged everything.

Both Greg and Kara were excited. They dared not say too much, but this was to be their first 'same room and whatever' experience with a couple. Greg had a car he'd hired to use during his stay in Brisbane that wasn't due back until Tuesday. He picked up Kara just after noon and drove to the hotel. They unpacked and grabbed a late lunch. As they planned to meet their new 'friends' at about 6.00 p.m., they thought it best to enjoy a large lunch. The time with their new 'friends' was planned for what would be at evening mealtime, and for sure, if things went as they imagined, they would have little time to eat. Well, no time to eat 'food' anyway! That morning before they left Brisbane, Kara bought cheeses, crackers, and fruit for a sharing plate as something for their hosts later that evening.

They enjoyed a lovely couple of casual hours. Sitting in an outside bistro, enjoying a casual chat about the success of the exhibition and other work ahead, they ate heartily. A perfect appetizer, to what would be the start of a whole new appetite for play. Mostly they talked about all the possibilities tonight might offer. It was thrilling, arousing and hot, imagining the things that could happen.

Greg and Kara exchanged ideas of what might turn them on and what they were not keen to do or see. They knew it was important that they both agreed on what each of them was okay with and what they weren't. Both were clear about not swapping partners for full sex. They agreed everyone had to stay in the same room, and if either felt uncomfortable, both would be leaving. They knew they would watch each other's backs the entire time.

Just after lunch, they drove around to strategically locate the actual home of their hosts for later that evening and check it out. It was located as per John's directions and looked pleasant as they had described. At least they knew where to go, and it all seemed legitimate. The anticipation and their talk of what might happen made them both become more and more excited and aroused as the time edged closer to 6.00 p.m.

When they pulled up to John and Anna's home, they had wine and the food platter on the back seat of the car. Rather than unpack everything, Greg wisely said, 'Let's meet them first and come and get the stuff from the car if it feels right. If it doesn't, we can at least head back to the hotel, enjoy the food and wine, and make our own fun.' Kara agreed.

John and his partner Anna met them at the door, greeting them warmly. 'Come on in. Welcome! I'm just heating the spa, it's here—' John pointed to the spa outside in the courtyard. '—if you feel like it. We thought you both might like it as an option. But, please, come on in.'

John, a surfie, was tall, slim, tanned, with blond hair, and had a broad smile. Anna had dark blonde hair and was a larger build than she had appeared in her picture, her large breasts were unrestrained. Her sparkling eyes told them she was keen for them to stay and play.

Greg and Kara looked at each other and nodded, as if to say 'Okay, let's do this and see where it goes.'

Kara said, 'We've brought some drinks and something to share to eat. We haven't really had dinner tonight, so we hope you don't mind?' She and Greg went to the car, took out the plate of food and a bottle of wine, and headed back inside.

'Well, here goes!' Greg said.

John grabbed some glasses and helped Greg pour a wine for Anna and Kara. They all sat in the lounge room, Kara on the lounge next to Anna, with Greg and John each taking the chairs. The usual introductory banter followed about their professions, their relationships, and how they entered the world of swing. After a time, Anna moved over to sit on the floor at John's feet. While her focus didn't stray from chatting or looking at Greg and Kara, she was ready to get the sexual vibe into active mode. Both Kara and Greg could see her open John's shorts, expose his penis and start to fondle him. He stiffened in front of them, while both he and Anna continued to casually chat away. It was a cue to start. Greg moved across to the lounge to sit next to Kara. As he watched Anna stimulate her man by hand, Greg stroked Kara's thighs, higher and higher under her shorts, and Kara could see his shorts starting to bulge. This was quite a turn on.

Anna turned to John and removed his shorts before rolling her tongue up and down his shaft, every few seconds enveloping her mouth over the whole of his long, thin rod, stopping to suck his tip and repeating the motion. Rolling, sucking, and licking.

Kara was so aroused by this, but a little nervous. They'd talked about this during sex, but it was such a contrast to anything she'd done before. Then came the moment of realisation that she was in this moment, experiencing a group sex encounter. She was no longer Kara. She was a wicked adulteress, a daring character in a film. This was her part. She had to play it right. She really was a horny, sexual woman. There were people around her who wanted to feel, taste, and enjoy her. A part of her wanted the same… yet the real woman wasn't that sure.

This is just play. It's sex. This isn't love but the real indulgent, hidden pleasure that you actually enjoy. Shut your eyes and just feel and go with whatever direction this takes. And she did…

Much to Greg's surprise, Kara stood up and walked over to Anna and asked, 'May I undress you?'

'Absolutely!' said Anna.

Kara moved up close to her, and as they stood in front of each other, Kara could feel both men watching intently. Kara unzipped her dress and slid it off her body, and without Anna wearing any underwear, this instantly exposed her large breasts and naked body.

'Would you like me to undress you too?' Anna offered.

'Sure,' whispered Kara.

As Anna undid Kara's shirt, she said, 'It's okay if you want to touch me.'

Kara reached out and ran her hands over Anna's shoulders before tracing down over her breasts and down each side of her body. After Anna had removed Kara's shirt and bra, she mirrored Kara's movements, feeling Kara's body and shape.

Kara turned to look at Greg and said cheekily, 'Hey, Anna, I think there's only one person who's not undressed. We need to do something about that, don't you think?'

Both women moved to where Greg was still sitting on the lounge. As Kara removed his shirt and kissed him, Anna stood close in front of him, leaned forward, and removed his shorts, releasing his erection.

Without warning, Anna took him in her hand, leading his knob into her mouth. John moved in close behind her, entering her from behind. Greg looked up at Kara, who was standing beside him with a look of surprise and checked for her reaction to see if this was okay.

Kara just smiled at him, mouthing, 'Go with it,' and moved to stand nearly behind John, running her nails down his back, massaging his butt cheeks, she could feel him clench as he thrust into Anna. Kara maintained eye contact with Greg the whole time.

Anna let out a loud moan as she came. John eased Anna back from between Greg's legs and turned to Kara, saying, 'I think it's your turn.'

Kara sat on the lounge next to Greg, and they kissed while Greg gripped her breasts. Then he whispered, 'You going, okay?'

'Yes,' she said. 'You?'

He nodded, and they both smiled.

At this moment, John knelt in front of Kara and said, 'I'd love to feel inside you. May I?' Kara glanced at Greg. He nodded as John started rubbing Kara's thighs and sliding his fingers inside her crotch. His fingers quickly found her, and feeling how wet she was, he slipped two fingers easily inside her, stroking the top wall of her vagina in a steady rhythm, attempting to stimulate her G-spot.

Anna had moved to position herself between Greg and Kara, taking turns kissing each of them deeply and forcefully. She kept one hand massaging Greg's shaft up and down and then back and forth across his balls. This was way more than the 'same room sex' experience they had originally thought would happen! Kara felt John's touch was not as sensitive or gentle as Greg's, and she noticed Anna was close to swallowing Greg with her passionate kissing, which she knew wasn't what he liked.

Kara signalled she needed to stop. 'Drink time,' she said with a smile. They all stopped for a break. Both Greg and Kara had a drink of water and then refilled their wineglasses, each taking a few sips. John and Anna had grabbed a drink, but now were back into it, John standing and thrusting into her from behind as she leaned over the back of a lounge chair. Anna groaned and gasped loudly, enjoying him as she convulsed in the sheer pleasure of being pounded hard.

When Kara and Greg moved to the lounge, Greg sat, and Kara straddled him. He slipped inside her. Their sex was intense and feverish as all four were watching each other, staring openly and revelling in the sound of flesh pounding and the moans and exultant cries that filled the room. Watching and being watched at the same time. It was an exhilarating experience, and Kara lost count of how many times she came while riding Greg and watching the other couple.

Throughout the rest of the evening, they continued in various combinations of stimulating each other—Anna and Kara, Greg and Anna, John and Kara, and their own partners. At one stage, Kara felt John attempt to enter her. Not willing to go that far, Kara gently moved away to signal that wasn't what was meant to happen, and John respectfully did not attempt any farther.

When John was ready to come, he moved Anna to lie on their massage table and mounted her. Witnessing the other couple lost in screwing each other hard and loud, Kara led Greg to the back of the lounge, saying, 'Do me hard.'

He bent her over the end of the lounge and screwed her hard from behind. They heard a groan escape from John, and he was soon done. Greg slid in and out of Kara, holding onto his rising orgasm. waiting for when he knew her body would quiver. Suddenly, Anna appeared on the lounge in front of Kara. She lay back on the cushions, her legs apart, allowing herself to be in hand and tongue's reach of Kara.

Kara glided her fingers over Anna's swollen lips and then slipped two of them inside her. She was so wet, still filled with John's pleasure. Enticed, Kara leaned forward and flicked her tongue over Anna's erect button. Greg's grip tightened around Kara's hips, and she knew what was about to happen. The anticipation of his orgasm, combined with the sensation of tantalising Anna, was enough for her body to lose control.

Kara shuddered uncontrollably beneath him. Greg loved this sight—Kara in front of him, touching and tasting another woman. He blew so hard inside her, filling her with his hot fluid. The groan which escaped him filled the room.

The four of them had spent close to three hours entertaining and pleasuring themselves and each other, taking soft swing to the edge. This was their first real couples experience, and it was memorable. Kara and Greg had remained connected the entire time, so the touch of another's warm flesh didn't evoke jealousy; it was accepted, the true meaning of compersion. While not every contact with the other couple was amazing by itself, and some bits were actually not that enjoyable, the unspoken thread of having realised their fantasies and thoughts of more future pleasurable possibilities resonated through every inch of Greg and Kara that night.

They had again felt the exhilaration that swinging gave them. Basically, it was just hot live porn and they both knew that they wanted more.

After dressing, saying their goodbyes and thank you to John and Anna, Greg and Kara walked to the car without saying a word. A few metres down the road, they both nearly simultaneously exclaimed, 'That was way more than same room!' and burst out laughing. They spent the night lying in each other's arms in bed, sipping cups of tea, and talking about every detail and their impressions and feelings about their most unexpected evening. Everything about these days together had been so unexpected, so easy and thoroughly enjoyable. Most of all, each of them knew that neither would say goodbye this time.

Greg awoke to the sensations and subconscious connection that was always present in a morning when awakening with a warm, beautiful woman next to him. But this morning was different. He was with Kara and not his fiancée. He looked at her, her dark curls filled her pillow, her naked body only covered by the thin sheet. The morning guilt was a painful stab, he just wanted to run and beg for a simple uncomplicated life, but he seriously doubted that it was possible now. Kara looked gorgeous as she lay sleeping, her beautiful, tanned body rising with each breath. He lay there watching her, as he tried to take in his situation. Their experience with the couple the night before had only consolidated their relationship. Kara slowly opened her eyes and a smile formed on her face. She could see he'd been awake for a while. She tried to analyse his feelings, knowing he would be struggling with his conscience. He could see her look of concern and he smiled to reassure her.

'Are you okay?' she asked with a genuine voice.

'Yes, sexy, it's just… you know… hard, I just wish it wasn't.'

She reached over and ran her fingers down his cheek.

'I'm sorry,' she said.

'Don't be, I love you and I know you love me, it's just…'

Kara sat up and kissed his lips so he didn't have to say any more. He pulled her to him and hugged her tighter than he ever had before. It was only seconds before they again were joined and the screams of pleasure filled the room.

The drive back to Brisbane was easy, the whole trip consumed with talk of the night before in detail. Greg's flight was today and Kara was to stay on another day and visit her friends. Kara dropped him at the airport and continued on in his hire car. The flight went quickly as his mind pictured on the new complication that was thrown at him. His experience in business taught him to never rush into big decisions, let the cards fall and see what hand you have to play with. He was also a great compartmentaliser and was sure he could put aside his renewed passion for Kara and the kinky world she presented, while his real world turned.

Now as he exited the airport in Adelaide, and headed home to where he now lived with his future bride, he was struggling. *How could I possibly hide this from Tess?* She will instantly sense that something was different, that he was distracted, as she was smart and astute and he was a bad liar. Just that thought alone ripped at his heart. Would he see her and breakdown in tears? No probably not but it was not going to be easy.

By the time the taxi arrived at their apartment he decided. He and Tess needed to talk.

He was greeted with a hug by his gorgeous fiancée as he walked in the door. She was busy still with wedding plans and her other little life duties that gave Greg the time he needed to put the past few days behind him and calm his thoughts.

Kara arrived back in Adelaide the next morning and spent the afternoon with her Aunt Sarah at her unit before heading back to Clare that same evening. Her thoughts tumbled randomly, filled with the replay of the weekend she spent with Greg. Him confessing how his heart was torn between her and Tess. Their uncontrollable, passionate, and exultant sex and their connection —held with the delicacy of gossamer, yet the strength and protection of arms that held so strongly as they indulged in the pleasures of swing. Kara's thoughts and feelings were a pendulum that struggled to find the space that told her this was not a good thing to continue to do, but she also doubted that neither of them could say 'never again' this time.

Chapter 28

ess had reflected hard on the tense couple of weeks leading
to Greg's departure and had regretted her outburst. She
wanted to express her genuine remorse for getting carried away
with the wedding, which really didn't need to be an extravaganza.
He was right. This was about the two of them and not anyone else.
While Greg said nothing more about the tense discussion before
he left, other than assuring her that whatever she wanted would
still be okay, she had felt the slight edginess and distance in their
phone conversations while he was away.

So, before he returned from Brisbane, she turned her thoughts
to saying sorry. She wanted to remind him of just how much she
treasured him in her life, more than her self-indulgent wedding
plans. His birthday was coming, and she wanted to really redeem
herself. She had churned through many ideas but hadn't yet found
something that would show the depth of what she felt for him.
She wanted to find something that showed how much she would
do for him in response to his most loving gestures and expressions
of love and care that she had carelessly disregarded in the fever
she'd got caught up in before he left.

Then she found it. The perfect gift.

Tess had been using Greg's laptop to complete the design of
their invitations and to revise the date back to April 30th of next
year. She had done a lot more research and found a delightful
winery, The Lane Vineyard in the Adelaide Hills, that boasted
award-winning wines, amazing views, and a restaurant that could

cater for about sixty people. Best of all, they were willing to host their special day on the day requested. It all felt right.

As she closed the emails to the print company, she spied the desktop icon link to the porn site Greg had shown her. She tentatively clicked on it, opening to a video of a threesome. There were two women and a man. They were massaging each other and kissing, and the women were taking turns stroking and sucking the guy. The next thing she noticed was that the site had been visited only recently.

Tess wasn't paying attention to the video as much as she was now thinking back to their fantasy stories about sex with others and the conversation with Greg about whether she would entertain doing their blindfold scene for real.

She suspected he had a genuine desire for this.

Tess spent the rest of the day thinking hard. She had been a little surprised and upset at first. Greg was hooked on adventurous sex. She loved the stories, the fantasy, and how much the idea of unconventional and illicit sexual encounters turned her on as foreplay and during sex, but she had never considered this as something she could actually do. She knew how much Greg loved her, so it wasn't her insecurity that worried her. It was that she was so completely satisfied with him, she needed nothing more. But she knew he got off on this, and since he still looked at these videos, they were a regular part of his life.

Tess thought hard. She loved the sexy thoughts, but this was something she just wasn't programmed to entertain in reality.

For the next few days, she thought hard about what situation she could create that might satisfy him and not make herself feel compromised. At last, she had it. Greg had told her that he sometimes enjoyed massages when he was working away that offered 'happy endings.' This had never bothered Tess; in fact, she was fine about it, especially as Greg had shared this openly with her.

It was now the end of August, and Greg's birthday was in two weeks' time. She jumped on the internet and set about her plans. Time to escape winter and celebrate in the sun. She booked flights to Phuket, Thailand, and some nice accommodation. She searched for a couple of other sites, too, and then sent some emails to confirm a booking for them at a Thai massage establishment.

One evening, about a week before his birthday, just as they were finishing dinner, she quietly slid a card across the table towards him. 'This is the first part of your birthday gift. You may need a little notice to make this happen.'

Greg was surprised. Tess was rather carefree and not that much into planning. That was his forte. He opened the card to find the e-ticket for a short escape to Phuket. But it was the wording in the card that got him most excited.

My darling Greg,

You have given me so much. It's my turn. Come away with me. I want to give you something for your birthday that hopefully fulfils some of your heartfelt desires.

Something that can't be wrapped. Only shared.

With all my love, Tess. x

Greg was completely overwhelmed. Tess had totally surprised him. Phuket was just the place for fun. He knew no matter what, she had chosen a place he loved. The next day, he alerted his team that he was taking a few days away.

All week he couldn't stop thinking about what the 'something that couldn't be wrapped only shared' part of his gift might be, and the options excited him. He couldn't wait. He hoped that Tess's message in his card was a promise of something sexy that involved more than just the two of them. That would be amazing. He tried not to think too hard, but it was difficult to think of anything else.

On Friday morning, they boarded the direct Qantas flight to Phuket Island. Once seated on the plane, Greg took her hand and wrapped his fingers around hers. As he squeezed them tight, he kissed her gently on the cheek and said, 'Tess, this is such a lovely birthday already. Thank you so much. I can't wait to find out what else you have planned.'

Tess just smiled. She knew he wanted to ask, but she wouldn't tell him anything. They held hands for most of the flight.

The plane arrived, and with only carry-on luggage, they were quickly through customs and in the cab for the forty-minute ride to the hotel. Tess had booked a suite for them at an exquisite five-star hotel on Patong Beach and had every luxurious amenity possible—exclusive pools with swim-up bars, in-house masseurs, restaurants, and water sport counters.

Greg, having experienced Phuket before, knew that there were many beautiful spots to see. The place appealed to his love of the outdoors, so he was quick to suggest to Tess that they grab a scooter and cruise around together for the day to let her see the real Phuket. After unpacking and strolling around the hotel to see its features, Greg grabbed his passport, a few bucks, and Tess by the hand and headed to rent a scooter.

After paying the seven dollar hire fee, they mounted their bike and headed for the hills. They went south out of Patong up a long, climbing hill away from the sunny beach, soon passing a mansion on the clifftop, a place Greg remembered from having attended a wedding there a few years earlier. The clifftop road had breathtaking views. He wanted Tess to see and feel what he loved—the natural beauty of the country combined with the carefree feel of wind through their hair as they climbed the hills.

A few times, Tess needed to tap him on his shoulder to remind him he was on a scooter in Thailand and not a MotoGP racetrack. The winding road through the hills was a little tempting for Greg to get lost in the ride's thrill and being free to explore. Greg had a plan for their tour. He took her past the big Buddha and down the other side of the mountain to another beachside town. Chalong Pier looked amazing, and after a long walk along the pier, they found a café, took a seat and ordered another coffee. They sat quietly, sipping their coffee and taking in the sights and sounds of the fishing boats, the people, and their whole surroundings. It was glorious.

Tess caught him noticing and pointing out the little massage shops that were scattered all over the place. 'Now, Greg, you know these aren't places you need to visit when I am with you.'

'I know that, babe, Sorry.'

On Saturday morning, his birthday, they took the scooter out again and continued their casual and random exploration of this beautiful island. They stopped to enjoy lunch at a little roadside pop-up cafe on a clifftop overlooking the Andaman Sea. The food was cooked on a little wok by the one-woman establishment and was just delicious. They both enjoyed a local beer and the easy pleasure of spending unhurried time together as they sat on the two metre strip that separated the road and the massive cliff face. Greg had slid into a relaxed birthday mood, buoyed even more by Tess, who was looking so happy and sexy.

'Hey, shall we head back to Patong now?' She was definite in her tone, prompting Greg to stand up.

'Sure, I'll fix the bill.'

He didn't see Tess checking her watch and smothering a little smile.

They jumped back on the scooter and headed back to Patong Beach. As they cruised down the main street, Tess asked, 'Hey, babe, do you mind parking somewhere here so we can walk? There're a few shops around here I'd like to look at, if that's okay?'

'Sure.' Greg slipped the bike into the first park.

Tess took his hand, and they walked down the street. Greg was fascinated by the many massage shops with girls spilling onto the street trying to lure them in. Then, to his surprise, Tess stopped outside one of the classier places and said, 'Happy birthday, babe.'

'Hello, Mrs Tess, we ready, as we said this morning,' said a cute local girl who greeted them both at the door. 'This way, please.'

Shocked, Greg stared at Tess and said, 'Now I know why it took you so long to get coffee this morning! You little…'

Tess just grinned. 'Shh now. Come on, let's get inside.'

The cute girl showed them to a room upstairs reserved for clients who were looking for more than just a foot massage. There were two massage tables arranged next to each other side by side in the centre of the room. The candles arranged around the room filled the air with the scent of gardenias. Greg noticed an array of oils on a small table. Clearly, they were both to be massaged at the same time. 'When did you organise this, you sneaky thing?'

'Oh, a little while ago. I had to find something special for your birthday.' A cheeky grin appeared on her face.

The cute little woman approached them. 'Please, remove clothes, we come back.'

Just watching Tess completely undress in a random room and lay beside him was enough to get Greg slightly aroused. Tess lay face down, turning her head to look at him, and she just smiled. He was undressed and leaning against the side of the table about to climb onto it when the two Thai women entered. They were both wearing light silk robes, which they removed as they approached—one moving to stand next to Tess, the other walking up to Greg.

'On table please, mister,' she said as she brushed her hand across Greg's thigh and lightly touched his slight arousal. Smiling wickedly, she sauntered off to get her oils ready.

Greg climbed onto the table, face down, and turned to look at Tess. The first woman was already anointing Tess's body with oil and gliding her hands across her body in a deep, slow, sensual massage. The sight heightened Greg's pleasure before he'd even been touched. This was amazing. He was watching another woman massaging his naked fiancée, her hands moving up and down Tess's back, across the smooth, rounded cheeks of her bottom, and over the full length of her legs. Hands and fingers gently squeezed her flesh and rolled in circular motions up and down her body.

Tess's eyes were closed, and her body melted with every stroke.

Greg lost himself in the moment, loving the fact that she had done this for him and that she was lying naked next to him with a naked girl running her hands all over her. He was barely aware of the hands that were adeptly massaging him. The woman's touch was skilful, light, yet deep and slow. Then he realised she was gradually focusing her hands closer and closer on the inside of his thighs before running her fingers the full length between his bum cheeks and stimulating every zone that would make him even more aroused. Eventually, it was time for them to roll over, Tess with a cheeky smile and Greg with an erection. The combination of this naked woman's touch and the whole sensation of the experience was working. Tess had been watching him the whole time as the woman stroked, caressed, and rubbed his body.

Seeing he was so aroused, she smiled. 'Are you enjoying this?'

The woman grabbed hold of his shaft and started stroking him with her oil-slicked hands. Greg reached for Tess's hand as the girl had her way with him, building her strokes to a faster rhythm from the base to just below his tip, sliding with a delicate grip up and down, over and over again.

Tess's woman was oiling and massaging her breasts, which she was loving. Her nipples were full and erect, and her breathing became faster. Greg watched as the woman bent down and whispered in her ear, 'Would you like down there?'

'No, that's okay. Thank you.'

On hearing Tess's response, Greg realised that she wanted to give him the pleasures of an experience shared with another, but she knew her limits.

So, she too, could truly enjoy the experience, he reached his arm at full length to touch between Tess's legs and could feel how wet she was. As he gently moved his fingers, he nodded to the woman, who quietly stepped away from Tess, slightly embarrassed. The lady's massage was finished as much as she could.

She noticed him reach out to feel Tess and did not say a word, just drizzled more oil and firmed her hold on him as she continued to quicken her strokes. Knowing and feeling Tess's arousal through his fingertips was all it took. Greg erupted all over the woman's hand, his sperm spraying out in at least four spurts over her fingers as an enormous groan escaped him. This was the only time his eyes had closed.

By the time he opened them, Tess was sitting beside him on the edge of the table. She leaned forward and kissed him softly on the lips. 'Happy birthday, darling,' she whispered with a smile.

'That was amazing. Thank you, babe.' He turned to look at the woman who was now cleaning him up with a warm moist towel and smiled. 'Thank you too. You were wonderful.'

'Thank you, sir.' With a half bow, she backed away to exit the room. As she reached the door, she paused and said, 'You a very lucky man. No Mrs has asked us to do this before.'

Greg and Tess smiled and hugged each other before proceeding to find their clothes.

They spent their evening eating dinner in their room and preparing for their trip home the next morning. They talked nonstop, recounting their afternoon's experience. Greg had thanked Tess over and over for the most thoughtful present. He also realised that this had pushed Tess to the limit of what she would reasonably entertain about fulfilling his fantasies. That was beautiful, that she had given him a gift and still held true to herself. That took a special courage and generosity. When he made love to Tess that night, it was slow, and tender.

When they arrived home, Tess felt so pleased that Greg had been so enamoured with her surprise birthday gift and their electricity had sparked once again, she now approached the wedding plans with gusto. There was plenty of time, and they were both open and relaxed about the wedding day that was shaping up to be just right for them both. They had talked lots on the flight home about what they both might enjoy, and now they were so at ease with what they had planned. For Greg, it was near complete. But he knew there was little time left, and he needed to tell Tess about Kara.

Chapter 29

*D*espite such an intimate connection and their couple's experience in Brisbane, Kara and Greg had little contact since their return home. They had spoken briefly when Greg called to say he was caught up with work and a few things. Kara didn't press the subject of home, letting that rest. She could sense the turmoil that emerged when he spoke with her after spending time with Tess.

She had firmly resolved that anything about his home life would need to remain his space for him to share or not as he felt the need or desire. Kara would always listen and share ideas, but nothing that would do more than encourage or challenge him in the moment. She would only discuss whatever he might need to best help him resolve matters with his work or his life away from home. Anything about his life with Tess, was not her place.

He was her lover and swing partner whenever it worked and felt right for them both. That was how they had left things and where Kara had felt comfortable enough to rest. She was happy to be the other woman if that meant she could be with the man she loved and adored. She knew there was still much to be enjoyed, so many kinky pleasures to be had.

Greg had become her closest friend—honest and open, each holding the other's innermost intimate secrets. This was what Kara cherished most. Then, Greg messaged her to say that they needed to talk as soon as she could. Kara's heart sank. She messaged him straight back asking him to call her. Her phone rang.

'Hello Greg.'

'Kara, you know I love you, don't you?'

'Yes, of course.' She could hardly speak. She knew his words were true, but his serious tone sent an uneasy tremor down her spine.

'Kara, I'm going to tell Tess about us, I thought I could have both of you... but I can't, it's killing me.'

Kara was silent.

'I'm so sorry, I should have never stepped into your shower,' Greg said.

'What are you going to tell her?' Kara asked, needing to sit down.

She heard the intake of breath before he answered—and she already knew. It was happening again. This time, her heart may not survive.

'I really don't know, I don't want to lose her, but...'

Kara couldn't bear to hear the words again. 'I'd better go, I hope it goes okay for you Greg.' And with that—Kara was gone, just like that.

Tess couldn't be happier. Everything was falling into place. She had things sorted with the date now firmly set for April 30th, the venue booked, a much smaller guest list, and most all other plans were confirmed. Both of them were quietly pleased at how things were taking shape, and the dramas were far behind them. The only thing Tess had been struggling with was the dress. What to wear? She wanted it to be beautiful and a statement piece, without looking like a traditional bride. Elegant, sexy, and breathtaking were the words that filled her mind every time she contemplated it, but she had not settled on any design or set style. She would know when she found it.

Eventually she decided she had to start a search. She had combed the internet and so many local bridal wear stores in Adelaide. She had decided she wanted a local designer and the dress should come from an Adelaide boutique, as both she and Greg were also local professionals and should support their home state businesses. As the shop of choice was in Hyde Park, she took a cab rather than hassle with the traffic through the city and parking.

Her mother, Monique, was meeting her there, as she needed some objective advice and her mum always had such an eye for style. Tess just knew that if she and her mum both agreed on a dress, it would be perfect.

Tess arrived in the cab and noting a coffee shop next to the boutique, she messaged her mother to meet her there. As they sipped their coffees, Tess explained about the dress she was looking for, and Monique saved the day with her impeccable insight, informing her, 'Darling, you are describing just the style of dress that I had. It sounds like you need a modern version of a classic nineteen-thirties-to-forties gown. So, let's find it, shall we?'

Tess could only laugh. She loved how her mum could read her. So, with Mon's guidance, she described the style to the attendants and then the designer, whom she insisted on speaking with. They brought out four gowns for Tess to try. They quickly started explaining that they would adapt anything to exactly what she wanted but would use these to find the closest style that suited her.

When she slipped on the third gown, she and Mon instantly knew she need not look any further. The minute she stepped out of the change room, Mon and everyone agreed she looked stunning. The dress was exquisitely beautiful, but it was Tess all over. It was a long line, fitted Charmeuse gown with a subtle fishtail hemline. The back fell from just above the knees and led into a long line half train. Backless, it accentuated her waist and smooth skin. The front was a round neck with a sheer Swiss organza lace bodice that fitted firmly to the top of her breasts.

It was sophisticated, elegant, and sexy. Tess was delighted. They chatted with the designer and manager for some time, confirming the exact fabric shade, complimentary shoe styles, and how to best wear her hair.

As they left the boutique, both Tess and Mon were thrilled about how finding the dress had been so much easier than they had both first imagined. Tess stopped and asked, 'Do you have time for lunch, Mum?'

'Well, we can either have lunch or I can run you home, darling. I had mentioned to Elaine that I would meet her at 2.00 p.m. for a coffee.'

Elaine was Mon's lifetime friend, and Tess knew that her mum would be dying to tell her all about their morning and the discovery of the dress.

'Well, lunch it is,' said Tess, 'but mind you, please don't tell Elaine every detail. It would be nice to surprise everyone!' She laughed. 'You can go straight from lunch, Mum, as its nearly one o'clock now, and I'll grab a cab back home.'

They walked a little further down Unley Road and stopped in one of the small cafes where they enjoyed a light lunch and Tess brought her mum up to speed on all the current wedding plans. Tess still had the draft invitation in her handbag and was so pleased to show her, along with pictures of the elegant little winery venue she and Greg had chosen. They enjoyed a special hour together, and as it neared 2.00 p.m., Mon exclaimed, 'Goodness, I'd better get moving, darling.'

As she stood and hugged Tess goodbye, Tess assured her, 'I'll sort the bill, Mum. You get going. Oh, and thank you so much. I think we've chosen well.'

Mon smiled and waved as she headed for the door of the cafe. Tess was so happy. She paid the bill and then booked a cab via the app on her phone.

Waiting outside, she was about to call Greg to tell him the dress was all sorted, when she thought she heard someone call her name.

She glanced around with some uncertainty. The voice was louder this time, followed by a gentle hand on the arm.

'Tess, it's nice to see you,' the much younger bronzed man said.

'Luke, what are you doing here?' She asked, looking around her.

'You look stunning,' he said, stepping toward her.

She took a half step back, but it didn't match his full step that put her in his arms. He kissed her cheek stalling long enough to take in her alluring fragrance.

'I miss you, Tess,' He said softly.

'Luke, stop it. Like I told you last week, it's over between us, I'm getting married, you know that.'

'I know, but that doesn't stop me wanting you, let me buy you a drink, a last one for old time's—or last week's sake.'

'I can't, I have a cab arriving any second.'

'Just one drink and you will never see me again?' he said just as a taxi pulled up in front of them.

Luke could see her indecisiveness and opened the taxi's front door and apologised to the driver that she had changed her mind. He held out his hand guiding her to the hotel next door.

'The usual?' he asked as they walked into the empty lounge area.

'Yes, thank you Luke.' Tess took a seat in a cubical in the corner of the room. She let her eyes roam toward him, taking a quick surveillance of the well-groomed, olive-skinned Adonis standing at the bar. The slick, tailored cut of his hair, like his form-fitting deep blue suit, was as smooth as he was.

Luke soon returned with a glass of her favourite Riesling and slid into the booth next to her.

'Thank you, you're looking immaculate as usual.'

She took the glass and he tapped his to hers, the clink of the glasses the only sound in the room. His brown eyes fixed on hers. His gaze was casual, yet intense.

She had to look away as she remembered the many times those eyes watched her as he made love to her. Her body tingled at the memory. She took a breath and said, 'I can't do this Luke.'

'Why, do you still have feelings for me?'

She looked up at him, 'You know I do.'

He placed his right hand on her cheek and leant forward to kiss her.

His kiss was soft, her eyes closed as his tongue traced her top lip. She didn't contribute but certainly didn't resist. It was only when his left hand was placed on her other cheek that she engaged in the kiss. Her mind pictured his young body again, naked above her, filling her with his youthful exuberance.

'No, no Luke,' she said her hand placed firmly on his chest. 'No, I can't do this, I'm sorry.' Tess went to leave, but Luke grabbed her arm.

'I know you want this as well, just one more time… please. You're wet, aren't you?'

Tess just looked at him, with her now flushed cheeks then, glanced around, making sure no one else could see or hear them.

'You know you've made me hard.' Luke said looking at his crotch.

Her eyes followed his and she could see the bulge she had enjoyed so many times. It took all her strength to leave in that moment, it could so easily have gone either way.

'You're really going to marry him, aren't you?' Luke called out as she reached the door.

'Yes, I am,' she said as she turned and left the hotel.

She felt the sudden urge to run but her heels would prevent that.

Tess regrouped as best she could. She paced down the street, her fingers now desperately punching to book a taxi and get home.

She looked up to see a taxi coming down the road. After hailing and climbing inside, her thoughts gave thanks for its opportune arrival.

It was only once inside the back seat of the cab that her breathing finally settled. *My God, that was close,* she thought to herself and pushed her thoughts back to 2.00 p.m. that day, desperately retracing to the message about her dress that she'd been poised to compose for Greg. She'd so wanted to put that far behind her and tell him all about the dress. Shit! *It's been ages since he's heard from me! He doesn't need to know any more other than the wonderful time spent with my mum. Damn it! He's probably at the airport by now!*

Her fingers were texting furiously as the driver of the cab pulled up at the traffic lights. She wanted him to know some good news before he returned home this evening.

> I've had a great time with Mum. We found the dress. All sorted. You'll be both surprised and impressed. This time for real, lol. With all my love, Tess xx

The taxi turned onto Greenhill Road and headed east. As they approached the next set of lights, she hit Send.

The encounter with Luke was fading as fast as the distance from him increased. Her thoughts were now only of the man she will marry in April.

The lights turned green and the cab moved away. Neither the driver nor Tess saw the truck that had run the red light.

The small Camry taxi was torn apart.

It was close to 9.00 p.m. when Kara was jolted by the ringing of her phone, she instinctively grabbed it from the coffee table. *Who on earth would be ringing me now?* she thought. She saw it was Greg Sheppard.

She sat upright and with a smile said, 'Hello Greg, what a pleasant surprise.'

It was the moment of silence that concerned her first.

'She's gone Kara… she's gone.'

Kara's Life: Pre-ignition

She was Kara Gilbert once more.

Gently rolling onto her back, and as she opened her eyes, she blinked in the realisation it was morning and where she was. Stretching out her arms and legs wide from her position in the middle of the bed, relishing in delight of having all the space to herself.

'Hmmm, I'm home,' she murmured to herself, smiling widely.

Before moving to rise, she started her panoramic scan from her silver lamp on the bedside table, across the photos of her dimpled daughter as a baby, her friend Sally and Aunt Sarah, then to the grey and blue hues of the Monet print on the wall. At the end of the white wooden bed was the grey cashmere throw, draped across her grandmother's carved chair.

'It's all still here.'

I so love waking up in this room, she thought as she did most days now. The light was streaming through the white wooden slats of the windows, left open to let in the world every morning. The day's first radiance brought even more warmth and glow into what had become her sanctuary.

She ran her hands over her body from her thighs, over her stomach, and up over her breasts before turning onto her stomach towards the window. She was so much happier about how she looked and felt. Sleeping naked was such a simple indulgent pleasure these days too. She turned her gaze to outside. Looking out to the garden, every leaf glistening with the first kiss of the morning sun. She planned her day.

The sound of the Verve's 'Bittersweet Symphony' blasted out of her phone, and she reached for it to silence the alarm. Time to leap into the day. She relished walking through her house naked, continuing to admire the spaces she had created that sang out with her love of colour and the contrast and blend of elegant, eclectic style as she headed to make that beloved first coffee.

Standing at the kitchen bench, cup in hand, she stared out to her garden. She loved how its colour smiled back at her, as if to say, 'Thank you for your effort and care.' She savoured the pleasure of the simplicity of her life these days, in contrast to before when she was Kara Werner—a woman she no longer knew.

Kara Werner's husband had finally passed away. Well, in reality, he was still very much alive, but in these last six months since the sudden and dramatic end to their twenty-three years together, Kara had officially laid him to rest. It was frightening at first. He still lived close, but she was no longer afraid of him. He couldn't influence or control her thoughts or decisions anymore. She'd created a new life for herself—a life of peace where she didn't have to run every thought or action through a filter of what 'he' might say or do or worry how he might react. There were always consequences—she had the scars inside and out as evidence. Thankfully, he could no longer hurt her. Kara was in charge of her own life at last.

At a little after 8.00 a.m., she stood in the shower, head tipped back, allowing the flow of hot water to wash away the night before and warm her energy for the day ahead. This used to be the only time at home when she could completely relax and enjoy herself. Now her time and decisions were hers alone to make. Every morning began with new possibilities.

In those first three years after the divorce, she had put her head down and trod water, focused on little more than working hard. It had taken her all that time to adjust to living alone. Now she could finally lift her gaze higher, proud of how she'd redesigned and invigorated not only the look, but the feel of her home, welcoming life and happiness into every inch. In doing so, she had cleansed the place, creating somewhere she belonged. Gone were the walls that for too long had hidden away the real story of her and her ex.

The flashbacks to her life before had subsided significantly, but there were always little reminders of what she had left behind. 'Evanescence' was thankfully only music to her and not a feeling of definition.

She thought back to when she was first on her own. She'd made such an effort as she knew it was important to stay connected with people, as much as she just wanted to hide away. This took lots of energy at first. Having been a highly recognisable couple, both professionally and in a wide number of high-profile circles, the end to her marriage raised considerable public notoriety and comment that continued for the first couple of years.

At times it was exhausting and difficult for her to keep putting on that brave face and go out in public or to social events that often resulted in her hearing those not-so-quiet whispers as she passed. In reality, they were in shock and couldn't understand how their separation had happened, or understand why now at the mere mention of her name to her ex, it would evoke a tirade of expletives and horrible stories about her. The whole town wanted to know what happened, questioning had she changed and what did she do.

So many times, she had those little sideline conversations to reassure and console friends who were confused and thought that association with her might be toxic. Dealing with this was hard work. Especially with her closest friend, Sally.

She'd landed at Kara's door, burst into tears and visibly shaking.

'Kara, I'm so sorry. I don't know what to do.'

'My God, what's happened?'

'He warned me. He baled me up and told me outright if I had anything to do with you, he would never speak to me or Paul again!'

Kara knew instantly it was her ex. He'd been doing this with everyone.

'Sally, it's okay. Our relationship hasn't changed. We are still friends. I haven't morphed into some new dangerous creature! You and Paul need to still be friends with him too. The only relationship that's broken is his and mine.'

'But he said he won't speak to us again!'

'That's up to him. I'm sure he wants and needs your company.'

Sadly, this became nearly the same conversation, over and over. It was tough, but she kept going. Some were so confused and fearful about what it meant for them they disassociated completely.

Then there were the emotional wounds and so much scar tissue. They were the toughest of all and had been slow to heal. But she was so fortunate. Her aunt—in reality her most special best friend and confidante—her four girlfriends, and her daughter, had been incredible in how they had rallied around her—advising, listening, and caring. They were such a blessed, steadfast comfort. She spent hours in their company—talking endlessly, shedding tears, dining, drinking, laughing, and going to new places with them. Thankfully, she also loved music and film, and it was through the lyrics and the characters and stories that Kara allowed herself to dream and escape when she felt so desperately alone.

But now Kara had reconnected with friends and made many new ones too.

She certainly felt much more like the young woman who had been lost since she was nineteen or twenty years of age. Like a jigsaw, Kara put all the pieces in place. She didn't need anyone or anything else. She could breathe easily and wore a smile every day. Sadly, she shared a similar story with so many women of her age, that she now found herself with two-thirds of her life lived, and had to start afresh.

She was nonetheless happy. But that was before she found the message that was about to transform her life.

A Message From the Authors

This is a book designed to arouse, stimulate, and excite. That's the purpose of romantic lustful literature. We hope this turns you on as much as it did me writing this story. We also hope you will read more, play more, and dare to share our book and stories with your friends. There is a bit of an underlying strange motivation for this fiction, which aims to challenge some myths about lust, love, sex, adultery, and relationships.

So, what is so different or important about this story?

This is fiction. A story for sure. However, its inspiration is based upon a collection of true-life experiences and encounters. About genuine, ordinary, decent people who are middle-aged or older.

While written through the lens associated with only the two main characters this story has from a collation of recollections and researched information from a range of couples and individuals who have shared their more secret lives with us, including their kinky desires, fantasies, real-life sexual encounters, and the many ongoing challenges they faced in their relationships through their years.

In our research, we found that people over forty, in their fifties, sixties, or even older, continue to be active sexual beings, aroused, horny, and adventurous. This challenges the myth often held by younger adults, that after middle age, you no longer enjoy sex, you don't suffer relationship problems, have intimate fantasies and desires, or seek out pleasures.

Often, many couples, as they mature, become comfortable enough to discard the traditional, societal moral codes that have stifled, rather than encouraged positive, healthy relationships. Challenging the accepted beliefs about monogamy, romance, and commitment for life, where sexual experimentation is a sinful pleasure only acceptable for younger adults, this story outlines a new paradigm—that sex for pleasure and love are not unanimous and that relationships be enhanced by having multiple partners, across many age groups and different genders for pleasure. That today, we may need to consider the confronting reality, that one person alone may not completely satisfy us. Most of all, sex is essential and awesome—at any age. Yes, older people really do it, want it, enjoy it and are good at it!

So, we thank you for reading Kara—for hopefully enjoying, and experiencing the romantic connection between two people lost to each other for decades with all its simple indulgent pleasure and fantasy. We hope you are tempted to keep reading more about Kara and Greg in *Kara: Lovers and Liars, Kara: My Shepherd,* and explore other titles by us and Midnight Authors.

Kathryn and Gary

About the Authors

Despite their contrasting lifestyles and professional careers, Kathryn and Gary's mutual desire to write, has resulted in a unique collaboration between these two South Australian authors. This unique combination has created a bold new genre of sophisticated erotic literature, which dares to explore the complexity of current day physical attraction, desire, sexual pleasure, and how modern-day relationships should be considered and fulfilled.

The male and female influence of their writing brings realistic insight into adult romance and encounters, through Kara and Greg's perspectives and emotions.

 Writing and engagement with people has been central to Kathryn's life for decades, with a highly successful and recognised career in education, research and the arts, which continues today. It wasn't until Kathryn's reconnection with the boy she first fell in love with as an innocent 12-year-old, that she found her true passion and talent as an author of adult romance. The real-life encounter with her first true love, became the catalyst into a wonderful renewal of self-acceptance and joy in writing, for pleasure alone—sparking the beginning of the Kara story.

Kathryn is the founding member of a small group of authors known as the Midnight Authors, who enjoy shaping their books for others, often in the midnight hours between their other careers. They support and encourage each other as they create their stories and navigate the challenges of self-publishing!

Gary Baxter's journey as a wordsmith began in his youth, where his natural gift for articulation and entertaining storytelling captured the attention of those around him. With an unwavering love for action novels and a burning desire to create stories that would enthral readers, he embarked on a mission that had been simmering within him for years.

As an accomplished car and motorcycle racer, instructor, entertainer and an esteemed figure in movie action vehicle coordination and stunt driving, Gary's thrilling life has fuelled his imagination and inspired his writing. From the roaring engines on the racetrack to the heart-pounding stunts on the film set, he channels his experiences into words that leap off the page.

Gary's writing has extended since the Kara trilogy into short stories, action and crime novels that will also captivate.

Kathryn and Gary are mature, new-age authors, who bring a refreshing style to romance that is riveting, arousing, and provocative.

www.ingramcontent.com/pod-product-compliance
Lightning Source LLC
Chambersburg PA
CBHW061926130726
47909CB00012B/1793